"Hurry, Daddy, hurry. She's getting so wet."

Royal frowned. "I'm sorry, sweetheart, but it's not safe to pick up strangers. You never know when—"

"No!" five-year-old Maddie screamed. "She's not a stranger. She's my angel."

Royal tried to speak sternly. "We don't know this woman. She's a stranger. Not an angel. Do you understand me?" Still, at the look on Maddie's face, he hit the brakes and reluctantly waved the woman inside. She quickly ducked in, slamming the door shut behind her.

She was soaking wet and minus any makeup, yet she was one of the most stunning women he'd ever seen. She smiled at Maddie as she attempted to dry off.

"You're a very pretty young lady. What's your name?"

"Madeline Michelle Justice, but Daddy calls me Maddie. What's *your* name?"

The woman paused and then smiled. "Angel. My name is Angel."

Dear Reader,

We've got a special lineup of books for you this month, starting with two from favorite authors Sharon Sala and Laurey Bright. Sharon's *Royal's Child* finishes up her trilogy, THE JUSTICE WAY, about the three Justice brothers. This is a wonderful, suspenseful, *romantic* finale, and you won't want to miss it. *The Mother of His Child,* Laurey's newest, bears our CONVENIENTLY WED flash. There are layers of secrets and emotion in this one, so get ready to lose yourself in these compelling pages.

And then…MARCH MADNESS is back! Once again, we're presenting four fabulous new authors for your reading pleasure. Rachel Lee, Justine Davis and many more of your favorite writers first appeared as MARCH MADNESS authors, and I think the four new writers this month are destined to become favorites, too. Fiona Brand is a New Zealand sensation, and *Cullen's Bride* combines suspense with a marriage-of-convenience plot that had me turning pages at a frantic pace. In *A True-Blue Texas Twosome,* Kim McKade brings an extra dollop of emotion to a reunion story to stay in your heart—and that Western setting doesn't hurt! *The Man Behind the Badge* is the hero of Vickie Taylor's debut novel, which gives new meaning to the phrase "fast-paced." These two are on the run and heading straight for love. Finally, check out *Dangerous Curves,* by Kristina Wright, about a cop who finds himself breaking all the rules for one very special woman. Could he be guilty of love in the first degree?

Enjoy them all! And then come back next month, when the romantic excitement will continue right here in Silhouette Intimate Moments.

Yours,

Leslie Wainger
Executive Senior Editor

Please address questions and book requests to:
Silhouette Reader Service
U.S.: 3010 Walden Ave., P.O. Box 1325, Buffalo, NY 14269
Canadian: P.O. Box 609, Fort Erie, Ont. L2A 5X3

Sharon Sala

ROYAL'S CHILD

Silhouette®

INTIMATE™ MOMENTS®

Published by Silhouette Books

America's Publisher of Contemporary Romance

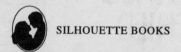

SILHOUETTE BOOKS

ISBN 0-373-07913-3

ROYAL'S CHILD

This edition published by arrangement with Harlequin Books S.A.

® and TM are trademarks of Harlequin Books S.A., used under license.
Trademarks indicated with ® are registered in the United States Patent
and Trademark Office, the Canadian Trade Marks Office and in other
countries.

Printed in U.S.A.

Books by Sharon Sala

Silhouette Intimate Moments

Annie and the Outlaw #597
The Miracle Man #650
When You Call My Name #687
Shades of a Desperado #757
Ryder's Wife #817
Roman's Heart #859
Royal's Child #913

*The Justice Way

Silhouette Books

36 Hours
For Her Eyes Only

SHARON SALA

is a child of the country. As a farmer's daughter, her vivid imagination made solitude a thing to cherish. During her adult life, she learned to survive by taking things one day at a time. An inveterate dreamer, she yearned to share the stories her imagination created. For Sharon, her dreams have come true, and she claims one of her greatest joys is when her stories became tools for healing.

With age, comes wisdom. But in gaining this gift, we often forfeit another. And that loss is an unswerving belief in things unseen.

Oh, to be a child again. For just one day. To walk in innocence and, on certain occasions, to talk to angels who sit on our beds.

I dedicate this book to the child in all of us.

Chapter 1

The fat man on the floor was holding his crotch and cursing in at least two languages. But Angel Rojas was impervious to his threats. She'd heard them all before. Instead of cowering beneath his anger, she pushed at his foot with the toe of her shoe in a warning gesture.

"Shut up, Louie. You can't fire me. I already quit."

His face green, Louie groaned. "You bitch! Your days in this town are over. I'll make damn sure you never work around here again."

His threats didn't frighten her, and harsh words had long since lost their ability to hurt her. Angel Maria Conchita Rojas had learned early on that the only people who could hurt you were the ones you loved. And the last person Angel loved had been her mother, who died when she was seven. By the time she was nine she'd run away from home, weary of the beatings her father kept giving her. As a teenager, she had run from one foster home after another. Angel had been running all her life and was afraid to stop. If she had, the devastation of her life might have overwhelmed her. She'd become adept at surviving in a male-dominated world and even more so at protecting herself.

But at the age of twenty-five, she was still waiting to find a place to call home. Her entire existence consisted of what she called pit stops. Fat Louie's Bar and Grill on the outskirts of Tuscaloosa, Alabama, was about to become a part of her history.

Angel felt like cheering. Today she'd reached a breaking point and done something about it. Lewd innuendos and groping hands were a thing of her past. With a heartfelt sigh of relief, she tossed her apron aside.

"You owe me two hundred and fifty dollars for the last two weeks' work. Don't bother to get up. I'll help myself."

Louie cursed again. "I'll have you arrested for stealing."

Angel turned, and the look on her face was warning enough. Louie was silenced.

"I personally know six other women, besides myself, who are willing to file charges of sexual harassment against you. Are you interested in calling my bluff?"

Wincing with pain, Louie struggled to get up. But there was something in her words he couldn't ignore. His complexion darkened as he waved a fist in her direction.

"Just get your damned money and get out." Then he cupped his crotch again and groaned.

Angel counted out her money and then grabbed her jacket and purse. By the time she got to the door, Louie was on his feet and still cursing her name.

She never looked back.

Royal Justice rolled out of bed and stood within the quiet of his bedroom. His heart was hammering against his chest as he glanced at the clock. It was almost five. In an hour or so the sun would be breaking the cover of darkness. His four-year-old daughter, Maddie, was asleep in her room down the hall, and although he couldn't hear a thing but the intermittent drip from a leaking shower head, he knew something was wrong.

Nearly five years of being a single parent had honed his instincts to razor-sharp perception. Without hesitation, he grabbed his Levi's, hastily dressing as he started out of his room.

Maddie was fine when he'd put her to bed last night, but he'd learned the hard way that time and children never stay static. Just as he reached the door of her room, the flesh crawled on the back of his neck. Shuddering, he paused, and it was as if a hand centered in the middle of his back suddenly pushed him forward. Frowning at his flight of fancy, he stepped in.

He knew before he touched her that she was sick. Maddie could tear up a bed faster than anyone he knew when she was healthy. When she was restless, it was impossible to tell head from foot. The covers were in a wad on the floor, and her pillow was nowhere in sight. He turned on the bedside lamp. When he brushed his hand across her cheek, her skin felt hot to his touch. She opened her eyes, but he could tell it wasn't him she was seeing. The image frightened him.

"I don't see her," Maddie mumbled.

"See who, baby?" Royal asked, but Maddie didn't answer. His hand was shaking as he cupped the side of her face. "Maddie? See who?"

"The lady. I don't see the lady."

He gritted his teeth and dashed into the adjoining bathroom, emerging moments later with a cold, wet washcloth. As he bent to wipe it across her burning face, she began to whisper.

"Daddy? Daddy?"

"Daddy's here, baby."

"I don't feel good, Daddy. My bed is spinning. Make it stop. Make it stop."

Royal clenched his jaw. He'd faced wild bulls, mad dogs and crazy hired hands without batting an eye, but anything regarding his daughter's well-being made him sick to his stomach.

"I know," he said softly. "Tell me where you feel bad."

She rolled into a fetal position without answering.

Royal's pulse shifted into high gear as he ran his hands along her arms. Her entire body was so hot and dry it almost felt like paper.

"Angel," Maddie mumbled, weakly pushing against the restraint of her father's hands. "I can't find my angel."

Royal's heart nearly stopped. "No!" he groaned, and thrust his hands into her hair and turned her until she was facing him.

The mere mention of angels made him crazy. He'd watched his wife, Susan, die and had tried to die with her. But that was before they'd put Maddie in his arms. Within a week of bringing his baby girl home from the hospital, he'd been too tired and sleep-deprived to think of anything but the next bottle to heat and the next diaper to change. At that point, Royal Justice would have had to get better to die. But that was then, and this was now, and he wasn't giving up any more of his family without a fight.

"Maddie, tell Daddy where you feel bad. Can you do that?"

Instead of answering, she fell into a feverish sleep.

He turned on the overhead lights, trying not to panic. Her long, dark hair was damp with perspiration and was sticking to her neck and face. He threw back the covers, then inhaled sharply as his gaze centered on a large, inflamed area on her thigh. Stunned, he bent closer, rubbing the area, testing the size and the heat emanating from within.

"Damn."

There was little else to say. His hands shook as he quickly checked the rest of her body, making certain there were no more spots like it. There were not.

It hadn't been there when he'd put her to bed. He would have bet his life on it. And then he remembered how impatient he'd been with her and how cranky he'd been when he'd tossed her pajamas on the bed. He thought back. The phone had rung. He'd left the room to answer it. By the time he had returned, she was already in her pajamas and in bed, begging him to read her a story.

Pain wrapped around a big dose of guilt as he remembered

that he hadn't read her the story, either. Instead, he'd given her a quick kiss good-night and promised to read her two stories tomorrow. All he could think now was, *Please, God, let there be a tomorrow for her.*

He looked at the huge welt again. The only thing he could think of was that something had bitten her. Probably an insect. But what? She'd been bitten by mosquitoes, stung by bees, even stung by a wasp, and not once had she experienced a reaction like this.

When she began to shiver, he panicked. He had to get her to a doctor, and fast.

"Maddie, I'm going to get dressed and then I'm taking you to the doctor. He'll make you feel better."

The fact that she didn't even argue about an impending trip to the doctor was sign enough for Royal that this was serious.

He was down the hall and in his room within seconds, yanking shirts from hangers and socks from his drawer. Within moments, he was dressed and in her room.

As he lifted her into his arms, he noticed something on the sheets where she'd been lying. As he looked closer, he identified the tiny carcass of a brown spider. In spite of the fact that it was flatter than normal and its long legs were curled in upon itself, the mark on the dead spider's back was impossible to mistake. It was a fiddleback, a brown recluse spider, highly poisonous to all and deadly to some.

He looked in horror at her lifeless little body, then grabbed a blanket from the foot of the bed and wrapped her in it as he dashed from the room.

A short while later he was in his truck and flying down the darkened highway toward Dallas with Maddie beside him in the seat. Although he drove with one hand on the wheel and the other on his daughter, her covers were already trailing on the floor.

"Daddy, Daddy, I'm falling," she cried, weakly pushing at the quilt her father had wrapped around her.

He splayed his hand across her stomach, assuring her that he was there.

"No, baby, you're not falling. Daddy's got you. He won't let you fall."

"Angel...my angel," she whispered, and kicked at the covers on her legs.

"Son of a bitch," he muttered, quelling an urge to throw up. His voice was shaking as he glanced down. "Damn it to hell, Madeline Michelle, you do *not* see angels, do you hear me?"

In typical Royal fashion, he had reacted to fear with anger. And for Royal, the fear was all the greater for the fact that he had nothing on which to focus except his daughter's condition. He couldn't eradicate the spider. It was already dead. He couldn't blame Maddie for the incident. For once, his maverick child had been a victim of circumstance, not of rebellion. And his great strength was useless in the face of such overwhelming odds. It was all he could do to concentrate on the drive to the hospital. He wouldn't let himself think of life without her. He couldn't believe that God would be so cruel as to take away his wife *and* his child.

A short while later, he stood at one side of the bed where Maddie was lying. He was in shock and numb to everything around him except the rapid rise and fall of her chest as her little lungs struggled to cope with the ravages of a rising fever. It wasn't until they moved her into intensive care that he started to crumble. He headed for a phone.

Roman Justice glanced at the digital readout on his alarm clock as he reached for the ringing phone. When he saw the time, he frowned. It was seven minutes after six in the morning. This was his private line. Few people other than family had this number. Instinct told him this wasn't going to be good.

"Hello."

"Roman, it's me, Royal."

Roman heard the panic in his older brother's voice and rolled out of bed. He was reaching for his jeans as he spoke.

"What's wrong?"

"It's Maddie. They just put her in intensive care."

Roman's heart dropped. It was all he could do to focus. Except for his wife, Holly, his niece was the most important person in his life.

His voice was rough and shaky as he buttoned his Levi's. "What the hell happened?"

"Spider bite. It was a fiddleback." His voice was shaky as he added, "It doesn't look good."

Roman flipped on the lights. "Where is she?"

"Dallas Memorial."

"Have you called Ryder and Casey?" Roman asked.

Royal took a deep breath and closed his eyes. "No. You do it. I don't think I can say this again."

Roman could hear the panic in his brother's voice. His hand tightened around the receiver. "Don't worry. I'll handle everything," he said. "Hang in there, brother. We're on our way."

Royal disconnected and leaned his forehead against the cool surface of the wall. The comfort of knowing his brothers were coming was small, but for now, it was enough. He straightened his shoulders, then lifted his chin and jammed his Stetson tighter on his head as he headed for intensive care. He didn't give a good damn about hospital rules. His daughter was only four years old, and he wasn't going to have her waking up in a strange place alone. There was no hesitation in his step. He wouldn't let himself believe Maddie might not wake up. She would get better. She had to.

He wangled his way through the closed doors of ICU and went to the nurse's desk.

"Please," Royal begged the nurse. "I won't move. I won't talk. I won't even breathe out loud. Just don't make me leave her."

The nurse was sympathetic, but the rules had been put in

place for the benefit of the patients, not the family, and for the patients' sakes, they must be obeyed.

"I'm sorry, Mr. Justice, but visiting time is over. Everyone else has to leave, and so do you. I can't extend special privileges just to you, and you know it."

"But what if she wakes up and I'm not here? What if she asks for something and no one hears her?"

"That's why we're here," the nurse said. "Now please."

"One more minute," Royal begged.

The nurse rolled her eyes then glanced at her watch. "I have to replace an IV. When I'm finished, you're out of here."

Royal went weak with relief. "Deal."

The nurse glared. "I do not make deals," she said, and walked away.

Royal didn't bother to watch her exit. He was too busy taking in everything they'd done to his daughter in his absence.

He looked at the needle in the back of her hand and winced. Maddie hated shots. He couldn't imagine how she was going to react when she saw it. He touched her forehead. It burned. His hands shook as he swept the hair from her face. Then he glanced up. The nurse was looking his way. He leaned down, desperate to get in one last word before he was forced to leave.

"Daddy's here, baby. Don't be scared. Daddy's here."

A soft sigh escaped Maddie's lips. Her fingers twitched, as if trying to grasp something just out of her reach. Then silent tears began seeping from the corners of her eyes.

"Can't find my angel," she whispered.

Royal's eyes widened in fear.

"Help me, Daddy. Help me."

He leaned his forehead against her arm, fighting the urge to weep.

"You just get better, sweetheart, and I'll help you find anything you want. Okay?"

Her eyelids fluttered as she drifted in and out of consciousness. Royal watched her struggling against the confines of the machines they had hooked her to and was almost glad she didn't know what was happening. As he watched, Maddie sighed and seemed to relax. He kept telling himself she was in good hands. And the longer he stood there, the more solid the belief became. His panic began to subside. She was in the hospital. The doctors would make her better.

"I love you, Maddie. Do you hear me? Daddy loves you more than anyone in this world."

"Mr. Justice."

He jerked. The ICU nurse was standing at his elbow, and the warning in her voice was impossible to miss. He straightened, giving her a hard look as he turned toward the door.

"Have you ever had a loved one in a place like this?"

The nurse blinked, taken aback by his anger.

"No, sir, I have not."

"Then I'll say a prayer for you that it never happens," he said shortly. "Because this is a parent's hell on earth."

When Royal exited ICU, Roman and Holly were waiting for him. Royal took one look at the fear on their faces and answered their unspoken question.

"As I said on the phone, it was a spider bite. They're pretty sure it was a fiddleback."

Holly pressed a hand to her lips and clutched her husband's arm. She and Roman had been married only a few short months, but in that time, Roman's niece had become as dear to her as if she was her own daughter. She couldn't bear to think of that tiny child suffering.

"Where did it bite her?" Holly asked.

"Her leg."

Roman looked toward the doors to ICU. The urge to see her was overwhelming. He couldn't believe such a lively child could be in such serious condition, and so quickly. He glanced at his brother, judging Royal's panic against his own.

"Royal?"

"Just pray," Royal said, and dropped into a chair. He stared at the floor, gathering the guts to say aloud what he'd been thinking for hours. His voice was shaking when he began to speak.

"She's pretty sick. Her fever keeps spiking. She's not out of the woods until they can get that under control."

Roman shook his head and slid into the chair beside his brother.

"I have never been this scared in my entire life," he muttered.

Royal managed a small grin. "Just wait until you have kids of your own."

Holly laid her hand on Royal's shoulder. "Is there anything we can do? If there's a specialist you need, all you have to do is ask. We'll get him here immediately."

Royal frowned as he glanced at the doors barring him from his child. "At this point, I don't think a specialist could help. Thanks for offering, honey, but there's not even anything I can do."

"Ryder and Casey are flying in," she added.

Royal leaned back in the chair and covered his face with his hands. He remembered last night and how Maddie kept begging him to read her a story. Guilt sat heavy on his shoulders as he took a deep, shuddering breath. Ah, God, if only this was just a bad dream and any minute he was going to wake up with Maddie begging him for breakfast. He bolted out of the chair and began to pace.

"I hate this," he muttered.

"Hate what?" Roman asked.

Royal wouldn't look at them, knowing they'd see panic in his eyes.

"The gathering of family. It makes Maddie's condition seem…"

He couldn't finish the sentence. He didn't have to. There was no way they could miss the point. Families gathered for various reasons. Births. Holidays. Illnesses. Deaths.

He shuddered. *Ah, God.*

All they could do was wait.

* * *

Seven hours into Royal's hell, his daughter woke up screaming. Royal was out of his chair in the waiting room of ICU before anyone had time to react. He was halfway through the doors when his brothers stopped him.

"Wait," Ryder urged, nervously eyeing the bed at the other end of the ward where he knew his niece was lying. Already nurses were hovering around her. "Don't make matters worse."

"They can't get any worse," Royal argued, and would have pulled away but for Roman's terse remark.

"Yes, they could," Roman said sharply. "She could be dead. Now let them do their work. If they need us, they know where we are."

Royal slumped. He knew his brothers were right. Already the sounds of Maddie's panic were subsiding. But that didn't help him. He needed to see her—to reassure her that all would be right in her world. He stood in the doorway, staring long and hard down the ward until one of the nurses began ushering him out.

"For God's sake, let me see her," he begged. "You heard her. She's scared to death, and with good reason. She went to sleep in her own home, in her own bed, and she wakes up in this place attached to needles and tubes and machines, and I'm nowhere in sight. At least let me assure her that I'm not far away."

Maddie's plaintive cries wrapped around them. The nurse hesitated.

"Wait here," she said and pivoted.

Royal held his breath. The need to see his daughter was making him sick. He had never been able to bear hearing her cry. Knowing she must be frightened half out of her mind made him crazy. His fingers curled into fists as he watched the nurses in conversation by Maddie's bed.

And then one of them turned and motioned for him to come

forward. His heart lifted. Within seconds he was standing at Maddie's side.

"Hey, baby girl, Daddy's here," he said. "Don't cry."

Maddie's wails dissolved into soft, gulping sobs. Careful not to disturb her IV, he leaned forward and gathered her into a hug.

"I want to go home," Maddie sobbed.

"And I want you there, sweetheart," Royal said softly. "But you got sick. Do you remember?"

Tears were streaming down her face as her head rolled from side to side.

"I don't remember anything but the lady," Maddie said.

Royal frowned. "What lady, baby?"

"The one who was sitting on my bed."

Royal spun toward the nurses. The head nurse smiled and shook her head.

"She must have been hallucinating. We don't sit on patients' beds."

Maddie sniffed as Royal wiped tears from her face. "Not them," she said. "The pretty lady in the blue dress. The one who's sending me an angel."

Royal frowned. Even now, knowing that Maddie seemed over the worst, the talk of angels made him nervous.

"You were dreaming, baby. Sometimes when people get sick they have real crazy dreams."

Tears welled. "It wasn't a dream."

"Another minute, Mr. Justice, and then I'll ask you to leave. Even if your daughter is better, the other patients in here are not."

Royal nodded.

"Don't go," Maddie begged.

"I won't be far," Royal said. "See those doors?"

Maddie turned her head, nodding as her chin continued to quiver.

"Guess who's out there?"

Maddie clutched her father's hand even tighter.

"Uncle Roman and Aunt Holly and Uncle Ryder and Aunt Casey."

Maddie's eyes widened at the mention of her favorite people, especially Roman. "I want to see my uncle Roman."

"And you will, baby, you will. Just as soon as the doctor lets me, I'll take you home. But you're going to have to take it easy for a couple of days. You've been a pretty sick little girl, okay?"

"Okay," she muttered, and her eyelids began to droop.

"Mr. Justice, please."

Royal nodded. The nurse was out of patience, and he was out of time.

"Close your eyes and take a nap, baby. I'll be back in an hour, okay?"

But Maddie's eyes were already closed. The medicine and her lingering weakness were taking their toll. Royal kissed her forehead and gave her cheek a last, lingering touch. By the time he got into the waiting area, there was a smile on his face.

Ryder stood up. "How is she?"

Royal nodded. "Better. The fever broke. I think the worst is over."

There was a general all-around hug between the Justice family, which lightened the mood considerably. But it was Roman who introduced some reality into the situation, reminding them that Maddie had a ways to go before being cured. His voice was quiet and filled with regret as he caught Royal by the arm.

"You know that bite is likely to leave a hell of a scar."

Royal nodded.

Holly frowned. "A scar? Surely a spider bite doesn't scar."

"This spider's bite does," Roman said.

Royal nodded. "It's a bitch, and that's for sure. Not only is it deadly, but the pain will be pretty severe and the flesh around the bite will probably rot away. But I don't give a good damn how it looks when it's over, because she will still be alive."

Casey slipped her hand in the bend of Royal's elbow and

hugged him close to her. Her voice was sweet and low, filled with the accent of her native Mississippi.

"We will say prayers."

Royal was blinking back tears as he looked around the small waiting area.

"Thanks," he said gruffly.

"For what?" they all said.

"For being here," Royal answered.

"Where else would we be?" Roman said. "We're family. We're all we've got."

Chapter 2

Within days of the spider incident, the entire house had been fumigated, and Royal had hired two cleaning women from town to put the house to rights. He'd watched them with a wary eye, making sure that every insect and spider they swept up was dead. Maddie's room smelled of lemon-scented disinfectant and furniture polish. Her favorite teddy bear was on her pillow, awaiting her arrival. As soon as he got his baby girl back, his world would be on track.

He stood in the doorway to her room, remembering the day she'd been born. It had been a mixture of heaven and hell. Watching his daughter claim life and watching his young wife die. His emotions had run the gamut. But he'd survived, and so had Maddie.

Now, as difficult as it was for him to accept, she was growing up. This fall she would start kindergarten. That meant half a day of school. For years he had chosen to ignore the fact that the routine he'd adopted was no longer going to work. He wouldn't be able to yank Maddie out of her bed, toss her into the pickup with a peanut butter and jelly sandwich and take

her to work with him. There would be no more fixing fence
with her unceasing chatter in the background or hauling hay
with her sitting by his side. Soon, her days would no longer
be all his. Somehow, he was going to have to find a way to
adjust.

Twice during his trips to the hospital, Roman had brought
up the subject of a permanent housekeeper, and each time
Royal had balked. He'd had a housekeeper when Maddie was
a baby. She'd lasted through Maddie's third birthday and then
moved away. The separation had been traumatic for them all.
Royal had vowed not to put Maddie through such loss again.
Over time they'd fallen into a routine that had suited them both.
Just the thought of finding someone new to intrude into their
world was an all-around pain-in-the-ass notion. Sharing space
with anyone except his daughter, no matter how good and kind
she might be, wasn't something Royal Justice did easily.

He glanced at his watch. It was almost seven. Holly had been
at the hospital with Maddie more than three hours. They'd
moved Maddie into a regular room, and she had not been left
alone. Someone from the Justice family was with her at all
times during the day, but it was Royal who stayed every night.
His steps were light as he grabbed his keys on the way out the
door. Tomorrow he was bringing her home.

Angel Rojas sat on the side of her bed, counting her meager
stash of money. Rent on her apartment was due, and even
though she knew truth was on her side, there would be no
justice for her in this town. Not with Fat Louie's angry influ-
ence. She flopped onto the mattress, staring at the ceiling in
quiet despair.

"Why do I keep getting myself in these messes?"

No one bothered to answer, because no one was there.

It was getting dark. One set of people were in the act of
shutting themselves in behind closed doors while others were
coming to life. And while the night called to some, there was
nothing within it that called to Angel. She'd seen it all and

committed a few more sins than she liked to admit, but turning tricks had never been an option.

She closed her eyes and rolled onto her side, then took a deep breath, making her mind relax. She was tired and heartsick and needed to rest. Today had been rough, but in the words of her heroine, Scarlett O'Hara, tomorrow was another day.

By sunrise she had made a decision. It had taken years for her to accumulate what constituted her worldly possessions, and parting with them was going to be painful. But she'd learned long ago not to dwell on a bad situation, and this was definitely one of her worst. If she had to leave town to survive, then she would do it. But there was no way she could take her things, too.

There was a living room suite bought at a yard sale. A bed and dresser that didn't match, and a table and three chairs she'd inherited from the previous resident of the apartment. Her entire wardrobe would fit in one small closet. The only thing she owned that she deemed of great value was a bookcase full of books she had spent years accumulating. She didn't own a car, she didn't have a credit card, and she didn't know where she was going. She gazed longingly around the small rooms, painfully realizing that this was no longer her home. Then she clenched her jaw, picked up the sign she'd made and walked outside. With a grunt, she stuck it in the lawn near the curb.

Moving Sale—Apartment Three

By five o'clock, she was sitting on the floor of an empty apartment and counting her money. Almost two hundred dollars to add to what she'd taken from Fat Louie, and she still didn't have five hundred dollars to begin a new life. Her hands were shaking as she folded her money and stuffed it in the bottom of her purse, then dropped the purse between her legs and closed her eyes.

"Please, God," she whispered. "Show me the way. All I want is a home."

That night she slept on the floor, and by daylight she was gone.

Later, someone remarked to Fat Louie that he thought he'd seen Louie's waitress hitchhiking west out of town.

Louie tongued his unlit cigar to the other side of his mouth, all the while cursing good riddance to the crazy bitch.

Meanwhile, Angel Rojas was doing what she knew how to do best—putting the past behind her and moving on.

"Maddie, want to come see the new kittens?" Royal asked.

"I guess," Maddie said, sliding off the sofa and dragging her feet as she followed him out the door.

Royal frowned. Ever since her return from the hospital, Maddie had been moping around the ranch like a calf that had lost its mother. Nothing seemed to interest her. Offers to let her cat, Flea Bit, into the house to play had fallen flat, and visits from her uncle Roman had failed to excite her. The doctors had quoted statistics, assuring Royal that some depression was normal after a hospital stay and that it would pass. But Royal didn't like statistics, and he wanted whatever was wrong with Maddie to be gone.

"What's wrong?" he asked, as they strolled toward the barn. He glanced at the angry red spot on her leg. Although it was healing nicely, it was far from well. "Is your leg hurting, baby? Want Daddy to carry you?"

"No," she said, and kicked up a cloud of dust without pausing.

Royal's frown deepened as he tried to find a topic that might excite her.

"Dumpling has a calico kitten with one blue eye and one brown eye, what do you think about that?" he asked.

Maddie paused and looked up. "Does that mean she sees blue with one eye and brown with the other?"

Royal grinned, scooped her off her feet and set her on his shoulders, careful to miss the sore part of her leg.

"No, it does not, and you know it," he said, chuckling as they started toward the barn. "What color are my eyes?" he asked.

"They're blue," Maddie answered. "Just like mine."

"Right. And when you look, is everything blue?"

"No," she said, and he heard her giggle. The sound was music to his ears.

"Then there's your answer."

He heard her sigh and felt her hands gripping the crown of his Stetson. Carrying her like this was hell on the shape of a good hat, but he'd willingly sacrifice a truckload of hats just to get back the girl she'd been.

They entered the shade of the barn. He set her in the midst of the hay where a mother cat was busy grooming her two-week-old litter. Royal shook his head in dismay as he counted the kittens. Five more to add to the growing number already in residence on his ranch. And then he shrugged. A working ranch could not have too many cats. As long as they stayed in the barns and sheds where the mice and rats might be, they were fine.

But there was Flea Bit, the cat who, thanks to Roman's interference, had taken up residence in the house. That damned ball of fur was underfoot every time he took a step. Then he looked at Maddie, squatting in the midst of the hay, tenderly stroking the new babies while muttering her sweet talk to the old mother cat. His heart tugged. He hoped to hell Maddie didn't ask to bring any of these cats to the house. There wasn't enough spit left in him to tell her no about anything. He squatted beside her, and when he tuned in on what she was saying, his frown deepened.

"I'm sorry I didn't come see you sooner," Maddie said, stroking the old cat's head in short, gentle strokes. "I got sick." She leaned closer, as if telling the cat a secret. "I saw a lady," she said softly. "She promised me angels." Her lower lip drooped. "But the angel didn't come."

Ah, Royal thought. The reason for her depression.

He dropped to one knee, cupping the back of his daughter's head.

"Maddie, look at me."

Maddie continued to stroke the cat's head as if her father was nowhere in sight.

"Madeline Michelle, I'm talking to you," Royal said softly.

When Maddie looked up, there was a stubborn, like-father-like-daughter thrust to her chin.

"What?" she muttered.

"You don't need to worry about angels anymore, okay?"

Her face fell. "But Daddy, the lady promised."

Royal tipped her chin so she was staring at him eye to eye.

"Maddie, there was no lady on your bed and there isn't going to be an angel coming. Angels don't live with people, they live in heaven, remember?"

She nodded, but he could tell she wasn't buying his explanation.

"What you saw…what you thought you saw, that was all part of your illness. Do you understand?"

Her lower lip protruded. "I saw a lady," she said shortly, and turned away, pretending great interest in the kitten with one blue eye and one brown eye. She lifted it into her lap, carefully judging its odd markings with a practiced eye and then abruptly announced, "I'm going to name him Marbles."

In spite of the fact that his talk had gone nowhere, he had to grin. "Why Marbles?"

"'Cause his eyes are the color of the marbles in the bottom of Uncle Roman's fish tank."

Royal rocked on his heels and grinned. "Marbles it is," he said softly. "How about the other four? Don't they need names, too?"

Maddie looked them over carefully, then shook her head. "No, only this one."

"Why?" Roman asked.

She looked at him, as if surprised by the stupidity of his question.

"Because Marbles is a people cat, not a mouse cat."

Royal rolled his eyes. "Oh, no, you don't," he said lightly, and put the kitten with the mother before setting Maddie on his shoulders for the trip to the house. "We're not making a house pet out of another cat, and that's final."

There was a marked silence between father and daughter. They were halfway to the house when Maddie leaned close to Royal's ear.

"Daddy."

"What, baby?"

"Do you think Flea Bit will sleep with Marbles?"

"If we're lucky, no," he muttered.

"What did you say?" Maddie asked.

"I said, it's hard to know," he answered, and said a mental prayer for forgiveness for the small white lie.

Tommy Boy Watson was looking for whores. At the age of thirty-seven, he was old enough to indulge his baser instincts if he so chose, but it wasn't the sex he was after. Since the death of his father, Claude, the extermination of whores had become his quest. He'd watched his old man go from being a successful trucker to an invalid, fighting the ravages of AIDS. The irony of Claude Watson's disease came from the fact that he didn't even know who'd given it to him or how many he'd passed it to before he became ill. He'd been a notorious womanizer, often taking advantage of the prostitutes hanging around the parking lots of truck stops and rest stops along the nation's highways. After Claude had been diagnosed, it had taken a month shy of three years for him to die, and he'd died blaming the lot lizards and not himself.

At four inches over five feet tall, Tommy Boy was almost a foot shorter and one hundred pounds lighter than his father had been. His biggest disappointment in life had been his size. He'd compensated with attitude. He'd done the job well. Tommy Boy Watson wasn't just tough, he was mean. And since his father's demise, a little crazy, as well. His pale green eyes seemed innocuous until you looked beneath his smile. Pure evil dwelled there. He wore a long, unkempt beard and tied his thin and graying hair into a ponytail. He favored baseball caps and kept all his keys on a heavy silver chain hooked to a belt loop. He was fond of the clink the links made as they rubbed against the rivets in his jeans.

Six weeks ago, he'd stood at his father's grave with a bottle of whiskey in one hand and a switchblade in the other and made a vow to get rid of every whore to cross his path. In his mind, it was the least he could do to avenge Claude's death. No other decent man should suffer the way his father had suffered. He'd been on the road since then, leaving the mutilated bodies of fallen women in his wake.

Last night he'd crossed the state line into Texas. It was the first time he'd been this far south. He didn't know whether he liked it, and it didn't really matter. He hadn't come for his health.

His gaze was sharp as he watched the people coming and going from the truck stop parking lot. There were plenty of women, but so far, none looked as if they were surfing for business.

Today it was hotter than normal, even for Texas, even for the middle of May, but it gave him cool satisfaction to know that he'd left the state of Oklahoma with one less hooker than it had had the day before.

He wondered absently if they'd found her body yet. His pulse accelerated as he remembered how easily the flesh beneath her chin had parted under the blade of his knife. Like hot butter. He shifted his stance and giggled just a little, not because he was happy, but because it had been so easy.

He thought of his little house on the outskirts of Chicago and wondered what the boys in the neighborhood were doing. This was Saturday. Tonight they'd be gathering at the local bar, watching TV and laying bets, like whether or not Jimmy Riordan could chugalug six raw eggs in his beer without throwing up. They always bet on something. For Tommy Boy, it was what made life worth living.

Then his smile faded as he remembered what he'd set out

to do. There would be time later for playing. After he was finished.

It never occurred to him to wonder when he might stop or how many dead women would be enough to assuage his anger over his father's death. All he knew was that his pain lessened with each slice of his knife.

Suddenly he straightened and pulled his cap tight across his forehead, shading his eyes from the blast of midday sun.

There. Just getting out of that old gray van. He saw her wave. He heard her laugh. He watched them drive away, leaving her standing alone in the parking lot. He watched her shift her duffel bag to her shoulder and start toward the restaurant. His pulse quickened. She was young, maybe mid-twenties. Her clothes were faded. Her legs were long. Her breasts... His breath caught at the back of his throat as he watched them bounce with the sway of her stride. His eyes narrowed. She looked Indian, maybe Mexican. He couldn't tell for sure, but there was all that soft-looking, warm brown skin, and enough black hair to strangle a man with. Resisting the urge to rub himself, he continued to watch her. It wasn't often that a whore excited him. Usually he felt nothing but disgust. His stare lengthened.

Yes. This was the kind of woman who'd tempted his father. This was a woman who could lead a man to his death with little more than a smile. When she disappeared into the restaurant, he smoothed a hand over the button fly of his jeans and started after her.

Angel was tired from the inside out. She'd been on the road for more than two days. It had been years since she'd done anything as foolish as hitchhiking, and although she'd started out apprehensively, so far her rides had been on the up-and-up. She glanced at the small sign near the restaurant door.

Bus Stop.

Lord, but what she wouldn't give for the money to travel in

style. Not that bus travel was all that stylish, but from the backseat of a stranger's van, it was looking better all the time.

She rubbed her palm over the outside of her duffel bag, imagining she could feel the small stash of money secreted in the bottom. Her feet ached and her forehead felt hot. She hoped she wasn't coming down with something. She couldn't be sick. Not like this. Not without a place to call home.

A blast of cool air hit her as she entered the restaurant and she paused in the doorway, letting her eyes adjust in the dim interior. It didn't take long to see that she'd have to wait. There wasn't a seat available. With a sigh, she headed for the ladies' room to freshen up. Maybe when she got back, some of the places would have cleared.

Her stomach growled to protest being empty. The scent of food and hot coffee almost did her in, but she kept walking. She didn't see the man who came in behind her, and even if she had, she would have paid him little mind.

But Tommy Boy Watson saw her as she disappeared into the ladies' room. He cast a quick glance around and slid onto a vacated stool at the counter. From where he was sitting, he had a perfect view of the ladies' room door. A cold smile tilted the corners of his lips.

Go ahead and wash your pretty face, bitch. I can wait.

Angel leaned toward the mirror over the sink and stared at her reflection. Her scalp itched, and her skin was sticky with sweat and the dust of the road. She closed her eyes and let her chin drop toward her chest in disgust. She felt dirty from the inside out. All she'd ever wanted in this life was a place to belong, and here she was in her mid-twenties, on the road and still looking for rainbows. She turned on the water, letting it run hard between her fingers before leaning down and sluicing the dust from her face.

She turned off the water and reached for a paper towel. As she did, she caught a glimpse of herself in the mirror again, and this time almost didn't recognize herself. With water dripping from her eyes and face, she looked as if she'd been crying.

It was a foreign thought. Angel Rojas didn't cry. Not anymore. The lack of expression on her face was frightening.

"God," she muttered. "Where have I gone?"

Then she shrugged off the thought and dried her face. There was no room in her life for regrets. Her belly growled again as she picked up her bag. Her feet were dragging as she walked into the restaurant. She found a seat and was soon immersed in reading the menu.

Tommy Boy was staring. He knew, like he knew his own name, that this woman was one who needed cleansing. He took a sip of coffee, picturing his father lying in this woman's arms, then picturing his father as he'd laid in his coffin. When he focused again, his face was filled with rage. Disease. Disease. They all spread disease.

"Want a refill, honey?"

He looked up. Startled by the waitress's intrusion, he glared. Realizing he had time to pass, he nodded.

He glanced at the woman in the booth again, watching her facial expressions as she studied the menu. When he heard the low murmur of her voice as she gave a waitress her order, his gaze snagged on the muscles working in her throat. And when she tilted a glass of water to her lips and drank, it was all he could do to wait. He had it planned. He knew just what he was going to say. It would be easy. After all, getting them into his truck was simple. They were bodies for hire. All he had to do was promise to pay for services rendered.

Angel stepped out of the restaurant and into the afternoon sunshine, wincing as the glare burned her weary eyes. She dropped her duffel bag and knelt beside it, digging in a side pocket for the sunglasses she'd put there last night.

"Hey, baby, did you lose something?"

Startled by the unexpected sound of a stranger's voice, she rocked on her heels and looked up. She had a moment's impression of long, greasy hair, a thin, straggly beard and eyes the color of a frog's belly. Her stomach knotted as she stood, but she refused to show fear. Instead, she slid her sunglasses up her nose, shouldered her bag and stared him straight in the face, taking momentary comfort in the anonymity.

"No, I didn't lose a thing."

The man grinned. "Just asking," he drawled. "Say, baby, I'm in the mood to party. How about it?"

The food she'd just eaten threatened to come up. "No," she said brusquely and turned away. To her shock, he grabbed her by the arm.

"Listen here," he said, running his hand up and down her arm. "I've got plenty of everything a pretty thing like you might need...including money."

It was impossible for Angel to misinterpret his intentions. His tone was suggestive, as was the way he smoothed his hand over his fly.

For Angel, it was shades of Fat Louie all over again. Her voice was full of anger as she yanked her arm out of his grasp.

"I've never been that hard up. Now get lost, mister, before I really get mad."

Tommy Boy was stunned. He hadn't expected a rebuff. The others had been all too willing to take some of his money. His lips narrowed angrily as he watched her stride away. It occurred to him that maybe he'd made a mistake, that maybe she wasn't a whore, after all. But a couple of minutes later, he watched her crawling into the cab of an eighteen-wheeler. He knew truckers weren't supposed to pick up hitchhikers. In his mind, the only reason that trucker had hauled her into his cab was to get a piece of tail.

"Damn her to hell and back," he muttered, and pivoted angrily.

By the time he got to his truck, he was in a blind rage. He gunned the engine, leaving a long black trail of rubber on the pavement behind him as he spun out of the parking lot and into the northbound lanes of Interstate 35, the opposite direction from the woman and the trucker. His head was pounding and his hands were shaking. The farther he drove, the more his head hurt. Sunlight bounced off the hood of his truck and into his eyes. He grabbed sunglasses from the dash and shoved them in place, cursing with every breath. Slowly, he became aware of a nagging little voice inside his head.

Go back. Go back.

He shook his head like a dog shedding water and focused on the highway traffic.

You let her get away. You promised to avenge me.

The familiar cadence of that voice gave him a chill. His father was dead. But it was still somehow Claude Watson's voice he heard.

Stop her. Have to stop her before it's too late.

Tommy Boy slammed on the brakes and made a sudden left on the interstate. Huge clumps of dirt and grass flew into the air as the tires on his truck tore through the center median. He bounced into the southbound lanes, barely avoiding a crash. Cars spun out of control, and a delivery truck full of bottled water skidded off the interstate and into the ditch to avoid a collision. Adrenaline rocketed into his system as he stuck his arm out the window and flipped off the cars behind him. Within seconds, he was out of sight, driving as fast as his black truck would go, desperate to find the whore who was getting away.

Chapter 3

Royal stood on the back porch, nursing a cup of coffee and planning his day. Sunrise had come and gone, and the day was bathed in light. Except for a couple of fading jet trails, the Texas sky was cloudless. He squinted against the glare of sun as he gazed east.

In the pasture next to the corral, the old cow he'd put there last week was bawling to be fed. He took another sip of coffee, contemplating the wisdom of hauling her off. It had been two years since she'd had a calf, her teeth were worn almost to the gums, and she had a monotonous tendency to jump fences. Then he grinned and discarded the notion. He admired an aggressive spirit, even in an animal, and he'd be damned before he sold her. She'd borne more than her share of calves over the years. So what if her fruitful days were over. She deserved a better ending than winding up in a can of dog food.

A door banged somewhere in the house behind him, and his attention shifted. Maddie must be awake. When the screen door squeaked behind him, he stifled a grin. One of Maddie's favorite pastimes was to sneak up on him. He braced himself for a great big boo. It never came.

He turned. Maddie was on her knees, cradling Flea Bit in her arms. Royal sighed. There would be cat hair all over her clean pajamas.

"Morning, sweetheart," he said softly, and set his cup on the porch rail. He knelt and lifted the kitten out of her lap and her into his arms. When she snuggled her nose against the curve of his neck, his heart tugged painfully. Even now, knowing that she was perfectly cured, he still hadn't recovered from the fear of almost losing her.

"You're awfully quiet this morning," he said. "Are you okay?"

Maddie nodded and wrapped her arms tightly around her daddy's neck.

"I had a dream."

Royal hugged her. "I'm sorry, baby. Did it scare you?"

"No."

"Then how did it make you feel?" he asked.

She hesitated, as if considering the question, then finally answered.

"Sad."

His frown deepened. "Want to tell me about it?" he asked. He sat in the porch swing and settled her in his lap.

She shrugged.

He let the question ride. In the past few weeks, he was coming to realize that Maddie was almost as hardheaded as he was. Instead of talking, they just rocked. The squeak of the chains from which the porch swing hung was persistent. But instead of an irritation, it was a comforting sound.

A light breeze had come up a short while ago and now it was slipping around the corner of the house, lifting the ends of Maddie's hair and cooling the heat of her warm little body as she cuddled against him. Royal glanced at the dark tangles they had yet to brush, then at the upturned nose she'd inherited from a mother she would never know. An emotion swelled within him, pushing up through his chest and tightening the muscles in his throat until it brought tears to his eyes. He jerked his head upward and closed his eyes, inhaling deeply to push back the feelings. Damn it to hell, but life just wasn't fair. Maddie was growing up, and the woman who would have rejoiced in it most was dead and buried.

Inside the house, the phone began to ring. And for Maddie, the sound was like magic. She came to life, bouncing off Royal's lap and heading for the door before he could even get out of the swing.

"I'll get it!" she shrieked. The door slammed to punctuate her announcement.

Royal grinned and got up to go inside. At least some things were back to normal.

In spite of the fact that the trucker Angel had accepted a ride with was well over six feet tall and pushing three hundred pounds, she felt safe. A priest had once told her the best way to judge character was to look in a person's eyes. When Angel had looked into the trucker's face, she hadn't seen a worn-out version of Grizzly Adams on uppers. She'd seen a friendly smile below a black handlebar mustache and warm brown eyes twinkling at her as he offered her a hand up in the cab.

"Where you headin', missy?" the trucker had asked.

"Where are you going?" Angel countered.

"South," the trucker said.

"That'll do," Angel drawled.

He laughed, and when Angel slammed the door shut, he began shifting gears. The big rig began to pick up speed. The farther they got from that parking lot, the better Angel began to feel. Even though the man who'd accosted her had only touched her arm, she'd known instant fear.

As the miles added up, she began to relax, although she kept glancing nervously in the rearview mirrors. She'd seen the man get in a new black truck, and although she knew it was silly to think he would follow, every time she saw a dark vehicle behind them, she tensed until she was sure it wasn't him.

"Lookin' for someone?" the big trucker asked.

Angel shook her head.

The man's eyes narrowed thoughtfully, although he gave her a smile.

"If you got trouble, missy, you'd best leave it behind you. That's what I always say."

With one last glance in the rearview mirror, she nodded.

"It is."

"That's good. That's good. Now then, we've got ourselves a decision to make. I'm pushing all the way to Houston tonight. You a mind to go that far?"

Angel blinked. Getting lost in a city that size wasn't what she had in mind, especially when she was still trying to find herself.

"No, I guess not," she said, although she was reluctant to give up the ride. "Just drop me off at the first convenient spot."

"What's your destination?" he asked.

"I thought maybe I'd try something on the outskirts of Dallas, around Arlington. It's summer. Maybe I can get work at Six Flags."

The trucker nodded. "Yeah, theme parks are the thing during vacation time, all right. You ought to do just fine."

A few moments later he pulled over. He pointed across her line of vision toward the west.

"See that highway off to your right?"

She turned and looked.

"Stay on that and it'll take you straight into Arlington."

Angel grabbed her duffel bag and paused at the open door.

"Thanks, mister."

The trucker's gaze quickly swept over the young woman, eyeing her feminine curves and old clothes. He knew what hard up looked like. He also knew what it felt like. His conscience kicked in as she began climbing down from the cab.

"Hey, missy."

Angel looked up.

"Hitchhiking is dangerous business."

She shrugged. "It's also cheap."

He laughed. "There's that, all right. Well then, be on your way, and Godspeed."

Angel watched until he was no longer in sight, then began making her way across the median to the other side of the highway. She glanced at her watch and was surprised to see she'd been riding with the man for almost an hour and had never asked his name. She saw a truck stop about a quarter of a mile ahead, and started walking. Her mind was on bathrooms and cold water and big, greasy hamburgers. For the time being, the pale, skinny man was forgotten.

Tommy Boy was sweating. The persistent whine in his head was eating into his nerves.

You let her get away. You promised to avenge me and you let her get away.

Tommy Boy's face was pale, and the pupils of his small, close-set eyes were fixed and staring. Every time he came to a crossroads on the highway, the knot in his belly gave another sharp tug. There were a dozen different highways the trucker could have taken. Without knowing his destination, he had no way of guessing where they had gone. But guilt rode him hard, and he kept on driving, stopping only to empty his bladder or fill up his fuel tank.

Once he spotted the back end of a rig like the one the trucker had been driving. Same company. Same color of trailer. He'd driven like a man possessed to catch up, only to find that he'd been chasing the wrong driver. Seeing the thin, bony face of a redheaded man behind the wheel had brought him to the point of tears. He'd eased off the gas and taken the first exit ramp off the highway, desperate to control his emotions. Moments later he was on the shoulder of the road, fighting the urge to throw up.

Time passed, and Tommy Boy was barely aware of the traffic. Finally he looked up. His mind was blank, his body, trembling. But the worst was over. To his everlasting relief, the voice had disappeared.

"Hell," he muttered as he started the engine. "What's one hooker? There's a dozen out there to take her place."

Having stated the facts as he saw them, he pulled onto the highway. Half an hour later, he realized the truck coming toward him on the other side of the road was the one he'd been chasing for nearly a day. When he saw the driver and that dark, bushy beard, he hit the steering wheel with the flat of his hand and laughed. The echo of his laughter was still with him when he realized the trucker was riding solo. Even though he knew the woman could be lying down in the sleeper, his instincts told him different. Somewhere along the highway, the trucker had dropped her off. Tommy Boy sneered. It figured. She was out there now, looking for another man to snare, another victim to infect.

Certain that fate was guiding him, he accelerated. He'd find her again. And this time, he wouldn't fail.

Angel entered the restaurant and paused in the doorway, eyeing the patrons and assessing the possibilities of her next ride. There were plenty of trucks in the parking lot, and every kind of traveling vehicle, including a half dozen fancy motorcycles parked off to one side. Surely someone would be going her way. But for now, all she wanted was a bathroom and food, in that order.

A short while later, she was finishing an order of fries and downing the last of her iced tea. She'd already spotted the people to whom the bikes belonged. With weather-worn skin as dark as burned toast, wearing denim, leather and boots, they were hard to miss. Some of them were with women. A couple were not. She'd already heard them talking about stopping in Arlington, so she knew they were going her way. When she noticed they were getting up to leave, her pulse kicked. It was now or never. She tossed some money onto the table to pay for her food, shouldered her bag and headed for the door.

The sun was bright in her face as she exited, but she waited to don her sunglasses. It was always better to ask for a ride when they could see your face.

"Nice ride," she said, as the group began to mount.

A couple of the women gave her hard looks. Another smiled. One of the men looked up. A long moment of silence passed between him and Angel, and finally he asked, "Need a lift?"

Angel stared hard and long at his face and at the expression in her eyes. Finally she nodded.

"Where you headed?" he asked.

"Six Flags. I'm looking for work." She paused and added, "And nothing else."

He nodded. "Fair enough." He turned and waved at the man to his left. "Juke, hand me your extra helmet."

In no time, Angel's bag was strapped on and she was settling in place on the Harley. The biker turned to look at her.

"I don't ride with strangers, so what's your name?"

Angel hesitated, but she could see no harm in the simple question.

"Angel," she replied.

The group broke into loud shouts of laughter as the biker got a silly grin on his face.

"What's so funny?" Angel asked.

"Your name," he said, and revved the engine.

She had to yell to be heard. "I don't get the joke."

"Hey, Demon, let's ride," someone called.

They pulled out of the parking lot in an orderly manner, two abreast. Angel caught a glimpse of herself in the windows of the gas station they were passing and knew a moment of panic.

Demon?

The man she was riding with was called Demon?

There was an instant when she started to shout at him to let her off. And then she caught a glimpse of something shiny and black from the corner of her eye and turned to look.

There. Pulling into a parking place at the pumps and getting out of the truck was the man from the diner. Instead of begging to get off, she found herself clutching Demon's jacket. Although she believed herself to be safely hidden behind the helmet's dark visor, she couldn't stop thinking about the coincidence of seeing him twice in one day and in locations that were so far apart.

Demon revved the engine.

It occurred to her that she could be putting herself between a rock and a hard place.

Dear God, please let this be all right.

She reminded herself that names could be deceiving. Demon was more than likely not a demon after all. Besides, she was called Angel, and she was about as far from holy as a person could get.

Royal got out of the truck with his arms full of groceries. Roman met him at the door, relieving him of part of his burden.

"Everything okay?" Royal asked.

Roman grinned, thinking of the can of shaving cream that had met an early demise. "If you're referring to your daughter, she's fine."

"I appreciate you coming to help me out," Royal said, as he set his sack on the kitchen cabinet. Roman followed suit.

"No big deal," Roman said shortly. "Besides, with Holly in Las Vegas visiting her father, I'd rather be here than in that apartment alone."

Royal grinned. "When you fell, you fell hard, didn't you, little brother?"

Roman arched an eyebrow but refused to be baited. "Don't be so damned smug. Your day is coming."

Royal snorted. "It'll be a cold day in hell before that ever happens," he muttered.

"Daddy, where's hell?"

Both men spun around. Royal had the grace to look shame-faced while Roman hid a grin.

"I keep telling you to watch your language around her," he said softly.

Royal glared at his brother, dug a package of Twinkies from the groceries and tossed it to Maddie.

"Here, squirt, take yourself outside to play while I put up the groceries, okay?"

Maddie caught her treat in midair and was out the door before her father could change his mind.

Roman rolled his eyes. "That's perfect," he drawled. "She curses and spits like a seasoned wrangler and now you're buying her off with enough sugar to keep her wired all night."

Royal sighed and looked away. "Yeah, yeah. Tell me something I don't already know."

Roman walked to the back door, watching as Maddie tore into the sponge cakes and broke off a piece for Flea Bit, who was scrambling around her feet. He smiled and turned.

"I'm sorry. That was none of my business," he said. "I don't know how you've done it—raising that baby all by yourself. You should be getting an award, not advice."

Royal looked away and frowned. "I know I'm not perfect."

"To Maddie you are, and that's all that matters," Roman said.

Royal shook his head. "Once I might have believed that, but no more. These days it's rare if I get a smile out of her. She's been moping around the house ever since she came home from the hospital. I can't seem to snap her out of it."

Roman stood, considering the reaction Royal was bound to have, and shook off the thought. Maddie was Royal's child. He had a right to know what was going on in her head.

"Come with me," Roman said. "I want to show you something."

Royal glanced out the door, assuring himself Maddie was still in sight, then followed Roman into the living room.

Papers were strewn all over the tabletop, the chairs and the sofa. A couple had drifted onto the floor.

Roman began picking them up and handing them to Royal

one by one. At first glance, Royal took the drawings to be nothing more than something Maddie had done to pass away time. The longer he looked, the more obvious it became that his assumption was wrong.

"What the hell?" he muttered, shuffling them in his hands.

"She said they were angels," Roman said.

Royal's belly jerked. "I thought she'd gotten all of that out of her mind."

Roman shrugged. "From where I'm standing, it looks to me as if that's the only thing on her mind."

Royal looked up, his face haggard with worry. "What am I going to do? And don't tell me to take her to a shrink! Four-year-old children do not need to see shrinks."

Roman shrugged. "That's not entirely true. Some do."

Royal glared but didn't answer. His gaze was drawn to the pictures. They were all the same theme repeated over and over with different backgrounds. A childish rendition of a woman in blue, surrounded in colors of yellow, and a dark-headed woman with wings.

"Did she say who they were?" Royal asked.

Roman pointed to the woman in blue. "That's the lady who sits on her bed."

Royal groaned. "This is getting way out of hand."

"And the brown one is supposed to be her angel."

"Brown angels?" He sighed. "I suppose this could set a trend."

Before Roman could answer, Maddie burst into the room.

"Daddy, Flea Bit wants some more Twinkies."

"I don't think so," Royal said. "It will ruin Flea Bit's supper."

Maddie rolled her eyes and started to pout, but Royal sidetracked her by holding up the drawings.

"I thought we'd talked about this," he said gruffly.

Although she didn't understand why, she knew she was in trouble. She gave her uncle Roman an accusing stare and then dropped her chin.

Roman sighed. In Maddie's eyes, he'd let her down.

Royal laid a hand on Maddie's head. "Madeline Michelle, I'm talking to you," he said.

She looked up, her eyes brimming with unshed tears.

Royal relented and dropped to one knee. "I'm not mad at you, baby. I just want to understand."

One huge tear slid down the side of her face, followed by another on her other cheek. Her voice was trembling.

"They're pictures of my lady and the angel."

Royal groaned. "Maddie, there isn't any—"

Maddie took a step back. "You're wrong! You're wrong!" she cried. "She's my lady, and you can't take her away."

Royal reached for her. "I'm not trying to take anything away from you, baby," he said gently. "But you have to understand the difference between real people and pretend people."

Maddie's lips were trembling, but her chin jutted in a mutinous thrust. If it hadn't been so tragic, Roman could have laughed. At that moment, father and daughter had never looked more alike.

"They're not pretend. They're real!" Maddie shrieked. "You'll see. The lady said my angel is coming. Then you'll see I'm telling the truth."

She ran out of the room, the Twinkies and the cat forgotten.

"Well, now, I think that went real well," Roman drawled.

Royal stood and glared. "Just shut the hell up."

Roman nodded. "I'm out of here. Call me if you need me."

Royal was left with the handful of drawings and a growing certainty that the situation was out of his control.

Tommy Boy Watson slid behind the wheel of his truck and shut the door. Washed in the silence, he leaned his head against the back of the seat and closed his eyes, savoring the adrenaline high he was on. The feel of her flesh was still with him, soft and pliant. It had parted beneath the blade of his knife like warm butter.

Silently. Swiftly.

Opening for him. Bleeding for him. Cleansing the filth from her body...and stealing her life.

It was night. It would be hours, maybe even days before her body was found. That suited him fine. He would be long gone before that could happen. He took a deep breath and opened his eyes. It was time to move on. Time to find the black-haired woman who got away. Maybe then it would be enough.

Angel was scared. The bikers she'd hitched a ride with were long gone, and twice since then she had seen a shiny black pickup truck like the one the skinny man had been driving. Each time, she'd been certain that she'd seen him behind the wheel. She kept telling herself she was being silly, that there was no way she was being stalked. But her instincts were telling her different. This was far beyond a coincidence. Fear was with her. The urge to run was overwhelming. But run where? Her plan had been to work at Six Flags. But instinct kept telling her to move on, to get as far away from Texas as she could.

The urge to spend some of her precious cash on a bus ticket was growing stronger, but her last ride had dumped her in the middle of nowhere. The highway stretched before and behind her like a flat gray ribbon. Added to that, the sky was darkening and threatening rain. She sighed. Rain. That would make this day just about perfect.

No sooner had the thought evolved than the first drops of rain began to fall. She rolled her eyes heavenward and hitched her duffel bag to her other shoulder, convinced that this day couldn't get much worse. And then a bolt of lightning split the sky with a crack, and she flinched.

"Okay, so I was wrong."

Hunching her shoulders against the sudden downpour, she started to walk.

Royal looked through the windshield to the darkening sky and frowned. "I was hoping we'd beat the rain."

Safely buckled into the restraints of a child's car seat, Maddie gave the darkening sky and the sudden downpour a minimal glance. She was too concerned with the free toy in the fast-food lunch her father had just bought her.

"What did you get?" Royal asked.

"Belle!" she crowed, holding it up for him to see.

He frowned. "Who's Belle?"

Maddie looked up in pure disgust. "Daddy, don't you know anything?"

He grinned. "Obviously not."

"Beauty and the Beast, remember?"

Recognition dawned. "Oh, that Belle."

Maddie rolled her eyes.

"Hey, you," Royal teased. "Give me a french fry and quit being so smart."

Maddie giggled and handed him two. "One for your mouth and one for your hand," she explained.

Royal was licking the salt from the ends of his fingers when he realized the dark shape he'd been seeing in the distance was a hitchhiker.

"Poor bastard. Hell of a day for a walk," he muttered, then stopped, remembering too late to temper his vocabulary.

To his relief, Maddie didn't bother to ask who the bastard was. She was busy craning her neck to look.

Royal continued to watch the hitchhiker as they drew closer. He hunched his shoulders against the downpour and ducked his head against the blast of the wind. He was almost upon him when he realized that the him was a her. A long black braid marked the middle of her back, and her clothes were plastered to her like wet tissue paper. She didn't have a spare ounce of fat on her body, and if it hadn't been for her womanly curves, he would have considered her far too thin. A fleeting notion of picking her up came and went, but then he thought of Maddie and moved into the left-hand lane to keep from splashing her as he passed.

Maddie jumped from her car seat and into the seat.

"Daddy! Daddy! Go back! Go back!"

Startled, he let off the gas. The pickup coasted as he looked in the rearview mirror. Had he hit something on the road and didn't know it? He searched for the hitchhiker through the pouring rain. To his relief, he could see her. Thank God, he thought. At least he hadn't hit her. He looked at Maddie.

"What's the matter with you?" he asked.

"That's her! You have to go back!" she screamed.

Royal stared at her, trying to fathom where the excitement had come from. She didn't get this worked up over Christmas.

"Sit down and buckle yourself up!" he ordered. "What's wrong with you, anyway? You're gonna make us have a wreck."

But Maddie was on her knees in the seat, looking through the back window.

"Hurry, Daddy, hurry. She's getting so wet."

Royal frowned. "I'm sorry, sweetheart, but it's not safe to pick up strangers. You never know when—"

"No!" she screamed, and started to cry in earnest. "She's not a stranger. That's my angel."

He hit the brakes before he thought, then cursed beneath his breath. The hitchhiker would take the red glow of brake lights as a signal. He looked in the rearview mirror again. Sure enough, she was jogging toward them.

"Now look what you've made me do," he muttered.

Maddie was almost hysterical with joy. It frightened Royal to see her elation. It was unnatural and out of control, and he didn't know how to stop it.

"Damn it, Maddie, you…"

She gave Royal a long, considering look. "Daddy, I don't think you should be cusping. My angel won't like it."

He rolled his eyes. "The word isn't cusping, it's cursing, and you're right. I shouldn't be doing it. But that doesn't change the fact that we do not know this woman. She's a stranger. Not an angel. Do you understand me?"

Maddie wasn't listening. She was busy gathering her food and making room for the woman to sit.

A chicken nugget rolled off the seat and onto the floor beneath Royal's boots. He clenched his jaw to keep from coming undone, and when the door suddenly opened, he pulled Maddie as close to him as he could, glaring at the woman in the rain as if this were all her fault.

"Where are you heading?" Royal asked, and before she could answer, a gust of wind blew a sheet of rain in the door. Maddie squealed and then laughed. Royal cursed and started waving his hand. "Get in, just get in!" he yelled. "We'll deal with destinations later."

The woman ducked her head and jumped inside, slamming the door shut behind her.

Suddenly there was nothing but quiet. Engulfed by the scent of chicken nuggets and french fries, they sat in mutual silence, each digesting a sudden change in circumstance.

Before a word could be spoken, Maddie leaned over and lightly ran her hand up and down the young woman's back.

Royal grabbed Maddie, scolding her as he moved her away.

"Maddie, where are your manners?" He glanced at the woman. "Sorry," he said.

She was soaking wet and minus any makeup, yet she was one of the most stunning women he'd ever seen. Hair as black as midnight, eyes so dark he couldn't see the pupils, and her skin was so smooth and so brown. He wondered if she was that brown all over, then jerked as if he'd been slapped.

"It's all right," Angel said. "I appreciate the ride…and the friendly gesture," she added, winking at Maddie.

Maddie beamed. "It's okay, Daddy. I was just looking for wings."

Water was running out of Angel's hair and onto her face as she threw back her head and laughed. The sound wrapped around Royal's senses like a warm quilt on a cold day. He shuddered, then glared.

"Sorry again," he said. "But it's a long story."

Maddie smiled at the woman and handed her the napkin from her lunch.

"You can dry off."

The woman smiled as she accepted the offer. "Thank you," she said. "You're a very pretty young lady. What's your name?"

"My name is Madeline Michelle Justice, but Daddy calls me Maddie."

Royal watched the woman make a futile attempt to dry off with the small piece of paper. He reached under the seat and pulled out a handful of clean paper towels he kept for emergencies.

"Try these," he said, then dropped them in her lap.

"Thank you," she said, and winked at Maddie, who was watching her every move in rapt fascination.

"What's your name?" Maddie asked.

The woman smiled. "Angel. My name is Angel."

Chapter 4

Maddie threw her arms around Royal's neck in wild excitement.

"See, Daddy? I told you! I told you!"

Royal was stunned into silence. How the hell had she known? He glanced at the woman who called herself Angel and gritted his teeth. There had to be a way out of this mess without insulting the woman or sending Maddie into a tailspin. Besides, he refused to believe that Maddie's search for an angel and this woman's name were anything more than a coincidence. A major one, he'd grant her that, but a coincidence nonetheless.

A little nervous about what was happening, Angel kept her hand on the door handle for reassurance.

"Why do I feel like I'm missing the punch line?" she asked.

Royal began unwinding Maddie from around his neck. He knew the truth, and it sounded crazy even to him. He could only imagine how anyone else would take it.

Maddie was so elated, he should have known she would make matters worse, but he wasn't expecting her to transfer her affections so quickly. Before he could stop her, Maddie had gone from his lap to the woman called Angel in record time.

Surprised by the unexpected affection, Angel caught the little girl in her arms to keep her from falling to the floor.

"Easy, honey," Angel said gently. "I'll get you all wet."

Maddie wasn't so easily deterred. "You'll dry. That's what Daddy always says." Then she touched Angel's shoulders one last time, as if assuring herself they were truly bare.

"Damn it, Maddie, back off," Royal growled, and scooped his daughter out of the woman's lap. Maddie would have argued, but a sharp look from her father changed her mind. She slumped into her car seat and had to be satisfied with staring at her angel instead.

"I didn't mean to get her in trouble," Angel said softly, and then waved at her dripping clothes. "I'm just so wet."

A muscle jerked in Royal's jaw as he tried without success to ignore how wet she really was.

"It's not that," he said. "It's just…oh hell," he muttered beneath his breath.

"Daddy! I told you! You can't say bad words in front of angels."

Angel looked startled.

Royal grimaced. "Yes, you heard her right. She thinks you're an angel."

Maddie crawled to her knees and leaned forward. There was no mistaking the intensity of her expression.

"She is my angel, Daddy. The lady told me she was coming, and see? She was right. Now you have to believe me."

Angel felt as if she was treading water and losing ground. She ran her fingers along the cool metal of the door handle to reassure herself that she was still awake. If she had believed in its existence, she could have convinced herself that she had crawled into a twilight zone between fact and fiction rather than a pickup.

"I'm sorry," Angel said. "If there's a problem, then I'm

out of here and no hard feelings. I can't get any wetter than I already am.''

"No!'' Maddie shrieked, and threw herself into Angel's arms. "You can't go. You can't. The lady said you would stay. The lady said you would take care of me.''

"God Almighty!'' Royal muttered, and started to forcibly remove Maddie from the woman's lap.

Their gazes met. The woman seemed to be begging him for something. He hesitated. It was all the time Angel needed.

She set the child in her lap so they were facing each other.

"Maddie…your name is Maddie, right?''

Maddie nodded.

"So tell me, Maddie. Tell me about the lady and why you think I'm an angel.''

Maddie sighed with relief. At last. Someone who was willing to listen.

"A spider bit me.'' She pulled up the edge of her shorts. "See, I have a scar.''

Angel frowned. Scarring from an insect bite was rare. She glanced at the father.

"It was a fiddleback. We almost lost her.''

"No, Daddy,'' Maddie said. "I wasn't lost. Just sick.''

Royal ran a finger along the curve of her cheek. "I know, baby. You were very sick.'' He glanced at the woman. "She had a very high fever. It was during the fever that she began having hallucinations. She kept talking about a lady sitting on her bed and telling her that an angel was coming.'' He sighed. "I thought when we brought her home she'd forget about it, but instead, it's gotten worse.''

Angel felt the little girl's fingers curling around her thumb. Touched by the trust, she looked at the small, grubby fist and a smear of drying ketchup and felt a tightening in the back of her throat. She blinked rapidly, then looked up.

"So a spider bit you. I'm glad you got well.''

Maddie nodded. "The lady said I would. But she said you would come to take care of me.''

Royal was surprised. This was something Maddie hadn't mentioned. He frowned, wondering about her sudden need to be cared for by someone other than him.

"What about your mother?" Angel asked.

"She's dead," Maddie said lightly, no more concerned than if someone had asked her the color of her hair.

Angel's heart went out to the child. She remembered what it felt like to be a motherless child.

"I'm sorry," Angel said. "My mother died, too."

That information brought a temporary silence into the confines of the truck cab. For a while, there was nothing but the sound of rain blowing against the windows and the underlying scent of cold food.

Royal wanted to dump the woman out and drive away. He wanted this to never have happened. But from the look on his daughter's face it was too late. Fate had interfered, and they were stuck with each other, at least for a time. The way he looked at it, the sooner he took the hitchhiker where she was going, the sooner his life would get back to normal.

He started the engine. "We're going about twenty miles west. You're welcome to ride that far."

Angel started to nod when Maddie came to life once more. Her lower lip was trembling, and her blue eyes were welling with tears.

"But Daddy, she has to come home with us."

Embarrassed, Royal started to argue when Angel took pity and said it for him.

"No, Maddie, you're wrong. I was on my way to—"

"No," Maddie said, as tears began to pour down her cheeks. "She said. She said you would stay with me."

"Who said?" Angel asked.

"The lady," Maddie sobbed. "The lady who sits on my bed."

"Sweet Lord," Royal said, and lifted Maddie into his arms. "Come here, baby. Don't cry. I'm sorry you're so confused, but I promise one of these days you'll understand."

"But, Daddy, I heard Uncle Roman tell you to hire another keeper. Why can't Angel be my keeper?"

A tender smile broke the somberness of Royal's face. "That's housekeeper, baby. Not keeper, although there are those who think I need one."

Angel grinned. There was something endearing about this big, tough man, although his piercing gaze made her slightly uncomfortable.

"Then you can hire Angel." Maddie turned tearful eyes toward Angel. "You can work for my daddy. He will pay you a lot of money."

Royal felt as if he was being backed into a corner. How do you explain to a child that you don't hire people off the street without insulting them? To his surprise, once again the woman relieved him of the burden.

"I'm sorry, Maddie, but that's not the way it works," Angel said. "Your father loves you very much, and he wouldn't let a stranger take care of his house...or you. Understand?"

Maddie's chin jutted. "I know that," she said loftily. "But you're not a stranger. You're my angel. I have pictures of you and everything."

Angel's eyes widened.

Royal sighed in disgust. "She's been drawing pictures."

"Oh, my," Angel said, eyeing the child with a new respect.

"We're having hamburgers for supper," Maddie said. "I like mine with ketchup and dill pickles."

Angel glanced at the drying smear of ketchup on Maddie's hand. "Ketchup is good. I like it on my french fries."

Maddie clapped her hands. "We gots fries. Daddy bought a big bag of them. You can have seconds."

"We *have* fries, Maddie," Royal said.

Maddie gave her father a disgusted look. "That's what I said. Now let's go home, Daddy. When my angel dries out, maybe then I can see her wings."

Royal groaned, and Angel was speechless. She was beginning to understand what this father had been going through.

"I don't know what to say," Angel said.

Royal knew he was going to regret it later, but he blurted the invitation before he could change his mind.

"According to the weather report, it's going to rain like this all night. I have never done anything this impulsive and foolish in my life, but I have an extra bedroom and a clothes dryer. You're welcome to both for the night."

"Yeah!" Maddie squeaked.

Angel felt as if she'd been pushed into a corner with no way out. In spite of the downpour and an overwhelming desire for hot food and dry clothes, her instincts were telling her not to get involved. Just as she was about to decline, a vehicle came flying past them, sending a spray of water onto the shoulder of the road and dousing Royal's truck.

"Crazy fool," Royal muttered, watching in disgust as the taillights quickly disappeared in the curtain of rain.

Everything Angel had been thinking came to an abrupt halt. She, too, watched as the shiny black pickup disappeared from sight. All she could think was that if she got out now, she would be at the mercy of the weather—and the driver of that pickup truck. This was past coincidence. That man was stalking her. She took a deep breath to calm her shaking nerves, and when Maddie's father looked back at her, she nodded.

"I accept your offer, but only for the night," she said, making sure that Maddie understood.

Maddie heard, but she let the warning go over her head. She wasn't concerned how it would happen. Her angel had come, like the lady had promised. Somehow, her angel would stay. She just knew it.

Royal nodded and started the engine. "Buckle up," he said. "It's time to go home."

Angel's heart tugged a little. Home. What a beautiful word. One of these days she would have a place of her own to call home, too. She glanced at the man as he pulled onto the highway and then focused her attention on the monotonous sweep of windshield wipers. A short while later, they began slowing and turned off the highway onto a blacktop road. Five minutes later, the rooftops of several buildings became visible through the rain.

Angel frowned. For some reason, this place seemed familiar, although she knew she'd never been here before. She glanced at the driver again, watching the expressions on his face as he drove on, checking fences, looking at cattle, pointing to an armadillo waddling through the runoff in a nearby ditch.

Angel flinched as if she'd been hit. There was so much power in his gaze and such a sense of pride in ownership. A vagrant thought drifted through her mind. Would he look at the woman he loved in such a manner? She let go of the thought as easily as it had come. Even if she was going to be angel for a day, she had no place in their world. She was only passing through.

She sighed. "So, Maddie's father… Since we're going to be sharing french fries tonight, I think it might be good if I knew your name."

Royal pulled the brim of his Stetson lower on his forehead, as if he was bracing himself for an unwelcome familiarity.

"My name is Royal Justice, and welcome to my home."

The steady rumble of the clothes dryer could still be heard toward the front of the house. But in the back, where the bedrooms were, it was silent. The rooms were dark, but Angel felt a measure of safety within their unfamiliarity that she hadn't known in years. She thought back to suppertime and the meal she'd shared with father and daughter, and smiled. Royal Justice was something else. At first glance, he gave the appearance of a big, tough cowboy. But she'd seen firsthand how easy his child could turn him to mush. Before the meal had started, the girl had let her cat in the house and smuggled it under the dining room table. It had been all Angel could do not to laugh. But when the cat, whose name she learned was Flea Bit, made the mistake of climbing up Royal's leg, Maddie's secret was out.

Royal let slip a mouthful of curses that even Angel hadn't heard as he calmly tossed the cat out the door. He'd given Maddie a hard, waiting stare, which she met with innocent silence. Angel lost it. Laughter bubbled up and out of her like a welling spring, surprising herself as well as Royal and Maddie. After that, the tension passed.

Angel sighed and rolled over on her back to stare at the ceiling. A faint glow of yellow from the night-light in the hall shone under the door to her room. She thought of the little girl sound asleep in her room down the hall, securely bundled within the confines of her favorite blanket. She couldn't imagine what it was like to feel that safe or that loved. Royal Justice was the king of his world, and Maddie was princess of it all.

Just for a moment, Angel let herself pretend she belonged in this place—with this man and his child—and then she snorted softly and discarded the thought. That sort of thinking was dangerous for a woman with no roots.

She focused on the sound of the rain pelting against the roof and gave a quick prayer of thanksgiving that she was sheltered, if only for the night. Soon she was sound asleep.

Hours later, she awoke to what sounded like an explosion followed by a roll of thunder so loud it rattled the panes of glass in the windows. She sat up in bed, her heart pounding wildly, and noticed that the light in the hall was out. But what panicked her more was the distinct scent of smoke in the air.

Instinctively, she reached for her clothes, too late remembering they were still in the dryer. The only thing she had on was a threadbare nightshirt that barely reached her knees. Before she could think what to do, she heard a child's terrified shriek. Her lack of clothes was forgotten as she bolted from bed and dashed into the hall.

She found herself up against Royal's broad, bare chest as he, too, came out of his room on the run. There was no time for embarrassment or apologies as they collided.

"Sorry," Royal said quickly, and grabbed her to keep from falling.

"What happened?" she gasped.

"That was lightning. Wait here."

She did as she was told, watching as he ran down the hall toward the sound of his daughter's cries. Seconds later, he emerged from Maddie's room, cradling his sobbing daughter against his chest.

Even though the house was in darkness, Angel could see enough to know that Royal was torn between fatherhood and responsibility to his property. The scent of something burning was still in the air. Obviously he needed to check on the house, but he didn't want to leave Maddie alone. Impulsively, Angel held out her hands.

"Give her to me."

Royal hesitated only briefly, then thrust Maddie into her arms.

"Here, baby, you stay with Angel while I check on some things. I'll be right back."

Maddie went without argument, clinging to Angel in trembling desperation and burying her face against Angel's neck.

"I'm scared," she sobbed.

"Me, too, sweetheart," Angel said, holding the small child tight. "But your daddy is big and strong, and he'll take care of you, just like he always does, right?" She felt the child nodding. "That's good, now let's see if we can find a flashlight or a candle. Do you know where the candles are?"

Another shaft of lightning shattered the darkness of the night. Angel flinched, but Maddie seemed calmer now that she had something on which to focus.

"There's a flashlight and some candles in the kitchen drawer under the phone."

"You show me," Angel said, and still holding the little girl in her arms, she made her way through the house to the kitchen.

"There," Maddie said, pointing to a cabinet drawer in the right-hand corner of the room.

Within a couple of minutes, the room was bathed in candle-light and the psychedelic pattern of a waving flashlight as Maddie aimed it about the room. The kitchen chair was cold against Angel's legs as she cuddled Maddie in her lap. Another roll of thunder rippled overhead, and she flinched, thinking of the man who'd run out in the storm. She pulled the child closer to her breasts.

"Are you cold, honey?"

Secure beneath her blanket, Maddie shook her head and snuggled closer.

The small child's trust was daunting. As she held her, the fragility of her body and the life that was just unfolding made her remember things she'd spent years trying to forget. She closed her eyes and rested her chin on the top of Maddie's head, thinking back to the time when she'd been four years old. If only she'd had a father like Royal, her life would have been different.

Her jaw clenched as she shook off the thought. Retrospection was not part of her makeup. She was practical, independent and more than a little antagonistic when it came to strange men. And she had not given motherhood much thought. Yet here she was, in a strange man's house, sheltering his child and wondering if the house was in danger of burning down around them. At that moment she knew that, given a chance, she would be good at the job.

She shivered as another gust of wind splattered rain against the windows. Even if lightning had hit the house, surely it would not burn in this weather.

The back door flew open and Royal ran inside, then slammed the door shut behind him.

Startled, Angel instinctively wrapped Maddie in a protective hold, and that was the way Royal saw his daughter—bathed in candlelight, swaddled in her blanket and a strange woman's arms. Breath caught in the back of his throat as he froze, stunned by the tranquility of the scene. He focused on the soft yellow halo of light behind them, and the thought crossed his mind that right now, Angel could very easily pass as a heavenly being. Then she spoke, and the moment was gone.

"Is everything okay? The house, is it...?"

Royal shook his head. "Everything's okay out there. I'm going into the attic to check on the wiring just to make sure."

Maddie frowned. "Make sure of what, Daddy?"

Royal hesitated. Lying to his daughter was not something he did, but at her age, she was still on a need-to-know basis.

"Oh, just to make sure that the storm didn't break any windows. We wouldn't want our Christmas decorations getting rained on, would we?"

A deep frown settled between her eyes. Christmas was her favorite holiday.

"Is it okay if we go back to bed?" Angel asked. "I think she's getting cold."

Royal nodded. "I'll put her to bed just as soon as I get back."

"I'll do it," Angel offered, and then felt as if she'd stepped over a line. "If you don't mind, that is."

The beam of the flashlight Maddie was holding suddenly stilled. Her voice shook.

"I don't want to go to bed in my room."

Royal cupped her cheek, tilting her face to his as he leaned down.

"You can sleep with me just as soon as I get back, okay, baby?"

She nodded and relaxed.

Royal's gaze slipped from his daughter's face to Angel. Her eyes were wide with unasked questions, but to his surprise, she didn't voice one. Her composure surprised him. She was the first woman he'd ever known who hadn't let loose with a barrage of questions in a situation like this.

"I won't be long," he said quietly.

Angel felt herself drowning in blue and then blinked. The notion passed, and Royal left. She shook off the feeling of lassitude and stood, still holding Maddie in her arms.

"Come on, sweetie, it's time to get some sleep."

Maddie sighed, but for once didn't argue. She bunched her

blanket beneath her chin and laid her head on Angel's shoulder. By the time Angel laid her in Royal's bed, her eyes were closed, but she still clutched Angel's hand.

"Don't go till my daddy gets back," Maddie begged.

Angel hesitated. It made her more than a little uncomfortable to be in the man's room, let alone sitting on the edge of his bed. Even if he wasn't in it, his presence was impossible to ignore. The covers were thrown back, indicative of his hasty exit, and the pillow still held the indentation from his head. But the little girl's plea was impossible to ignore.

"Okay," she said softly. "Now close your eyes."

Maddie did as she was told, but moments later another bolt of lightning hit the ground somewhere between the house and the barns. Maddie shrieked and began to cry.

Angel slid into bed and wrapped her arms around her, shushing her as she cuddled her close.

"You're safe, little girl. You're as safe as you can be. Feel my arms around you, holding you tight?"

Maddie shuddered on a sob, but nodded.

"I promise I won't let you go until your daddy comes back, okay?"

"Okay," Maddie whispered, and scooted as close as she could get.

Angel smiled and pulled the little girl into the curve of her body. Above their heads she could hear the soft thump, thump of footsteps as Royal moved about the attic. Secure that someone else was taking care of business, Angel closed her eyes. Just to let them rest. Just until he got back.

And that was how Royal found them—wrapped in each other's arms and sound asleep in the middle of his bed. He didn't move and he couldn't speak. All he could do was stare at the image before him.

The woman's long black hair spilled across his pillow. His child lay within the shelter of her arms. Emotion hit him without warning, like a kick to the gut. He reached for the door facing, using it as a brace to steady his knees.

This was what it would have been like had his wife, Susan, not died. Tears burned the back of his throat. Was it the absence of a woman in her life that had caused Maddie's dreams? Could the yearning have been so strong that it had caused her to imagine the lady on her bed? And even if that was so, how did that explain the promise of an angel or of her arrival into their midst?

Royal drew a deep breath and stepped inside, staying only long enough to pull the covers over both of them. He couldn't look at the woman without wanting to stare, and he wouldn't let himself linger over Maddie for fear that he'd wake them both up. He paused in the doorway, looking back one last time before he closed the door.

The storm passed. Clouds were moving across the full face of the moon, dragging dark shadows along the moonlit ground as they blew. The sleepers were bathed in the luminescence of a heavenly glow, and for a moment, Royal could almost believe Maddie's claim of an angel come to earth. But then he shook off the notion and walked out of the room.

Angel woke up before dawn. The presence of a warm body beside her was startling, but only for a moment. She looked into the sleeping face of Royal Justice's daughter and remembered. She'd spent the entire night in Royal's bed.

This was just great. The thought of that man watching her sleep was unnerving. There was something about his unblinking stare that made her want to turn tail and run. It wasn't as if she was afraid of him. Angel wasn't afraid of anyone. She amended the thought. Except that man in the black truck.

Maddie sighed in her sleep. Resisting the urge to kiss her soft cheek, Angel pulled the covers over her bare legs and slipped out of bed, careful not to wake Maddie up.

For a moment, she stared around the room, searching for clues to the personality of the man who slept here. Nothing seemed obvious. It was large enough to accommodate the king-size bed. Except for an oversize picture of Maddie over the headboard, the walls were white and bare. But for a small wagon full of wooden blocks and a pink feather boa wrapped around the wheels, it was neat and orderly, just like the man who slept here.

She shuddered, as if coming out of a trance, and headed for the door. She needed to get her clothes and get herself packed. If she was lucky, she might make Dallas before noon.

She moved through the rooms on bare feet, pulling at the hem of her nightshirt and hurrying as she neared the kitchen. Never had she felt as vulnerable as she did right now. Only a few more steps and she would retrieve her clothes. Dressed, she could face anything—even the man in whose bed she'd slept.

Chapter 5

Royal was making peanut butter and jelly sandwiches when Angel entered the kitchen. She groaned. It had been too much to hope she would be the only one up. It had been bad enough last night to face the man in this threadbare nightshirt, but in the early morning light, she might as well have been naked.

"I'm just going to the dryer to get my clothes," she muttered, and darted toward the utility room.

"The electricity went off before they got dry," he said.

His announcement stopped her cold. She rolled her eyes, then folded her arms across her breasts as she turned to face him.

"Then I'll have to wear them wet. I can't leave looking like this. Besides, they'll probably be wet again before the day is over."

Royal frowned. For some reason, the thought of her out on a highway at the mercy of strangers made him angry. And then he reminded himself they were strangers to each other. She was a grown woman. She didn't need anyone to take care of her. He dropped a spoonful of grape jelly on a layer of peanut butter and smeared it around the slice of bread.

Angel watched in fascination, admiring the way the filling clung to the bread and wondering where he'd spent the night.

"Um, last night, the lightning...was anything damaged?"

"No, we were fortunate, but the phones are still out and so's the power," he answered.

She nodded and tried to think of something else to say.

"Mr. Justice..."

"Royal," he corrected.

Slightly embarrassed, she felt the need to apologize. "I didn't mean to fall asleep last night. Why didn't you wake me?"

He kept spreading jam. "It was late. You and Maddie were sound asleep. I didn't see the need."

"But I was in your bed."

He stopped and looked up. "And I was in yours."

The intimacy of that statement hit them at the same time, and neither moved or spoke. Royal was the first to break eye contact, and he did it by slapping a slice of bread on top of his gourmet creation and sliding it onto a plate.

"Since the power's out, this is going to have to serve as breakfast." He grinned. "Maddie won't care. Except for her uncle Roman's pancakes, this is her favorite breakfast, anyway."

It was his smile that did it. It changed everything about him in a way Angel hadn't expected. Just for a second she saw the boy he'd been and probably the man he could be with someone he loved, and she knew a swift moment of fear.

"I hate to ask, but I need something to wear," she said.

"I laid some things out in your room," he said shortly. "Wear whatever suits you until your own things are dry."

"But I thought you said the power was out," Angel said.

"It is."

"Then what..."

Royal interrupted. His voice was low and angry. "It's some

of my stuff, damn it. Just get dressed.'' He stabbed the knife into the jar of peanut butter and reached for another slice of bread. ''I think better when there's more between us than a few cotton threads.''

Stunned, Angel alternated between punching him in the nose and laughing in his face. But then he looked up. Their gazes met and held. She was the one who broke. She bolted from the room as Royal dropped the knife into the jar of peanut butter and stomped out the back door onto the porch. There was a smear of peanut butter on the end of his thumb. He sucked it off as he stepped off the porch, intent on checking on the animals, when he heard a car coming down the driveway. It was Roman, probably coming to satisfy himself they had not blown away in last night's storm.

''Great,'' he muttered, thinking of what Roman would make of the half-naked stranger in his house.

''Hey,'' Roman called, as he got out of the car. ''I tried to call. Your phones are out.''

Royal nodded. ''I know. So is the power.''

Roman's gaze raked the familiar lines of their old family home. ''Everything okay in there?''

Royal snorted. ''About as good as could be expected,'' he muttered.

''What did you say?'' Roman asked.

''Nothing,'' Royal said, and jammed his hands in his pockets.

Roman's eyes narrowed thoughtfully. Of all the Justice brothers, Royal was the most open with his thoughts. There was something going on Roman didn't understand. Royal was the kind of man who cursed when he was angry and laughed when he was glad. He wasn't given to hints, yet Roman would swear his brother was hiding something.

''Maddie all right?'' he asked.

''Maddie's fine,'' Royal answered.

''No more visions of ladies and angels?''

Royal resisted the urge to roll his eyes. "Not anymore," he growled.

"Uncle Roman!"

Both men turned at the childish screech of delight. Roman grinned and held out his arms as Maddie bounded toward him. He caught her in midjump and swung her against his chest, nuzzling her neck and stealing kisses along the side of her cheek. Her giggles of delight brought smiles to both men's faces, but the smiles slid sideways when the back door opened again.

Royal groaned and gritted his teeth as Angel came out on the porch. She was wearing one of his T-shirts and a pair of his sweatpants. Everything was too long and too big. She should have looked like an orphan. Instead, those dark, bedroom eyes were wide and questioning, and her long, black hair was mussed and hanging to the middle of her back. She had the look of a woman who'd spent the night in a willing man's bed. Royal cast a quick glance at Roman and then looked away. Technically, that was exactly what had happened. The only problem was, the willing man had been sleeping elsewhere.

Roman glanced at Maddie, unconsciously tightening his hold in a protective gesture as he looked over her head at his brother.

"I don't believe I've had the pleasure," he drawled.

Royal's jaw clenched. Roman's sarcasm was too thick to stir.

"That's my angel!" Maddie shrieked, and wiggled to be put down.

Roman let her go, not because he wanted to but because she'd given him no option. To his shock, she ran and anchored herself to the woman's leg.

"She's going to be our keeper," Maddie said, smiling at Angel.

Angel cast a nervous look at Maddie's father and shrugged as she bent to pick Maddie up. This was his daughter, his problem. If he wanted to explain, it was his prerogative.

Royal frowned. He should have known Maddie wouldn't be happy to settle for one night.

"Roman, this is Angel Rojas. Angel, my brother, Roman."
Roman tipped his hat without smiling. "Miss Rojas."

She met his cool stare with one of her own. "Mr. Justice."

Maddie's next innocent remark only added to the furor. "We found her in the rain!" she said. "She came, just like the lady said she would."

Roman's eyes widened in disbelief as he turned to Royal. "You *found* her in the rain?"

Angel was tired and uncomfortable, and thanks to Fat Louie and that nut who'd been following her, she was pretty much fed up with men in general. The fact that Royal's brother kept looking at her as if she was a bug in need of squashing was the last straw.

"I wasn't lost," Angel snapped. "I was hitchhiking. They offered me a ride. The rest of this stuff about angels is over my head."

Her unexpected anger silenced whatever Roman had planned to say.

"But your name…"

"Is really Angel. Angel Maria Conchita Rojas, to be precise. I was born in Las Vegas. My mother died when I was small. I was raised in foster homes. I owe no man and no man owns me. And, as soon as my clothes are dry, I'm out of here."

Roman had the grace to blush. "Look, Miss, I didn't mean to—"

"Yes, you did," Angel snapped, then she looked at Royal. "I came out to tell you that the power is on. As soon as my clothes are dry, I will be out of your hair."

"No!" Maddie shrieked, and wrapped her arms around Angel's neck. "You can't leave! You can't leave! The lady promised you would stay and take care of me." She started to sob.

The words tugged at Angel's heart. In her anger, she'd forgotten to temper her words for the little girl's sake.

"But sweetheart, I told you yesterday that your daddy can't just hire a stranger to take care of you. He loves you more than anything in this world, and he would want only the best for you.''

''You're not a stranger to me,'' Maddie sobbed. ''I saw you in my dreams. I have pictures of you. Wait here. I'll show you.''

She wiggled out of Angel's arms and dashed into the house. Angel glared at Roman without speaking while Royal shoved his hand through his hair in an angry gesture of defeat.

''This is one hell of a mess,'' he growled.

''It's none of my business,'' Angel said, ''but I'd watch my language if I were you. Especially around Maddie.''

Royal's face turned an angry red as Roman grinned. To his surprise, Roman found himself liking this woman for no other reason than her spunk.

Before anything else could be said, Maddie came running. The screen door hit the wall with a bang as she shoved a handful of pictures into Angel's hands.

''See! See? I knew you! I knew you!''

Angel glanced at the pictures, a little surprised to see that Maddie's childish drawings depicted what could only be described as a dark angel. Most people, and especially children, thought of angels having blond hair and long white robes. This angel had brown skin and long black hair. Angel frowned as she looked at them. One picture had the angel wearing braids. That was the way she most often wore her hair. She glanced at Royal, surprised by the understanding on his face.

''Well,'' she said softly.

He nodded.

''This is my favorite,'' Maddie said, pulling one out of the stack Angel was holding.

Angel smiled as she looked, then she gasped. The smile froze on her face. Her hands started to shake. Without thinking, she dropped to her knees and pulled Maddie close.

''Oh, my, little girl. Oh, my.''

Maddie looked at her father. ''See, Daddy. She likes my drawings a lot.''

Angel stared at the child, unable to tear her gaze away. It wasn't that she didn't believe such things were possible, but she'd never expected to be part of such a miracle. And a miracle it was. She hugged Maddie gently, then got to her feet, handing the drawing to Royal without explanation.

"Wait here," she said, then took Maddie by the hand and went into the house.

Roman moved closer to look at the drawing Royal was holding. On one side of the page was the figure Maddie called the lady. She was the same in every picture. A woman wearing a long blue dress. On the other side was the figure Maddie called her angel. She was barefoot. Her long black hair was loose around her face, not in braids as in most of the other pictures, and she was wearing a bright pink dress with blue and green decorations around the bottom.

"What?" Roman asked.

"Don't ask me," Royal muttered. "I haven't been in control since yesterday when we were coming back from town. It was raining like hell. I saw a hitchhiker. Didn't even know it was a woman. Before I could pass her, Maddie was screaming for me to stop. I kept on driving. Maddie got hysterical, begging for me to go back. She said it was her angel, the one the lady said would come."

Roman inhaled slowly as the skin crawled on the back of his neck.

"Damn."

Royal grimaced. "You have no idea. Before I knew it, she was in the cab and Maddie was crawling all over her."

Roman's eyes widened. "Maddie doesn't like strangers."

"You forget," Royal drawled. "Maddie claims she's not a stranger. And then there's her name. Hell, when she told me it was Angel, I got a knot in my stomach that still hasn't gone away. While I was trying to think what to say, Maddie went berserk. The next thing I knew, I was inviting her to spend the night. At least until the rain had stopped."

Roman shook his head. "Man, Royal, what are you going to—"

The back door opened, and he never finished his question as Maddie and Angel came out hand in hand.

"Look, Daddy. Now do you believe me?"

Royal stared. First at the woman standing before him, then at the picture, then up again.

"It's still a little damp and needs a good ironing, but you get the picture," Angel said softly, as she smoothed the dress she had taken out of the dryer and slipped on.

Royal was stunned. "Oh, Lord," he whispered.

"Oh, Lord is right," Angel said. "I'm beginning to think He had something to do with this after all." She squeezed Maddie's hand as she continued. "I bought this dress with the first money I ever earned." Before either man could respond, she added, "It was honest work."

Roman couldn't think what to say. There was no disputing the fact that the pink dress she was wearing was old and fading, but the wide band of blue and green embroidery around the hem of the skirt was impossible to mistake. With her hair around her face and her feet brown and bare, she was the angel in Maddie's drawing come to life.

Royal looked at the drawing and then at Angel, shaking his head in disbelief.

"How?" he muttered.

She shrugged. "Ask your daughter. She seems tuned in to what's happening."

Maddie beamed. She didn't really understand everything that was being said, but she sensed her father's capitulation.

"Angel is going to be our new keeper, isn't she, Daddy?"

Royal didn't know how to answer. Common sense told him this might be the most foolish thing he'd ever done, but instinct was leading him in another direction. He didn't understand a damn thing that was going on, but in his gut, it felt right. He took a deep breath and then stared Angel Rojas straight in the face.

"Are you interested in the job?" he asked.

Angel's chin lifted defiantly. "Are you offering?"

Royal almost grinned. Damned if he didn't like her spunk.

Roman couldn't remain silent. Ever the private investigator, he interjected, "What about references?"

Angel's stare hardened as her gaze moved to Royal's brother. It was all she could do to keep her voice civil.

"Well, shoot," she drawled. "I must have left my résumé in my other pocket. However, I can give you names and places of where I've worked. You can call any or all of them about me."

Royal interrupted Roman before he could answer. "This is my daughter, my house, my business," he said shortly. "If there's any calling to be done, I'll be the one doing it."

Roman recognized the anger and authority in his brother's voice and took a mental step back.

"Well, now," he said softly, looking at Maddie. "I think it's time I went back to work. Come here, Little Bit, and give me a goodbye kiss."

Maddie giggled as Roman lifted her and swung her around before kissing her soundly on the cheek. Then he nodded to his brother and started toward his car. Just before he got inside, he paused and turned, as if he'd forgotten something.

To Angel's surprise, he was almost grinning as he tipped his hat to her.

"What was that all about?" she asked Royal as Roman drove away.

Royal gave her a long, considering look. "That was my brother's way of butting out of my business."

She nodded and then gave Royal a cool stare. "So, do you want those names and phone numbers or not?"

"Yes, I suppose I do."

His answer was just shy of rude, and Angel could have taken affront, but she chose to consider the source. Royal Justice seemed to be a man who made his own rules, and that she understood.

"I need a pen and some paper," she said.

"I'll get them!" Maddie cried, and bolted into the house, leaving Angel and Royal alone on the porch.

"Do you know what you're doing?" Angel asked.

A muscle jerked at the side of Royal's jaw. "Hell, no."

"Then why do it?" Angel asked.

Royal almost grinned. "I learned a long time ago that when it comes to dealing with women, I don't have to understand. I just follow my instincts."

His answer surprised her, and because she sensed it was an honest one, it compelled her to answer in kind.

"Look, Mr. Justice..."

"Royal," he corrected.

She took a deep breath. "Royal."

He nodded.

"As I was going to say...I am overwhelmed by your daughter's insight, and I promise I will not deceive you or let Maddie down. If the time comes when I think I should go, I'll tell you."

For a moment, Royal was silent. Finally, he nodded.

"Fair enough," he said. Then his features hardened. "But I warn you, mess with what's mine and you'll be worse than sorry."

A shiver slid down the middle of Angel's back. "Fair enough," she echoed.

Royal shifted, then headed for the house. "So, let's go see where Maddie has gone. If she found the peanut butter and jelly sandwiches, she's already forgotten what she went inside to do."

The city limits of Abilene were dead ahead when Tommy Boy Watson began to slow down. He'd been driving almost nonstop since passing through Dallas and points west. He'd seen the inside of more truck stop cafés than he cared to think about, and still no sign of that dark-haired whore. He had the beginnings of a headache, and his butt was numb from sitting so long in one place. His left leg, which he'd broken some years back, was aching in the place where it had healed. He hated to admit it, but he was going to give up the search. He kept telling himself it would be all right. That there were plenty of others like her out here on the highways for him to take out. Thanks to his efforts, the population of highway hookers was already down. Eight less, to be exact. He wiped his nose with the back of his sleeve and grinned.

And he was just getting started.

Ahead, the familiar sight of a Texas highway patrol car was visible. Tommy Boy admired cops. He often dreamed of being one. To Tommy Boy, there was power in packing a gun. He liked the look of bulletproof vests beneath their starched uniforms, thinking it gave them the appearance of wearing armor, like the knights of old.

He tipped his hat as he passed the parked patrol car. To his delight, the trooper nodded. Although the connection they'd made was impersonal, he was still grinning when he pulled into the parking lot of a small motel. In his mind, their occupations were similar. The police protected the public from criminals. Tommy Boy protected innocent men from the wiles of evil women.

All he needed was some food in his belly and a good night's rest. That would put that damned black-haired witch out of his mind once and for all. Besides, there were plenty of whores still left who needed cleansing.

Having decided on a plan of action, Tommy Boy paid for his room and strolled across the parking lot to a nearby café. To his delight, when he got inside, he saw two troopers sitting in a booth, eating their meal. Their clean-cut appearances and steely-eyed gazes gave him a sense of well-being. He shifted his stride to a swagger and nodded and smiled as he passed them by, then took a seat where he could watch them eat. Although he admired them, he also felt a sense of superiority. To his knowledge, only four of the eight women he'd killed had been found, and there wasn't a single clue pointing to him.

There sat those cops, dressed to shine and legally packing, and they still had no idea they were within spitting distance of the man responsible. He grinned.

"What'll it be, mister?"

Tommy Boy looked up as the waitress slid a glass of water in front of him.

"What's good?" he asked.

"Me, if you're lucky," she drawled, and then giggled.

His hackles rose. Another pushy woman. Weren't there any decent women left in this world?

"I'll have a burger and fries and coffee. Plenty of coffee," he said shortly.

The waitress shrugged and walked away.

"Bitch," he muttered. Moments later she was back. She poured his coffee without comment and slipped away as quietly as she'd come.

His food came, and he ate it without relish, merely fueling his body. He gave the waitress another glance as he paid for his food, but she didn't bother to meet his gaze. He shrugged. It was just as well. He wasn't in the mood for cleansing. Not tonight. He craved sleep, not justice.

As he strolled across the parking lot to his room, he prayed that the night would be his and his alone. He didn't need any visions from Daddy. Daddy had to understand. He was doing his best. He was keeping his promise. It was all he could do.

Chapter 6

Royal stared at the list Angel Rojas had given him, taking careful note of each job she'd held. The dates went back as far as eight years, and he had yet to find a person who had anything but good to say about her. And yet each time he'd asked why she left their employ, none of them could give a clear answer.

It would seem that there was a bit of Gypsy in Maddie's angel, and he didn't like that. He didn't want to set Maddie up to get hurt. How would Maddie react if, one day, the angel up and flew the proverbial coop?

He looked at the list again. There was a discrepancy in the time frame. The two-year gap between her last job, at a sheriff's office in West Virginia, and her presence at his ranch bothered him.

The sound of laughter caught his attention, and he glanced out the office window. Maddie was in the porch swing, lying on her stomach and trailing a piece of rope between the slats, while Flea Bit did body flips trying to catch the frayed end.

Royal grinned, admitting only to himself that the damned cat did have its moments.

Then he remembered the list. Before he gave Angel the go-ahead to hang up her clothes in his house, he needed some answers. Two years was a long time to have been out of work. There were too many things that could have occupied her time. She could have been married...or living with a man. He frowned again, letting his mind wander into all the possibilities as to why a relationship fails. But he was guessing. It didn't have to be a man. For all he knew, she could have been in jail.

Angel's clothes were clean and dry and spread out on the bed. She didn't know whether to put them in her bag or hang them in the closet. Everything hinged upon the final nod from Royal Justice. She'd given him the list of her past employers over two hours ago. He'd taken it without comment and disappeared into his office. Now she waited.

It surprised her to realize how much she would really like to stay, but she'd learned years ago to do without things she couldn't have. Part of her had to admit that in spite of Maddie Justice's dreams, maybe this wasn't meant to be. Maybe Royal Justice would think she wasn't capable of caring for his daughter. She didn't have any experience in child care, but Angel didn't see that as a problem. Maddie was not a baby, she was a little girl—and Angel was a big girl. Somewhere within that concept there had to be common ground.

She stood with her arms crossed and her face blank, waiting for a man she didn't know to pass judgment on her past.

She stared out the window at the vast array of grassland that was the Justice ranch. Horses dotted the landscape, as did a herd of cattle on a distant hillside. The outbuildings were painted. The corral was in top repair. From where she was standing, there wasn't a single thing Royal Justice had left undone. He was a man in control of his world.

Then she thought of his child. Whatever had driven Maddie Justice to this moment was beyond his control. And Angel knew that scared him. She'd seen it in his eyes. The uncertainty, the lack of understanding for a child who had visions. In a way, she sympathized. For a man so obviously used to being boss, he was struggling to find his center with a daughter who conjured up angels in dreams. But she had to give him credit. Not many men would have stopped on a highway in a thunderstorm to pick up a stranger, especially on the word of a child.

Impulsively, she turned her back to the window and gazed around the room. It was without frills, but a place in which she could easily become comfortable. And then she sighed. She was past expecting miracles in her life, and even though she was at a loss to explain how Maddie had drawn a picture of her before they'd met, there was a feeling within her that said here was where she belonged. At least for the time being.

Yes, she believed she could come to love the child. As for the work—caring for the house would be simple, easier in fact than a lot of jobs she'd had. But caring for the man? She wasn't sure it was something she could do, or for that matter should do. He was obviously well-to-do, single and far too handsome for his own good. Not, she reminded herself, that she was an easy mark. It had been years since she'd been stupid enough to fall for a good-looking man's lies, and it would be a cold day in hell before it happened again. But that didn't change the fact that she was human—and lonely. As lonely as a woman could be.

Then a knock sounded at the door, and her thoughts scattered. She dropped her arms to her sides and lifted her chin, as if bracing herself for a blow.

"Come in."

Royal opened the door.

"Got a minute?" he asked. "There's something I want to ask you about your list of references."

"Ask away," she said. "I told you before, I have nothing to hide."

Royal leaned against the doorjamb, trying to find a tactful

way to ask what amounted to a personal question. He reminded himself his daughter's welfare was at stake, took a deep breath and let go.

"So far, everything checks out," he said.

Angel exhaled slowly, unaware until he said it that she'd been holding her breath. But he stood staring at her with that cold, blue gaze.

"Why do I feel like you left out a but?"

Royal thrust the list in her hands. "You tell me."

She looked at it, frowning. "Tell you what?"

"Have you ever been married?"

Her eyebrows arched in surprise, but she answered without hesitation.

"No."

He glanced at the list, then at her. "The last name on this list is for a county sheriff in West Virginia."

She didn't see where he was going. "That's true. So?"

"So that was two years ago. What have you been doing since?"

Understanding dawned. Her attitude shifted from accommodating to defiant within seconds.

"Working at a place called Fat Louie's in Tuscaloosa, Alabama."

Royal frowned. "Then why didn't you put the owner's name and number on the list?"

"Because the only recommendation that bastard would give me is to go straight to hell."

Royal arched his eyebrows and remained silent, waiting for her to continue.

"Don't you want to know why?" Angel asked.

"Do I need to?" he asked.

Angel laughed, but it was a harsh, ugly sound that made the hair on the back of Royal's arms stand up.

"Who knows what men need?" she said, then she sighed and shoved her hands through her hair, combing the thick, dark

lengths from her face. "Sorry," she muttered. "He's a bastard."

"What happened?"

Angel gave Royal a long, considering look. "Why don't you
call him and ask? I'd be curious to know how he explains the
fact that I left him rolling on the floor with his hands between
his legs."

Shock swept through Royal, followed by a rage he hadn't
expected. He kept staring at her, imagining her fending off the
unwanted advances of some unknown man, and the thought
made him sick.

"Why?" he asked.

Angel closed her eyes, picturing the endless months of fending off her boss's unwelcome advances. When she looked at
Royal, there was a truth on her face that he couldn't ignore.

"Because I got sick and tired of getting caught in corners.
Every time I turned around he was grabbing at me, running his
big fat hands all over my body and making innuendos about
what it would take for me to keep my job."

Royal's anger shifted to a darker, deeper place. "Did
he—?"

Angel's face was devoid of expression. "I believe they call
it sexual harassment. I called it quits. He crossed a line. I put
him on the floor."

"But why didn't you press charges?" Royal asked.

She snorted beneath her breath. "And who would believe
me? Despite reports to the opposite, don't you know that it's
always the woman's fault for leading the poor man on? Besides, people look at me and think wetback. It doesn't matter
that I was born in Nevada. My skin is not lily-white. My eyes
are dark, my hair is black. I have no family—no permanent
home. I might as well have *illegal* tattooed on my forehead.
People like me rarely find justice in a white man's world."

Royal's face was flushed with anger. "Wait here," he said
shortly. "I won't be long."

Before Angel could speak, he was gone. She dropped to the

corner of the bed and closed her eyes. Wait here? Where else could she go?

A few minutes later Royal blindly punched in the numbers the long-distance operator had given him, trying to picture what a man named Fat Louie would look like. When the phone began to ring, he took a deep breath and tightened his grip on the receiver. A few seconds later, a man's voice rumbled in his ear. It sounded thick and harsh from lack of sleep or too much of something from the night before.

"Fat Louie's," the man said.

"I need to speak to the owner," Royal countered.

"That's me," Louie muttered. "Who's asking?"

Royal stilled. Had the men been face to face, Fat Louie Tureau would have known to back off. But they weren't, and the anonymity of a stranger's voice wasn't enough warning for Louie to hold his tongue.

"Royal Justice. I'm calling about a woman named Angel Rojas. I understand she used to work for you."

A string of profanity, coupled with a harsh cigarette hack, reverberated in Royal's ear. About the only distinguishable words he heard were "the bitch" and "her kind."

Although Royal narrowed his eyes, his voice remained calm. "Exactly what do you mean by…her kind?" he asked.

Fat Louie spit. Royal heard the sound and almost hung up right then. Even if Angel had been lying through her teeth, this man was offensive enough to terminate the conversation. Still, Royal had Maddie to consider. He waited.

"Damn wetback," Louie growled. "Do 'em a favor and they just up and quit on you."

"I wasn't under the impression that she's an illegal."

"Well, maybe not," Louie muttered. "But it don't hardly matter. She's still a Mex, and she quit without notice."

Royal had known plenty of bigots in his life, and without ever having laid eyes on this man, Fat Louie from Tuscaloosa, Alabama, was about to win the prize.

"Did she give a reason she terminated her employment?" Royal asked.

There was a pause.

It was enough for Royal. And when Fat Louie suddenly came back with a question instead of an answer, Royal knew she'd been telling the truth.

"What did *she* say?" Louie asked.

The corner of Royal's mouth turned upward just a little. "That she left you rolling on the floor and holding your crotch. Is that true?"

Another string of curses erupted. It was all Royal needed to hear. Without waiting for Fat Louie Tureau to answer, he hung up the phone and stalked out of the office. He went to her room and stood in the doorway. He glanced at her clothes laid out on the bed and then at the expression on her face.

"Do you have enough hangers?" he asked.

Her shoulders slumped, but only slightly, as if giving herself permission to relax. She glanced at the bed and then at the open closet door.

"Yes, I believe that I do."

He nodded. "Good. As soon as you get your things hung up, why don't you meet me outside? I'll walk you over the place. You need to know where things are located, especially Maddie's favorite hiding places. And we can talk money and days off then."

The urge to giggle was strong, but Angel nodded, waiting until Royal had walked away before allowing herself a small smile.

Royal wasn't as easy in his mind about what he'd just done as Angel had been in accepting it. All he could think as he walked outside to where his daughter was playing was that he hoped to God he wouldn't live to regret this.

Tommy Boy Watson pulled off the blacktop onto the graveled shoulder and got out. He stretched lazily then tilted his head to gaze at the stars. They were thick and bright: tiny pinpoints of white, blinking lights on a blanket of black velvet. The air was warm and humid. His blue and white striped shirt clung to his body like wet tissue paper to the side of a glass. But he didn't care about comfort. He didn't care about anything except that he was all right with the world.

A few miles north, the horizon was aglow from the lights of Abilene. He'd never been to Abilene before, but he was headed there. His belly growled, and he remembered he hadn't eaten a bite since early this morning. He rubbed a hand over his face, wincing at the two-day growth of whiskers. Tonight he'd get himself a room, then a steak. A great big steak. Sleeping in his truck was okay now and then, but tonight he was celebrating. Tonight he would shower and shave and sleep in a real bed. Tommy Boy liked a clean shave.

Somewhere to his right he heard a calf bawl, and he jumped. Then a few moments later a cow answered. He relaxed. No big deal, just a calf that had lost its mother. He shook a cigarette out of the pack in his pocket and lit one up, savoring the night, the silence and his smoke. When he was finished, he dropped the stub into the dirt, then ground it out with the toe of his boot until it was indistinguishable. He turned toward his pickup truck. It was time to get to business.

He let down the tailgate and pulled the tarp-wrapped body onto the ground as if it was so much trash. With a few quick tugs on the tarp, the lifeless body of Carol Jo Belmont, late of the Big Wheel Truck Stop, rolled into the ditch.

Anxious to be on his way, he folded the tarp and laid it in his truck, weighting it down with his spare tire to keep it from blowing away. He would need it again, of that he was certain. A few minutes later, he pulled onto the blacktop and drove away without looking back. By the time he'd reached the city limits, he was exhausted. But it was a good exhaustion. The kind that comes from knowing you've done a good day's work. He smiled. His daddy would have been proud.

By the time a week had passed, the trio at the ranch had settled into their routine. After a couple of days of hovering around the ranch house making certain Angel could cope with his daughter's antics, Royal began to relax. It would seem that Maddie's angel wasn't afraid of work. The house had never been cleaner. And coming in to hot meals, meals he didn't have to cook, and having clean clothes in his closet that he didn't have to wash were blessings he hadn't expected. But there was still the discomfort of living with a stranger.

On the other hand, Maddie had never been happier. And Royal was seeing a change in her he wouldn't have believed. His little tomboy was turning toward things of a feminine nature.

Royal glanced at his watch and cursed beneath his breath. In less than fifteen minutes, he was supposed to have Maddie at Paige Sullivan's birthday party, and he still had to change his clothes. Frowning, he screwed the lid on the bottle of leather cleaner and hung up the bridle he'd been working on. Life with Maddie had been a lot simpler when she was a baby. A female's maturation was difficult enough for a man to handle without all the added social events that seemed to come out of nowhere. Granted, she and Paige had been playmates and friends almost from the day they could toddle, but back then it hadn't been such a big deal. They played together when Royal and Tom, Paige's dad, had business to deal with, and that was that. But in the last year, Maddie had learned how to dial a phone, and to his disgust, so had Paige. At the age of four, Maddie had already been given a five-minute phone curfew. He was beginning to wonder what it would be like when she started school. More friends. More calls. And for a man who understood horses better than he did his own daughter, more worries. He didn't even want to think what his life would be like by the time Maddie was old enough to date. Then he reminded himself to concentrate on the present, and right now he was late for a date with his very best girl.

He entered the utility room, glanced into the kitchen and saw

Maddie and Angel sitting at the kitchen table. Without paying attention to what they were doing, he bent to pull off his dirty boots.

"Hey, peanut, sorry I'm late. Just let me change my shirt and shoes, and we'll be ready to go to Paige's birthday party."

Oblivious to her father's presence, Maddie's gaze was fixed on the still-wet, rose-colored polish gleaming on her nails. She mumbled okay.

Angel looked up. From where she was sitting, she could just see her employer's backside as he bent to pull off his boots. One soft grunt, then another. It would be fair to say her attention wavered.

She bit her lip and looked away, making herself focus on the last two tiny nails she had yet to paint.

"Just another minute and we'll be through," she told Maddie, and smiled at the intent expression on the little girl's face.

Maddie blinked and nodded, but only slightly. Angel's caution to remain still had turned Royal's child into a small, living, breathing statue. The female fascination of having her fingernails painted for the first time in her life had overtaken every outside stimulus. Except, of course, the completion of the project and gloating to her friend, Paige, about the acquisition of an angel.

Unaware that her presence was going to be Maddie's small coup, Angel dipped the brush into the bottle, then pulled it out, carefully removing the excess polish on the lip. Then she took Maddie by the hand and leaned forward, bent on finishing the task they'd started.

Sock-footed, Royal produced almost soundless steps as he entered the kitchen. Whatever he'd been about to say slipped out of his mind. He inhaled slowly, fighting an unexpected surge of tears as an errant thought came and went.

So this is what little girls do when left to their own devices.

Spellbound by the innocent beauty of their profiles as they bent to the task, it was all he could do to breathe. He looked at his daughter and saw her—really saw her—as the individual she was and not an extension of him.

She was wearing a dress he didn't recognize. It took a few moments for him to remember Ryder and Casey had given it to her for Christmas last year. To his chagrin, he realized this was the first time she'd worn it. His conscience pricked.

Her hair was in a braid. That made him feel better. He braided her hair, too. Then he looked closer. This was a fancy braid, with five plaits rather than three. And the ribbon in her hair…it matched the pink and white dots on her dress.

He knew a moment of loss, as if he'd stepped off balance. It was one of the few times in his life he could remember feeling helpless. He narrowed his eyes and shifted his gaze from his daughter to the woman who was holding her hand. Emotion hit him belly first. It was jealousy, pure and simple.

If it had been possible at that moment to turn back time, he would have done it. If only he'd taken a different road home that day in the rain, this wouldn't be happening. This woman wouldn't be giving his daughter things he couldn't. But Maddie looked up, and every selfish thought he'd been having died. He couldn't remember ever seeing such joy in her eyes.

"Daddy, look! Angel is painting my fingernails. I'm going to be so beautiful."

He shook his head as if coming out of a trance. And when he bent to kiss the top of her head, the smile on his face was only a little bit sad.

"You already are," he said softly. "Now hold that smile. I'll be right back." He started out of the room, then stopped. As difficult as it was to say, there was something he had to get said. "Hey, Angel."

She looked up.

"Thanks."

"For what?" she asked.

He cocked his head toward his daughter. "For that."

"It is nothing," she said quietly.

"Not to her," he said.

Angel could feel the power of his gaze even after he was gone. There was something in his eyes she kept dodging—a message she wasn't sure she should read. She screwed the lid on the polish and leaned back in her chair.

Lonely. That was what she'd seen. Royal Justice was just possibly the loneliest man she'd ever met. Although he had the love of his family and his daughter, this was a different kind of lonely. The kind that comes from not having anyone to share yourself with.

She wasn't sure he knew it. And if he did, she knew he'd never admit it. But it was there just the same. She knew because every time she looked in the mirror, she saw the same emptiness on her face.

A few minutes later he was back, and the indecision she'd seen in his eyes was gone. The take-charge man was back.

Royal breezed through the kitchen on his way out the door. "Come on, girl, you're gonna be late, and don't forget your present."

Maddie stood like a queen rising from a throne. Her pink and white dress belled around her legs, and the ribbon at the end of her braid was bouncing against the middle of her back.

"You carry it," she solemnly announced, pointing toward a neatly wrapped package. "My nails are still wet."

He stopped, flummoxed by the inability to cope with all this femininity.

"Oh...uh, sure," he muttered, and went to the cabinet to retrieve the present.

Maddie sailed out the door ahead of him as if she was going to war, marching with her head held high and waving her hands in the air to dry them as Angel had shown her.

As Royal was pulling the door shut behind him, he could have sworn he heard a snicker. But when he turned, Angel was busying herself cleaning up the cotton balls and polish.

"We should be back in a couple of hours," he said shortly.

Angel answered without looking up. "Yes, sir."

Royal frowned. "Don't call me sir," he growled.

"All right, Mr. Justice."

His frown deepened. "And don't call me mister, either."

Angel stopped. She knew she'd pushed him enough.

"Okay."

"Okay what?" Royal asked.

Angel flinched. Saying his name, even to herself, seemed too personal. But he was the boss.

"Okay… Royal."

Royal nodded. "Like I said, we won't be too long. Consider the next two hours free time for yourself."

She nodded.

He started out the door and realized she wouldn't know where they'd gone. He couldn't imagine why, but there was the outside possibility that she might need to reach him. But when he looked back, she was gone.

"Daddy! Come open the door for me! I'll mess up my nails," Maddie yelled.

Royal rolled his eyes. "Damnation, Madeline Michelle, you're pushing your luck," he yelled.

A magazine lay half open on the floor where it had fallen from Angel's lap as she'd drifted off to sleep. The digital clock in Royal's bedroom blinked, sending out a new number to indicate the passing of time. Outside, a light breeze blew, cooling the afternoon heat. Down in the barn, Dumpling, the old mamma cat, lay dozing in the hay while her babies nursed and slept. Peace pervaded.

Sonny French took the wrong road home, which was understandable considering the amount of liquor he'd been consuming. It did occur to him to wonder why his driveway had a curve he didn't remember, but by the time his mind had considered the thought, it was too late for him to miss the tree. He hit it head-on, bouncing his truck over a ditch and through the tightly strung wires of a five-strand fence and scattering the herd of cattle that had been grazing there.

It came through the depths of Angel's sleep. First the thud, then a crunching of metal, then the frantic bellows of animals gone wild. She came off the couch in one motion, staring in sleepy confusion and wondering if she'd been dreaming in stereo. But then she realized she could still hear the cows and ran to the window. Even from the house, she could see the crumpled front end of a vehicle jammed through Royal's fence. In the pasture beyond, cattle were bawling and milling in nervous congestion. She didn't recognize the pickup but was relieved to see it wasn't Royal and Maddie.

She ran for the phone, only to discover there were no emergency services in the area and wasted time looking up the police number. To make matters worse, when they asked her for directions to the accident, she realized the only thing she knew to tell them was Royal Justice's ranch. As luck would have it, the dispatcher on duty knew the place well, and promptly dispatched an ambulance and a sheriff.

Angel dropped the phone onto the receiver and dashed out of the house. By the time she got to the wreck, she was in adrenaline overdrive. The driver was slumped over the wheel with blood dripping from his forehead. Smoke poured from the crumpled hood of the truck, but Angel could tell it was steam rather than fire. Unwilling to move him for fear of injuring him more, she turned in a panicked circle, unsure what to do first.

To her dismay, the cattle had run to the opposite end of the pasture and were now coming toward her at a steady walk, curious to see what had invaded their space. She took one look at the length of fence that was down and groaned. She had no idea how to reach Royal and it would be several minutes at best before help arrived.

Panicked, she started toward the break in the fence. An expert on cattle she was not, but the least she could do was try to keep them from getting out until help arrived.

"My head," Sonny groaned.

Angel pivoted. One good thing. At least he was alive. She darted toward the cab.

"Don't move, mister. An ambulance is on the way."

"Don't need no ambulance," Sonny drawled. "Jus' need my bed. My good ol' bed." Then he groaned again and passed out.

Angel's eyes narrowed angrily. She'd seen the empty beer cans in the floor of his truck. Stupid man. She turned toward the pasture. The cattle were getting nearer.

"Now what?" she muttered, and once again started toward the broken fence.

But this time, as she circled the truck, she spied something in the pickup bed she thought she could use. Without hesitation, she crawled in on her hands and knees, grabbed a cattle whip from beneath a jumble of trash and jumped out.

The long handle was coated with a film of greasy dirt. The whip on the end wasn't much more than a yard long, but its tip was forked like a snake's tongue. She tried popping it over her head and almost popped herself in the butt.

Dancing sideways to dodge her own wrath, she began moving toward the converging herd with the whip over her head, waving it in the air and, when she got up the nerve, giving it a sharp crack to one side. After a few tries, the motion became easier. A flip of the wrist, then a sudden jerk back. That's all it took. She looked nervously at the cattle. Now if they just got the message, she'd be all right.

Chapter 7

The party was a huge success. Within five minutes of leaving Paige Sullivan's house, Maddie had slumped sideways in the seat and gone to sleep. Royal drove with one hand on the wheel and the other on her. The tires on his truck hummed as the miles sped away, and he thought as he drove that there was something inherently comforting about living in ruts. He'd been driving down this particular stretch of highway most of his life. He knew every bent tree and rusty fence post, every windmill, every owner of every acre he passed. He even knew the identity of the old fellow on the tractor in front of him.

Old Man Hargis drove, as his daddy used to say, like the dead lice were falling off him. Instead of being impatient with the snail's pace, he grinned. It was just as well the old fellow didn't drive much faster than he walked, because his eyesight was worse than his hearing.

Finally the road ahead cleared, giving him room to pass. He glanced at Maddie, giving her seat belt a tug to make sure she was still buckled in, then whipped out from the trail of Hargis's diesel smoke. At peace with the world, Royal waved at his elderly neighbor as he passed, then slipped into his lane, leaving the old man far behind.

He thought back to the party. It had gone well. As always, he was the only male parent, but he'd long gotten over the oddity of being the only male present. In fact, there'd been times in his past when he'd secretly enjoyed all the female attention. Even if they were only friends. Even if they were all married to some of his buddies. A little fussing never hurt.

But that was before Maddie's blossoming. Today their appearance at the party had been the topic of conversation.

Maddie was wearing a dress.

The women couldn't believe it.

And Maddie's nails were bright with new pink polish.

Their eyes were round with wonder.

And then there was the hairdo and the fancy pink ribbon. The list went on and on. Add to that Maddie's announcement that their new keeper was an angel, and Paige Sullivan's fifth birthday had become the second most important event of the day.

Royal sighed, picturing the gossip around supper tables tonight, then leaned back and grinned. He had to admit, Maddie had dropped a bomb on them all with that one. He'd let her talk. And why the hell not? Her explanation was better than his. He still didn't know what to say about what he'd done.

Out of habit, he took a hand from the wheel and smoothed it over his daughter's head, then her shoulder, patting her gently before turning his attention to the road.

God, he loved her. More than breath. More than life. And today she'd glowed. He'd never seen her that way, so confident of herself as a female rather than just a child. He had Angel to thank. When he got home, even if it tied a knot in his tongue, he was going to do just that.

Four miles from home, he topped a hill. In the distance he could see the flashing lights of an ambulance as it dipped and disappeared into the valley below. He frowned and glanced at

Maddie again, thankful she was asleep. If they came on a wreck, he didn't want her to see.

He accelerated slightly, as if being in his own space would give him a sense of safety from the outside world.

Three miles, then two, then one, and when he turned the curve in the road just above the ranch, his heart dropped. Damn it to hell, but that ambulance had turned down the drive to the ranch.

He thought of Angel, alone in the house. Of all the accidents that could happen. Of all the possible reasons for an ambulance call. His stomach did a flip-flop as he realized she could be hurt. The thought made him nervous, then guilty. If he'd been there, he might have prevented whatever had happened.

He turned down the driveway and topped the hill above the ranch. Nothing could have prepared him for what he saw. A wreck! Someone had run through the fence! Then he recognized the truck.

"Well, damn, Sonny French's truck. I'll lay odds he was drunk when it happened," he muttered, not realizing he'd spoken aloud.

Maddie stirred, then sat up, blinking sleepily. "Daddy, are we home?"

"Almost, sweetheart," he said. "But it looks like someone wrecked their truck in our fence. I'll have to stop and see. You stay inside, okay?"

By the time Royal rolled to a stop, Maddie was out of her seat belt and on her knees, bracing herself against the dashboard as she gazed through the windshield. She squealed.

"Daddy! Angel's in the pasture with the cattle. You told me never to get in the pasture with the cattle. You've got to go get her! Hurry!"

Royal's gaze shifted from the flashing lights of the ambulance and Sonny's wrecked truck to the pasture beyond. He could only stare in disbelief. The sight of one slender woman with a whip and a herd of milling cattle made him wonder what else she'd endured in his absence. As he watched, she raised the whip in the air. Although he couldn't hear it from here, Royal knew by the way the cattle moved that it had cracked.

"Look at her, Daddy. I didn't know Angel could do stuff like that."

"Neither did I," he said softly, then gave his daughter one last warning. "You stay in this truck and you do not get out until I say so. No matter what! Do you understand me?"

Maddie's eyes were round. "I promise, Daddy. I won't get out until you come and get me. Besides," she added, "I wouldn't want to get my new dress all dirty."

It was an amazing admission from a child who willingly shared bites of peanut butter sandwiches with a cat.

"Right," he muttered, jumped out and ran.

Angel's knee was skinned and bleeding from crawling into Sonny's truck, and her ankle was sore. She was limping, compliments of a gopher hole and an errant cow. There was fresh manure on her shoes and some mud on her shorts, but she'd done it. The ambulance was here, and not a single cow had gotten out.

The herd bull was standing between her and the herd. Every now and then he would lower his head and paw dirt, which made her nervous. The urge to run was strong, but she'd stayed this long. She wasn't going to run now. He took a couple of steps forward, then stopped and bellowed.

"Don't tell me your troubles," she muttered. "Just because you have a tail and long ears doesn't make you any different from the other males I've known, and I put the last one on the floor."

To make herself feel better, she popped the whip above her head. The loud, reassuring crack was enough to send the bull into the herd. She exhaled a shaky breath and then heard someone calling her name.

She turned. Royal was coming toward her at a lope. Relief

flooded, along with the overwhelming urge to cry. He was home!

Then she froze. What in the world was wrong with her? She didn't need anyone to take care of her, and there was no need to cry.

So she watched him run toward her, and in that moment she began shaking from the sensation that she'd stood like this before, seeing the long stride of his legs and the way his body moved within his clothes. Feeling the air around her shifting to make way for his presence. Watching him silhouetted against the afternoon sun and knowing that when he reached her, her world would never be the same.

And then he was there, cupping her shoulders and staring intently into her face.

"Angel! Are you all right?"

She shaded her eyes and looked up, staring blindly into a dark, anxious gaze.

"Yes, I'm fine."

He squeezed her shoulders. The contact was brief and little more than one stranger to another, but her heart quickened as if waiting for more.

"I am so sorry you had to deal with this on your own." He moved past her to stare at the cattle.

"I managed."

It was her quiet, almost noncommittal tone that made him turn. And then he looked at her. Really looked. At the dirt smudge on the curve of her cheek and her skinned and bleeding knee. At her shoes caked with drying manure. At the mud splattered on her bare legs and the edges of her shorts.

He grinned. "Yes, ma'am, you sure as hell did." He looked at the whip. "Where'd you get the popper?"

She pointed with her chin. "Out of the back of that truck."

Royal's eyes narrowed thoughtfully. "You're one resourceful lady, aren't you, Angel Rojas?"

She shrugged. "What is that old saying? Necessity is the mother of invention?"

Royal nodded, then reached for the whip. "Give it to me," he said gently. "I'll handle it from here."

She relinquished the whip with a sigh and they both turned to look at the sound of another siren.

"That would be the sheriff," Royal said. "Why don't you go crawl in the truck with Maddie where it's cool? Wait for me there. I'll drive you to the house in a while."

She nodded and started to walk away.

"Hey, Angel."

She turned.

"Good job," he said.

She blinked, then shuddered. The sensation of déjà vu was even stronger.

"Thank you," she said, and started walking.

The closer she got to the wreck, the faster she went. By the time she reached his truck, she was running, her sore ankle forgotten in her need to get away. But she didn't get in the cab with Maddie. Pointing to her muddy clothes and dirty shoes, she let down the tailgate and sat on it with her legs dangling. A few minutes later the sheriff took her version of the incident for his records, and followed the ambulance and the wrecker as they removed Sonny and what was left of his truck from the ranch. There was nothing left but a large, gaping hole in Royal's neatly strung fence.

Angel glanced at the pasture, debating with herself about going out to help. But Royal seemed to have everything under control. A couple of minutes later, a red truck topped the hill. Behind it came a shiny new blue one. Then another and another. It would seem that word had spread fast about Sonny French's latest fiasco.

Before she knew it, several men were helping Royal fix the fence. Within thirty minutes, it was over. The men left, one at a time, tipping their hats and giving her polite but curious glances as they drove away. She felt like a fly in the icing on top of a big white cake. Noticeable—and not long for this world.

And then she heard Royal's deep, husky growl as he bid the last neighbor goodbye. He was on his way to the truck. Still shaken by her earlier sensations, everything inside of her coiled as she waited for his approach. Then he was standing in front of her, frowning, and her defenses went up.

"I thought I told you to get inside where it was cool," he growled.

"I was too dirty," she said.

He glanced at her knee, where the skin was peeled. The urge to tend it was strong. Instead, he found himself pushing when he should have been pulling back.

"Dirt washes off," he said shortly. "Next time do what I say."

Angel's chin jutted and her lips firmed as she slid off the truck bed and onto her feet.

"Now you listen to me, you—you...your royal highness. It'll be a cold day in hell before I do something I think is wrong just because a man told me to do it. And if you're going to have a problem with that, then let's just consider me fired."

Having said her piece, she started down the road toward the house, leaving Royal standing in the dirt, too stunned to speak. Not since his mother, God rest her soul, had a woman ever put him so neatly in his place.

Royal highness? He clenched his jaw. She had some nerve. But as hard as he tried, he couldn't get mad. Instead, he watched in disbelief as she strode toward the ranch with her head held high and that long black braid swinging like a pendulum down the middle of her back.

"Daddy, I want to walk with Angel."

His daughter's voice yanked him out of his shock. He inhaled sharply and turned toward the truck.

"Madeline Michelle, don't lean out the damned window!" he yelled. "You'll fall on your head! And you're not walking anywhere. You don't want to get dirty, remember?"

Maddie shrugged and dropped back in her seat as Royal slid behind the wheel and started the engine.

"Let's race her," she said, pointing to Angel.

A mental image of driving past Angel and leaving her choking in their dust flashed through his mind. Royal looked at
Maddie, then burst out laughing.

"Let's not," he said, then put the truck in gear. "I think
I'm already in enough trouble. How about we just give her a
ride?"

"Okay," Maddie said.

Royal pulled up beside Angel, letting the truck coast as he
leaned out the window.

"Hey, lady, need a lift?"

Angel glared at him and stumbled when she saw the look of
devilment on his face. She'd been expecting anger, not a chal-
lenge.

She stopped, forcing him to step on the brakes to stay even
with her. There was nothing between them but the sound of a
well-tuned engine idling smoothly.

"I can't," she finally said. "I'm fired."

He gritted his teeth, enunciating each word distinctly. "No,
damn it, you're not fired."

Angel almost fainted with relief, but she'd die before she'd
let it show. She waited. There was more he had to say.

Royal glanced at Maddie, who was listening to the conversation with far too much interest. He sighed and turned to Angel.

"How about if I said I was sorry?" he asked.

Her lips twitched. Her only sign of pleasure. Still she remained silent.

"Well?" Royal growled.

"Well, what?" Angel asked.

"Hell, woman, what do you want besides an apology?"

There might have been cow dung on her shoes and blood
on her leg, but she wasn't lacking in attitude.

"The apology would do nicely…if I'd heard it. All I heard
you ask was, would I like you to say you were sorry. I didn't
hear you *say* you were sorry."

Royal didn't know whether to curse or laugh. Thinking of home-cooked meals and clean laundry, he grinned.

"My mistake," he drawled. "Miss Rojas, I am abjectly sorry for behaving in an inappropriate manner. Would you accept my most heartfelt apology?"

She snorted as she started toward the back of the truck.

"Overkill is hardly your style," she announced, and slid onto the tailgate. When she was settled safely in place, she yelled, "I'm ready."

Royal glanced in the rearview mirror. All he could see was the stiff tilt of her head and shoulders.

"Hang on," he yelled, and then accelerated gently.

They rode the rest of the way to the ranch house in silence. Even Maddie was unusually quiet. After he had parked, Royal got out, then lifted Maddie out of the seat.

"Change that pretty dress before you go out to play," he warned.

"Okay," she said, and tore into the house, leaving Royal alone with the keeper.

Angel slid off the tailgate, wincing slightly at the jolt to her ankle. Royal saw it and caught her by the arm before she could escape him.

"Easy," he said softly, when her dark eyes flashed him a warning. "I'm just trying to help."

Angel sighed and nodded. "It's been a long day."

Royal resisted the urge to sweep her into his arms and carry her into the house. He offered her an elbow to lean on. She hesitated, then took it gratefully.

"Thank you again for all you did," Royal said.

Suddenly uncomfortable with the intimacy, she shrugged off his thanks.

"It happened. I was here. It was nothing," she said shortly.

"And you hurt yourself for me," Royal said. "Your ankle hurts, I think, although you don't seem to trust me enough to say so, and you have shed blood on my behalf." He pointed to her knee. "I think that deserves some special thanks."

She looked up and blushed, then looked away.

Royal stumbled. A man would need a blazing fire not to get lost in eyes that dark. And her skin—it looked like velvet, soft, brown velvet. Yep, he'd been right. That day in the rain...he should have kept on driving.

"Well, then," he mumbled. "Let's get you cleaned up, then we'll take a look at your bumps and bruises and see what we can do, okay?"

"I'm sure I'll be fine," Angel said.

Royal stopped. A frown deepened the grooves on his forehead.

"So am I," he said. "But indulge me...please."

Angel finally gave in. Not because he had weakened her resolve, but because he was so hardheaded it was easier to agree than to argue.

"Do you need any help?" Royal asked.

Angel bent, pulled off her shoes and left them on the front porch.

"No, but thank you," she said quietly.

She could feel the heat of his gaze between her shoulder blades all the way to her room. Before she opened her door, she thought about turning around just to see if he was still watching. But then she changed her mind and bolted inside. She didn't want to know.

A short while later, Angel emerged. Fresh from a shower, in clean clothes, she felt ready to tackle anything. When she walked into the kitchen, her opinion changed. Royal was waiting. Make that anything except Royal Justice, she thought. There was antiseptic on the table and a large box of Maddie's favorite bandages.

"Beauty and the Beast?" she queried, pointing to the box.

He never cracked a smile. "Maddie insisted."

"She does a lot of that," Angel said.

Royal's composure slipped, and he grinned. "Yeah, Roman says she's a lot like me. Now if you wouldn't mind, I will see to your knee and then get out of your hair."

Angel reached for the sack of cotton balls he was holding. "Oh, I can do that my—"

His fingers tightened around the plastic. "I know that," he said shortly. "Indulge me."

She sat, wishing she'd put on something other than shorts. They weren't tight, and they were completely modest, but his hands on any part of her body seemed a bit like waving a lit match over a dynamite fuse—just to see if it would catch.

Royal bent to the task, frowning as he dabbed an antiseptic-soaked swab to the wound on her knee. Even though it had happened some time ago, it was still seeping, evidence of how deep the abrasions were.

Although she hadn't moved, there was a muscle jerking above her knee. He was hurting her, and he knew it. Without thinking, he lowered his head and blew, just as he would have done for Maddie.

When his head dipped toward her knee, Angel froze, and when his breath touched her skin, whatever she had been thinking curled up and died. She groaned and he looked up, certain he'd caused her more pain.

"I'm sorry," Royal said. "It's deeper than I thought."

He was talking. She knew it because she could see his lips moving. But there was a roar in her ears that she couldn't get past. She swallowed twice, trying to think what to say, but the words wouldn't come. To save herself, she closed her eyes, blocking out the sight of his face. It was all that saved her.

When it came to a woman's pain, Royal was a pushover. Right or wrong, he'd been raised to believe that it was a man's duty to take care of what his father had called the weaker sex, although he had long since figured out that the only thing weaker about most women was their physical strength. When it came to endurance, they could beat a man hands down every time.

And he was living proof of that theory. Here he was, down on his knees and putting medicine on what amounted to a rather insignificant wound, and he was almost sick to his stomach. If she cried, he'd be lost.

His fingers were trembling as he gave the wound one last dab. His breath was shaky as he blew on it again. He rocked on his heels, waiting for it to dry, and reached for the box of bandages.

"Wanna pick?" he asked.

Startled by the question, Angel opened her eyes. The box of decorative bandages was in her lap. It was the icebreaker she needed. She smiled as she pulled a bandage out and handed it to him.

Royal managed a grin, opened it and pulled it out of the wrapper with a flair.

"It's Belle. Good choice."

Before he could stick it on, Maddie came running. "Let me. Let me," she cried. "I can stick it on."

Royal took one horrified look at his daughter and bolted to his feet. Her clothes, the ones she'd just put on, were dotted with fresh grass stains, and there was a dark, smelly smudge on the seat of her shorts. As she reached to take the Band-Aid, he grabbed her hands, turning them palms up and staring in disbelief.

"What the hell have you been doing?" he yelled.

A frown furrowed her forehead. "Playing with Flea Bit and Marbles," she mumbled.

"Playing what, the apocalypse?"

The analogy was over her head, which only deepened her frown.

"We wasn't playing any pocky lips. We played hide-and-seek. I won."

"I'd hate like hell to see those poor cats," he muttered, then handed Angel the Band-Aid almost as an afterthought and grabbed Maddie by the arm, intent on marching her to the bathroom to clean up.

Angel reacted before she thought. All she could see was a

little girl in trouble for nothing but playing and a father who yelled before he talked. She grabbed Royal by the arm.

"Wait," she urged. "It's only grass and dust. It will wash...and so will she."

Her even tone was all the quiet Royal needed. Almost instantly, he calmed. He looked at Maddie. The obstinate look on her face was proof enough he'd reacted in exactly the wrong manner. Instead of arguing with Angel, he took a deep breath and dropped to Maddie's level.

"Sorry," he said gently, poking the end of her nose. "But you sure made a mess."

Maddie nodded in agreement. "I'm sorry, Daddy, but I was just having fun."

Royal hugged her then grabbed her hands, turning them palms up again.

"If you want to help doctor Angel, you have to wash your hands first. You don't want to get germs in her sore knee, right?"

Her eyes widened thoughtfully. "Right," she agreed, and gave Angel a nervous look, afraid the bandage would get applied without her assistance. "Wait for me," she begged. "I'll be right back."

"I'll wait," Angel promised as Maddie ran out of the room.

Again they were left alone. Royal ran a hand through his hair and exhaled softly.

"Thanks again," he said quietly, reached for his hat and walked out the back door.

The quiet slam broke the silence in which Angel was sitting. Down the hall, the sound of running water was evidence that Maddie was doing as she'd been told. Angel looked at the Band-Aid she was holding and set it on the table. She took a deep breath and exhaled slowly. Finally, she was alone.

Her knee still stung where Royal had applied the medicine. Her hands were getting sore, she supposed from gripping the filthy handle of Sonny French's whip for so long. Her ankle was throbbing, and her head was starting to hurt. But none of that was as bothersome as the unsettled feeling in her belly. She didn't know whether to start crying or throw up. Something was happening she didn't want—hadn't planned. She'd taken this job for a number of reasons, none of which included a physical attraction to the boss. But it was happening just the same.

She covered her face with her hands. "Oh, God, don't let this happen."

The sound of running footsteps warned that Maddie was on her way. She lifted her head and fought for composure.

"I'm ready!" Maddie announced, showing her clean hands as proof.

"Looks good to me," Angel said, and handed the little girl the bandage.

Chapter 8

Tommy Boy Watson had taken a liking to Texas, so much so that after he'd done the deed in Abilene, he'd moved toward the outskirts of Amarillo. Yesterday he'd stopped at a café to eat some lunch and overheard the two men in the booth behind him talking about a sweet little waitress named Darcy at the Little Horn Café. He'd listened absently until he'd heard them mention that twenty bucks would put her in a willing mood. At that point he stopped chewing. One added that he'd heard for fifty dollars, she could send a man to the moon.

Low laughter followed a couple of suggestive comments as Tommy Boy resumed chewing his food. He swallowed, washed it down with the last of his sweet iced tea and reached for his check. He had a sudden urge to see if this Darcy really was on the menu at the Little Horn Café. If she was, he figured it was time to do a little editing.

He tossed some money on the table and dug his keys out of his pocket. He strolled out of the café, picking his teeth and jingling his keys. He liked making plans. But he liked following through on them even more.

* * *

The Justice homestead had been in the family for over a hundred and fifty years. The original house, built by Royal's grandfather, had been little more than a bedroom with a cooking shed attached. When he married, they'd added two rooms downstairs and two up to accommodate his growing family. By the time Royal's father, Micah Justice, had taken over the running of the Justice ranch, the only thing left of the original building was the massive stone fireplace and the eight-foot hand-hewn log that was the mantel.

Angel knew the story. Royal had related it proudly after dinner one night. She listened with interest as he went through the generations, watching the pride on his face as he looked at Maddie, knowing she would be the link to keeping the Justice family alive.

Today, as Angel ran a lemon-scented dust cloth along the mantel, she was thinking of her history. Of the family she'd lost and the family she longed to have.

She moved to the tables, then the windowsills, applying polish and rubbing it in, savoring the rich sheen that came out in the wood and taking pride in her work. Some would look down upon work such as this. But to Angel, anything she got paid to do was worth doing well.

A week had passed since the wreck. Her knee had healed. Her heart had settled into its normal place. She'd chalked her emotional reaction to her employer as nothing more than the heat of the moment. She'd been slightly afraid of the cattle. Royal had come and taken the fear out of her hands. Gratitude. That's all it was. She'd been grateful, not attracted.

Having settled that firmly in her mind, she'd managed to stay in the background of Royal's world for the rest of the week. She cooked. She cleaned. She did everything a housekeeper should do except become a part of the family. As much as she enjoyed Maddie's company, she had an innate resistance to letting anyone get too close. In her entire life, the only person she'd ever loved without reservation was her mother. And she'd died, leaving Angel to the whims of a drunken father and a welfare system that didn't work. Angel had grown up the hard way, and in doing so had grown up hard.

Her appearance was attractive. Dark hair, dark eyes and the warm complexion of a sun worshiper. Some might even call her beautiful. Her behavior, while obstinate and willful, was never cruel. But she kept her feelings close to her heart where they would be safe. She'd learned the hard way that if she didn't give love away, then there could be no chance of rejection. And yet she'd agreed to stay with a child who believed she'd been sent from God.

It wasn't as if she really loved them, Angel told herself. They were good to her. It was easy to be good to them. It didn't have to mean anything.

She gave her cleaning rag another dose of lemon oil polish and knelt beside the massive dining room table to clean the legs. As she was working, she heard the back door slam and the familiar sound of Maddie's footsteps running through the house. She grinned. Maddie never walked when she could run.

"Angel! Angel! Where are you?" Maddie called.

"In the dining room," Angel called, and rocked back on her heels as Maddie burst into the room. She barely had time to register the fact that Royal was right behind her before Maddie thrust a handful of wildflowers toward Angel's face.

"These are for you!" Maddie said.

Angel looked at the wad of squeezed and broken stems in the little girl's fist, then at her face, then at the man behind her before looking at the flowers.

"Oh, my," she said softly, and reached for the wilting bouquet, inhaling the scent of crushed grass and sweet blossoms as Maddie thrust them in her hand.

"Do you like them?" Maddie asked, then before Angel could answer, she began pointing and talking. "These blue ones are my favorites. They're bluebonnets. Did you know that's a Texas flower? And these are Indian blankies."

"Blankets," Royal corrected.

Maddie nodded without missing a beat. "Yeah, blankets. My daddy likes them best. They're not really blankets, you know. They're just flowers. I don't know why someone gave them that name. I think they look like clown flowers 'cause they're red and yellow like Ronald McDonald and he's a clown and—"

"Damn, Maddie, give it a rest," Royal growled, then tugged at her ponytail to take the sting from his words.

Maddie giggled, but she stopped talking, which was what Royal had intended.

Angel lifted the flowers to her nose, inhaling the separate scents. Some were sweeter than others, and the colors were as varied as a Texas sky at sunset. To her surprise, tears came quickly, blurring the colors and Maddie's face.

Maddie saw the tears and took a hesitant step back, leaning against her daddy's leg for comfort. She looked at Royal.

"Daddy, did I do something bad?"

Angel groaned beneath her breath and before she thought, reached for Maddie and pulled her into her arms.

"No, baby," Angel said softly, hugging the little girl close. "You did something good."

"I did?"

Angel nodded. "Oh, yes, and do you know what it was?"

Maddie shook her head.

"No one ever gave me flowers before."

"Ever?" Maddie asked. "Not even on your birthday?"

"No. Not even on my birthday." She hugged her again and kissed her on the cheek. "That's why these are so special. Thank you a hundred times. Maybe even a thousand times."

Maddie beamed and spun out of Angel's arms. "We need water! Daddy said we need to put the damn things in water." She headed for the kitchen.

Royal's face turned red as he offered her a hand up. "I didn't mean that the way it—"

Angel eyed the wide, callused palm and the long fingers before getting up on her own.

"I know," she said, smiling slightly as she bent to smell them one more time. "I'd better help Maddie find a vase."

Royal shifted uncomfortably. "Yeah, Maddie can make a mess faster than anyone I ever knew."

"She's just a child," Angel said.

Royal nodded, watching the look of awe on Angel's face as she kept touching first one flower and then another. To him they looked like hell. Maddie had sat on part of them once and dropped all of them twice since they'd been picked. They were covered in dust, and if he wasn't mistaken, there was a small green worm climbing up one of the stems. A floral tribute it was not. But it had come from his daughter's heart. He kept thinking how close he'd come to ignoring Maddie's request for him to stop along the roadside where the flowers had grown.

All he could think was that this moment would never have happened and Angel would still have been waiting for her first bouquet.

"Angel?"

"Yes?"

"Was that true? Are these the first flowers anyone ever gave you?"

A wry grin tilted the corner of her mouth. "Yes. Doesn't say much for my popularity, does it?"

He frowned. "I'd come near saying the men you've known have been sadly lacking in class, that's what I'd say."

Then, embarrassed that he'd given so much of himself away, he pivoted, muttered that he'd help Maddie find that damned vase and stomped away.

Angel stood, staring at the stiffness in his posture and the haste with which he left, and tried to decide if he'd been angry with himself or with her. Finally, she shrugged. It didn't matter. Right now, nothing mattered but these flowers and the love in which they'd been given.

At that moment, a little crack began to form in the shell around Angel's heart. But she didn't hear it, and if she had, wouldn't have recognized the sound. It would be a while yet before Angel Rojas became familiar with the sound of joy.

That night the flowers were the centerpiece for the dining room table, and long after the lights were out and everyone else had gone to sleep, Angel still lay, wide-eyed and sleepless, thinking about the way Maddie's arms had felt around her neck. Remembering the silky-soft texture of the little girl's skin against her cheek. Tasting the faint, salty taste of sweat as she'd kissed her.

A longing for something more than she had began burning within her. She felt empty and lonely in a way she'd never known. With a groan, she got out of bed and walked to the window. She stared across the yard toward the building beyond. The blue-white glow of the security light gave an icy appearance to all that she saw. She shuddered and spun to stare at the room before her.

Thanks to her sleepless night, her covers were in tangles, and although her shoes were near a chair and she knew her clothes were in the closet, the room had taken on an unfamiliar feel. It was as if she'd walked out of a nightmare into a place where she didn't belong.

She wrapped her arms around herself and closed her eyes, whispering a prayer her mother had taught her many years ago to take away bad dreams. But when the prayer was over and she opened her eyes, the feeling was still with her.

She bit her lip and sighed and headed back to bed. Just before she laid down, a thought occurred. She dropped the covers she'd been holding and hurried out of her room.

The red Spanish tiles in the hallway were cool beneath her feet. Out of her room, she felt vulnerable. Anxious not to be discovered, she hastened her steps, all but running to get to the dining room table.

Then she was there, sighing with relief when her fingers curled around the cool, smooth surface of the mason jar that doubled as a vase for Maddie's flowers. She scurried down the hall clutching the vase and her bouquet.

As she crossed the threshold to her room, her anxiety decreased. She sat on the side of her bed, lightly fingering the velvety petals. Peace settled. She gave the petals one last touch, then laid down, pulled the covers up to her chin and closed her eyes. The last thing she remembered was the hum of the central air-conditioning and the sound of her heartbeat in her ears.

The next morning began with a knot in her shoelace that she couldn't untie and went downhill from there. When she went into the kitchen to start breakfast, Royal was already up and the coffeepot was half empty. The anger on his face was evident as he talked on the phone, and although Angel did not know who he was talking to, she felt sympathy for them just the same.

"Look, damn it. I ordered that fertilizer over a month ago. You promised delivery last week, and it's still not here. I don't give a rat's ass who you're trying to blame. What I'm saying to you is, if it's not here today, then consider my order canceled."

Angel winced as he slammed the phone down. She was debating about leaving the room when he realized he was no longer alone.

"I'm sorry," she said quickly. "I didn't know you were—"

Royal shoved a hand through his hair in frustration, mussing the dark, spiky strands into instant disarray.

"No, I'm the one who should be sorry," Royal muttered and had the grace to look ashamed. "Sometimes I lose my temper."

Angel stifled a grin. That was the most obvious understatement she'd ever heard.

"Yes, I know."

Royal stilled and gave her a long, considering look. "Was that sarcasm I heard?"

She didn't flinch, returning his stare look for look. "Do you have a preference for breakfast?" she asked.

Royal tried to glare, but it was hard to get the point across when being ignored. He moved a step closer, taking some small delight in the fact that she took a step back.

"Yes, I have a preference," he said softly.

Angel's eyes widened and her heart started to pound. She wanted to run but couldn't find the will to break free of his stare.

"I'm hungry as hell," he continued, took another step toward her and lowered his voice to just above a whisper. "But I don't know what I want."

God give me strength, Angel thought, and wondered if she could deck him as she had Fat Louie. And then wondered if she would. There was something about the man she had tried without success to ignore.

"Do you have any suggestions?" Royal asked, knowing he was pushing every button she had and wondering, as he continued to bait her, why it mattered.

Angel doubled her fists and took a deep breath. But before she could react, he turned and poured himself another cup of coffee and strolled toward the back door as if she wasn't even there.

She went limp with relief and cleared her throat, thankful that her voice wasn't as shaky as her legs.

"Do you intend to eat breakfast or not?" she asked.

Royal turned, the cup halfway to his lips, and grinned. "Surprise me." He walked outside and let the door slam shut behind him.

The urge to throw something was strong within her as she stomped to the cabinets and yanked out a bowl. He wanted a surprise? She would give him a surprise. He'd think twice before he pulled that macho stuff on her again.

Royal glanced at his watch and then up the driveway, nodding with satisfaction as the man from Wilson's Seed and Feed circled the pasture, applying liquid fertilizer. It was almost two. His belly grumbled. He'd missed lunch, which was probably just as well. His mouth was still burning from breakfast. He knew the moment he'd started the game with Angel that he was taking his frustration out on her. But who would have known she'd take it so personally?

Hell, his lips were blistered and bound to peel, and he wondered if tongues peeled, too. He'd had hot food plenty of times in his life. In fact, he prided himself on being able to eat real Tex-Mex cooking with the best. But he'd never in his life eaten anything as hot as the omelette she'd put on his plate.

The first bite was already in his belly before he knew what had happened. He hiccuped and reached for his coffee, then changed his mind and poured himself some of Maddie's milk.

Maddie had continued to eat her cereal, unaware of the undercurrents between Daddy and her angel.

The milk had helped, but only slightly. He stared at the remaining omelette on his plate and then at Angel, who was shaking more pepper sauce onto hers. His eyes narrowed. Damn her. What was she trying to prove, that she was tougher because she could eat liquid fire? Infuriated that she was making him eat his words, he picked up his fork and took another big bite.

Angel didn't look up. Not because she was afraid of what she'd done but because she was afraid she'd laugh in his face. He was hurting, and she knew it. The hiccup was proof that his stomach had experienced an instant rebellion. But he was tough, she'd give him that. She heard the scrape of his fork against his plate and knew he'd taken another bite. She reached for a piece of toast and began to butter it with smooth, even strokes. Then she picked up the rack.

"Want some toast?" she asked.

Royal's eyes were running streams of pure tears, and he was in the act of digging a handkerchief from his pocket to stop the flow. He stuffed the handkerchief under his nose and yanked the rack of toast out of her hands.

"Thanks."

Angel met his glare with an innocent stare. "Don't mention it...again," she said softly.

He started to speak and choked and coughed instead. All he could manage was a nod, but he'd gotten the message. He'd pushed. She'd pushed back. He wasn't sure, but he didn't think he would be pushing her again. At least not like that. When it came to revenge, Maddie's angel didn't play fair.

But Royal wasn't the kind of man to dwell on the past. So he'd made a mistake. It wouldn't happen again.

He glanced toward the house in the valley. Maddie was little more than a dot on the landscape, but he knew it was her. He could tell by the way she kept darting to and fro that she must be playing with one of those cats. He didn't see Angel anywhere. But that didn't mean she wasn't there. He'd seen the look on Angel's face when Maddie had given her the flowers. It was an instant friends-for-life gesture if he'd ever seen one.

And then he frowned. But where did that leave him? After the stunt he'd pulled this morning, were they going to be enemies forever? Something within him rejected the thought. He did not want Angel Rojas for an enemy. His frown deepened and he looked away. But what did he want from her? He'd hired her as a housekeeper. Why did he keep pushing her buttons? Why couldn't he just let her be?

Angel sat in the porch swing, watching as Maddie played with Flea Bit and telling herself she should go inside and get supper started. She'd baked a cake earlier and she knew it was cooled enough to ice, yet moving from where she was sitting was the last thing she wanted to do. It was peaceful here. Peace was something she hadn't known in years. She brushed a fly from her face and smiled, then laughed as Maddie held up the cat for her to see. It was wearing a pink bonnet from Maddie's Cabbage Patch doll, and Angel could see something that looked suspiciously like cotton balls running the length of the animal's belly. She bit her lip and sighed. Oh, Lord. So that's where the bag of cotton balls went. She didn't even want to know how Maddie had stuck them on. If the cat was lucky, it was with glue. At least that could be cut away. If she'd taped them on, poor Flea Bit might be wearing them for quite a while.

She stood and walked into the driveway where Maddie was playing.

"What have you done to Flea Bit?"

Maddie danced the cat on its back legs and waved a front paw at Angel.

"Flea Bit's a clown. See? He has a hat and little fuzzy balls."

Angel bit her lip to keep from laughing. That remark was priceless. Aside from the cotton Maddie had glued to the cat, Flea Bit did have little fuzzy balls and, she hoped, a sense of humor.

"Yes, I see," Angel said. "But don't you think he's played enough? It's getting awfully hot out here. Why don't you take the costume off Flea Bit and come up on the porch. I'll get him some milk and you an ice-cream cone, okay?"

"Yeah!" Maddie cried, and tore the hat off Flea Bit's head.

Angel winced and made a grab for the cat before Maddie started pulling at the cotton she'd glued to its belly.

"Be careful, sweetheart. Here, let me help you."

To Angel's surprise and relief, she saw the cotton balls had been stuck on with mud rather than glue. A little dab of water from the hydrant by the porch and Flea Bit was as good as new.

"Go wash your hands," Angel said. "Then you can have your ice-cream cone."

Maddie frowned. "The ice cream always melts on my hands. I wanna wash my hands after I eat."

Angel shook her head. "So we'll wash them twice. Now scoot."

Maddie started to argue, but the idea of ice cream was enough to snuff out the thought.

"Be right back," she yelled, and dashed into the house.

Angel held the cat in the air, giving it a careful inspection to make sure it had suffered no harm. Everything was still in place.

"Poor kitty," she said softly, and set it on the porch. "If you have the guts, hang around a minute. I'll get you some milk."

The cat must have understood, because it was waiting beside the door when Angel came out with the small dish of milk.

"I'm ready for my ice cream," Maddie announced, displaying her still dripping hands for Angel's inspection.

"You sure are," Angel said, and started inside to get Maddie her treat. Maddie surprised her by hugging her bare legs.

"What's that for?" Angel asked, a little surprised and a little bit touched.

"'Cause I love you," Maddie said, and left Angel standing as she dashed into the house.

Angel watched through the screen door as Maddie shoved a chair to the refrigerator, opened the freezer door and began digging through the contents for her favorite flavor of ice cream.

Angel kept telling herself to move, that Maddie would make a mess before they even started, but she didn't trust herself to speak. There was a knot in her throat and tears burning the back of her eyes and she could still feel the imprint of Maddie's body against her legs.

Love. Oh, Lord. This wasn't in the job description.

Something clattered to the floor, and Maddie ducked beneath the open door of the freezer to see if Angel was watching. It was all the jump start Angel needed.

"Wait, Maddie. Let me help," she said, and hurried inside.

Royal closed the last gate, then turned and watched as the truck from the feed store drove away. He glanced up, gauging the gathering clouds against the fact that all the liquid fertilizer had been spread. And by the looks of the sky, none too soon. It would be just about perfect if they got a good rain tonight.

Not too much. Just enough to soak that fertilizer right into the ground.

Then he looked at the house in the valley, squinting against the glare of a setting sun and wondering where everyone had gone. Probably inside where it was cool. The day had turned out much hotter than predicted. He gave the darkening sky one last look and headed home. He should be just about able to finish the chores before anything hit.

Angel was swirling the last spoonful of white icing on her cake while Maddie was at the kitchen table, coloring in one of her coloring books. It was a quiet, homey scene, idyllic from a bystander's point of view.

The evening news was being broadcast, and Angel listened halfheartedly to the portable television on a nearby sideboard, trying to make sense of what the newsman was saying in conjunction with the running commentary being given by Royal's princess.

"Look," Maddie cried, and held up her book, waiting for praise.

Angel glanced at the picture. "Wow, Maddie. That's very good. I'll bet when you start to school this fall you'll be one of the best in the class at coloring."

Maddie nodded, as if to say, of course she would, and turned to a new page, anxious to begin her next masterpiece.

Angel's attention moved to the sixteen-inch television. She frowned as the picture of a young brown-haired woman was flashed on the screen.

"...found in a culvert by a passing motorist who'd stopped to change a flat tire. Amarillo authorities have identified her as Carol Jo Belmont, who was last seen at the Big Wheel Truck Stop. Her throat had been slashed and—"

The back door opened and Angel pivoted, the icing-coated knife clutched in her hand. It was Royal.

"Daddy!" Maddie squealed and abandoned her crayons for her father's arms.

The instant pleasure on Royal's face was, for some reason,

difficult to watch. She turned and laid the knife in the sink then reached for a paper towel to wipe her hands. When she turned, her composure was firmly in place.

"You're already back. I'm afraid supper's not quite ready."

"That's all right," Royal said. "From the way the clouds are building, I think I'd better finish the chores first."

Maddie suddenly tightened her hold around Royal's neck.

"Is it gonna rain, Daddy?"

Royal nuzzled her cheek with his nose. "I hope so. The grass needs a drink."

She frowned and wiggled to be put down. "I'd better make sure Marbles and Flea Bit will be all right. Maybe they should come inside with—"

"No, ma'am, maybe they better not," Royal stated firmly. "But you can come with me if you want to. You can put them to bed and tell them good-night, okay?"

Cakes and coloring books were quickly forgotten as Maddie dashed outside. Royal gave Angel a tentative glance.

"That looks good," he said. "Is it safe?"

She flushed and turned away in embarrassment, but she knew what he meant. Obviously the Habenero peppers had gotten his attention. She lifted her chin and turned, refusing to let him know that he often intimidated her. Innocence dripped from her voice as she stared him straight in the face.

"Why? Shouldn't it be?"

Royal grinned and held up his hands, as if to say, I give up. "Just asking," he said, and glanced at the television. "Been giving any weather bulletins?"

She shook her head.

"Put it on channel four," he said. "They update better than the others."

Angel nodded and switched channels. The bulletin she'd been listening to was forgotten as she turned up the volume and turned on the stove. It was time to finish the meal.

Chapter 9

Supper was over, and Royal was giving Maddie her bath. Angel could hear the rumble of his voice and the childish squeals of Maddie's laughter as the evening routine played out. She knew that when it was over, there would be water on the floor and wet towels hanging from every hook, but it was something they both seemed to enjoy. While the hilarity was good, it reminded Angel that she was the outsider in this house.

At first she hadn't cared. In fact, she had welcomed the evenings to herself. The times when Royal was present and the duties of Maddie's keeper returned to the father, where they belonged, had been a welcome respite. But during the past few days, her feelings had begun to change. Instead of looking forward to the break in her routine, she began to dread it. Today was no exception.

She picked up a magazine and tossed it down, knowing she wouldn't be able to focus. Instead of turning on the television, she moved outside, choosing the old swing under a nearby oak tree rather than her usual place on the porch. She brushed off the seat, turned and sat, testing the length of her shorts against

the wooden seat. Satisfied that they were long enough to pre-
vent any splinters, she relaxed. Immediately, her shoes slid off
her feet.

The rope from which the swing was hanging was thick but
soft. Her fingers curled around its surface as she leaned back
and pushed off. At once, the sensation of weightlessness took
over, and she closed her eyes, letting herself go free. As she
did, an old memory surfaced, one of standing at the side of a
playground, watching as the other children in her class laughed
and played. Even then she'd been set apart, by her ethnicity
and the fact that the people she lived with were not her own.
So she'd stood alone, wanting a turn on the swings but afraid
to ask.

It had hurt then, not being one of the crowd. But now, after
so many years on her own, it was her saving grace. She cele-
brated her differences. She did not mourn them. And she'd
learned to appreciate her gifts rather than covet what she could
not have.

Motion stirred the air, blowing bits of her hair into her eyes
and then away from her face, plastering her T-shirt to the thrust
of her breasts and caressing the backs of her bare legs as she
continued to pump.

Back and forth.

Up and down.

Faster and faster.

Higher and higher.

When she opened her eyes, the world was flying past her in
a blur of blue and gray shadows. She dropped her head forward
and pulled up her legs, letting the momentum of her body move
the swing.

Peace came then. With nothing but the soft whoosh of air
against her ears and the beat of her heart for a rhythm, she
began to slow down. Only after the swing was motionless did
she become aware that she was no longer alone.

She felt his presence rather than saw him. When she looked

up, he was standing on the porch steps with his hands stuffed in his pockets, watching.

She shuddered.

Dusk hid all but the outline of his body and face from her gaze, and yet she sensed the intensity of his scrutiny. She didn't know whether to acknowledge his presence or make her excuses and leave. She did neither. When he came off the steps, her first instinct was to stand. And when he started toward her, the urge to run was strong. He moved quietly but with purpose, his strides certain and even. She tightened her grasp on the ropes and tried to tell herself that it was safe. But the closer he came, the faster her heart began to beat and the shorter her breaths became.

Lord help me. "Was there something you needed?" she asked.

Royal paused. Her question was a verbal stop sign if he'd ever heard one.

"Maddie wants you to read her a story."

Angel's voice rose an octave in pleased surprise. "She does?"

"Yeah," Royal said. "I told her this was your time to yourself, but that I'd ask."

Angel stared at him through the growing dusk, trying to draw a conclusion as to how he felt about his daughter's request. But it was getting too dark, and he was standing too still.

"I don't mind...if you don't," she said.

Her answer surprised him. "Why would I mind?"

She shrugged. "Well, I know how much you enjoy this time with her. That it's your special time together. I don't want to intrude or force myself into the situation."

Royal sighed, and Angel heard it. His voice was tinged with exasperation as he answered.

"Look, if it bothered me, I wouldn't have asked you. Okay?"

She nodded, and realized he probably couldn't see her.

"Yes, sir," she said quickly, then slipped on her shoes and started toward the house.

Royal stepped in her path, then cursed beneath his breath when he heard her frightened gasp.

"Damn it, woman, quit calling me sir," he said shortly. "And stop shaking like a cornered rabbit. I am not going to hurt you."

Before Angel could answer, he pivoted and stalked away. Thankful for the cover of darkness, she lifted a shaky hand to her face and started toward the house. When she got to the door, she turned and looked into the yard, past the illuminated circle beneath the security light. Motionless, she stared into the darkness.

Nothing moved, but he was out there somewhere. Was he watching her, as he had before? She breathed slowly, as if by doing so she could hear his approach. Then she sighed. Maybe she was reading more into this than was there. He had a right to observe her behavior. After all, he was her employer. Then why, she wondered, did every instinct she had tell her it was more than observation? Why did she feel as if he was waiting to pounce?

She shivered then stepped back, and without taking her eyes from the darkness, closed the door between them.

Royal stared at the house and the woman who stood in his doorway as he leaned against the hood of his truck. When he realized she was looking for him, the skin crawled on the back of his neck. The intimacy of such a search made him think of things better left alone. Half the time these days he didn't know whether he was coming or going.

The other day he'd gone to town to get horse feed and came home with everything but. He made appointments and then forgot to keep them. Even worse, he was getting short-tempered with Maddie for no reason at all. She was just a little girl. She shouldn't have to suffer for whatever was going on in her daddy's head.

As he watched, Angel moved. He took a deep breath, holding it as she took a step back—exhaling as she closed the door between them. The tenuous tie between them was broken. He shuddered. There was a hunger within him that was growing more and more difficult to control.

At the oddest times, her image would move through his mind and he'd catch himself thinking of the way her body swayed as she walked, of the way she chewed on her lower lip when she was thinking, of how her right eyebrow arched when she was about to let her temper fly.

He grinned. Damn, but she did have a temper. He was still trying to get over the slander of ''royal highness'' and had nightmares about Habenero peppers in his toothpaste. He ran his tongue over his lower lip. It was well now, but it had peeled, just as he'd predicted.

He'd learned a lesson that day. He still wasn't sure what kind of a friend Angel Rojas might be, but he could vouch firsthand as to how fierce an enemy she would make.

In a way, that was where their bond was strongest. He lived his life without following rules, railing against fate when it suited him and defying propriety to get something done his way. He respected independence. He admired passion. And from where he was standing, Maddie's angel had more than her share.

A faint rumble sounded in the distance. He looked at the sky, noting the absence of moon and stars. Clouds were gathering. Against the horizon, a single streak of lightning split the sky, like a fragile thread of silver. But it was soundless, too far away for worry. Chances were the rain would miss them.

He glanced at his watch. The luminous dial was a vivid reminder that morning always came far too soon. With a sigh, he pushed off from the truck and started toward the house. By now the story had surely been read. Maddie would be asleep. She always fell asleep in the middle of her bedtime story. And if he was smart, when he got inside the house, he'd go straight to his room and stay there. No more playing around with an angel's fire. Someone could get burned.

* * *

Amarillo wasn't all it was cracked up to be, at least not to Tommy Boy. It had been raining nonstop for the better part of two days. He'd been forced to stay holed up in this piss-poor room, waiting for the weather to clear. Yesterday he'd called his bank to check the balance in his checking account. It was getting low. Either he called a halt to his quest or he started working part-time jobs. He frowned as he considered his options. The promise he'd made to himself was getting out of hand. When he'd started this quest, the need to cleanse had burned within him. But with each woman who died, a little part of his anger died, too.

Nine women later, there was always the worry that the authorities might somehow connect the deaths. If that happened, his anonymity would be severely threatened. If the national media got wind of a serial killer, it would be over. He couldn't afford to let the FBI get involved. And yet there was a part of him that reveled in challenging the system, of getting away with the deeds. And the women who died had deserved it.

He'd traveled the same routes his daddy had taken. Unknowingly, he might have already taken out the woman who'd infected him. The possibility was remote, but it was there. He liked to think it had already happened.

He aimed the remote at the television set and clicked until he found a station broadcasting weather, then frowned. The northwestern part of the state was under a weather alert. There was a line of thunderstorms running from west of Amarillo all the way past the Fort Worth Dallas area and as far south as Austin. He cursed beneath his breath and aimed the remote, silencing the box. As long as this weather pattern held, the women in the business of selling sex would be somewhere else rather than the open lots of truck stops.

Since that was the case, he might as well make the best of it. Consider this a mini vacation. Bunching a pillow beneath his head, he rolled over and closed his eyes. The steady rhythm of raindrops splattering against the window soon lulled him to sleep.

Angel fought her covers as she dreamed her way toward morning. Lost in a nightmare in which Fat Louie played the lead role, she struggled to find her way out. One pillow was bunched beneath her cheek. The other had fallen to the floor. The lightweight blanket that had been covering her feet had slipped between the mattress and the footboard of her bed, and the sheet was wrapped around her legs. Sweat plastered her nightshirt to her body. The knit fabric clung to every curve, and her hair, still in a braid, had bunched at the back of her neck. In her mind, the sensations had translated themselves into Fat Louie's breath and Fat Louie's hands. She was fighting him now as she had fought him then. Closer and closer he came, pushing her into a corner, grabbing at her breasts and her backside. She doubled her fists to fight back—just as the light came on in her room.

"Get up!" Royal said quickly. "We've got to get to the cellar. I'm going to get Maddie. Meet me in the hall."

Angel was still trying to assimilate the fact that she was in this house and in this bed instead of stuck between Fat Louie and the wall of the restaurant kitchen when Royal disappeared.

"Wait!" she mumbled as she crawled out of bed, but he was already gone.

It was reflex that made her grab some clothes. What was it he'd said? Something about the cellar?

Then she heard it, the ominous howl of wind that comes with nature out of control.

Tornado.

It had been years since she'd heard the sound, and she'd been nineteen and living in Kentucky. That night a whole town had been destroyed, and eleven lives along with it. Now she had a real fear to face, not one of her dreams. Without hesitation, she began pulling on shorts and a T-shirt and looking for her shoes. Before she could find them, the power went out, plunging the house into darkness.

She turned. Guided by a slice of lightning that flashed outside her window, she headed for the hallway as Royal had told her to do. Her heart was pounding, her legs shaking as she called out.

"Royal!"

Suddenly he was there, coming toward her with a blanket-wrapped bundle in his arms.

"Here," he said, thrusting a flashlight into her hands. "Take this and lead the way."

Angel grabbed it and switched it on. She aimed the feeble beam of light ahead of them, mentally tracing the path they would take down the hall, into the kitchen and then to the cellar off the back porch.

She wished she'd been able to find her shoes, but it was too late to worry about that. Royal was at her heels. She could hear the rapid sounds of his breathing and Maddie's terrified sobs as they ran through the darkened house. The wind was louder, the howl a deep and eerie wail, like the sound of a runaway train.

She looked back once and almost stumbled.

"Hurry," he said.

He didn't have to say more.

Then they were at the back door and on the porch. Angel aimed the flashlight into the downpour and gasped as the wind blew the rain in her face. Royal was at her back, giving orders that she followed without thought.

"Trade," he said quickly, and shifted his daughter into Angel's arms before yanking the flashlight out of her hands.

Angel clutched Maddie with tender strength, sheltering her as much as she could as they dashed into the storm. Royal took her by the arm and dragged her toward the cellar, and she knew that, but for him, she would not have been able to stand. Another flash of lightning tore through the night, followed by a blast of thunder so loud it shook Angel's bones. Maddie started to scream. Angel wanted to join her. Instead, she stood with Royal, praying as he struggled to open the cellar door against the force of the wind.

Then it was open and he turned, bracing himself and shouting something to her that the storm took away. But she didn't need him to tell her what came next. Clutching Maddie, she ran down the steps and into another kind of darkness—one so thick that it felt devoid of any air. Before she had time to panic, Royal was behind her. The door slammed, and the sudden light from his flashlight was like the supernova of a star. She blinked and turned away, letting her eyes adjust to new surroundings.

Water dripped from the hem of her T-shirt onto her feet. A new fear arose as she remembered she was barefoot. Cellars were notorious for harboring scorpions and snakes. If they were here, she didn't want to know it.

Maddie fought against the covers over her head. Angel helped her emerge, then laid her cheek against the top of the little girl's head, rocking her in her arms as if she'd been a tiny baby.

"Ssh, ssh, baby, it's all right. It's all right," Angel crooned. "We're all together and we're safe. That's all that matters."

Adrenaline was starting to wane, and the muscles in Royal's arms were beginning to shake. There'd been a minute when he hadn't been sure he could get the door open. His fingers were trembling as he swiped them across his face to clear his vision. All he could think was thank God Angel had been here. He would never have been able to open the door with Maddie in his arms.

He looked at them, woman and child standing in the dim glow, and reacted without thinking. He moved. Seconds later he had them both in his embrace.

Surprised by the action, Angel flinched. But the feeling was so welcome. So right. They'd battled nature and won. They were protected from whatever was happening above them.

Maddie was still sobbing, but quieter. Angel ventured a look at Royal and knew she'd made a mistake. She was pinned by a smoky stare. Her mouth parted, but the words died on her lips.

Royal shivered. "Are you all right?"

"Thanks to you," Angel said, and looked away.

Royal cupped the back of his daughter's head. "Baby?"

Without looking up, Maddie held out her hands. Royal lifted her from Angel's arms and held her close against his bare chest.

"What's happening?" Maddie sobbed.

"It's a storm, sweetheart. But like Angel said, we're safe, and that's all that matters."

"What about Flea Bit and Marbles and Dumpling? What will happen to them?"

"They're probably safe and dry in the hay barn," he told her. "Remember, that's their favorite place."

Satisfied, Maddie quieted. The silence within the cellar lengthened as the storm continued to gather in strength.

Angel felt restless. She had questions, but unfortunately Royal Justice couldn't answer them as easily as he'd answered his daughter's. She kept thinking about the way it had felt to stand in his arms. His strength was evident, his compassion obvious, but something else had happened that she hadn't expected. Something she hadn't felt in so many, many years. Safe. She'd felt safe.

Needing to take her mind off of everything, including Royal's bare chest, she took stock of her surroundings. There were shelves directly before her with a couple of dozen empty fruit jars shoved to the back. There was a small jar of matches and a couple of empty lanterns on a lower shelf, which would do them no good. Three folding chairs leaned against the wall, and the concrete floor, while rough and damp against her bare feet, was clean—and as far as she could see, critter safe.

Before she had time to explore any further, the cellar door suddenly rattled on its hinges. Frightened, she spun around, looking to Royal for reassurance. She could tell he was battling some fears of his own.

"It's bad, isn't it?" she whispered.

He glanced at Maddie, who'd fallen back to sleep in his arms, then nodded.

She thought of the ranch and of his home. Of the barns and sheds and the miles and miles of fence. Of the animals, exposed to the elements. The loss could be devastating.

"I'm sorry."

"None of this is your fault."

"I know. That's not what I meant. I'm just sorry this is happening."

He nodded. "So am I."

Another blast of wind came, and to their horror, the heavy door began to lift. The sound of the storm was once again upon them. Wind funneled into the opening.

Angel screamed as the flashlight slid off the shelf.

Royal thrust Maddie into her arms and leaped forward, catching the door before it opened all the way.

"Get back!" he shouted, pointing to the farthest corner of the cellar. "Get back and get down."

Angel plastered herself into the corner and pressed Maddie's face against her shoulder to protect her from flying debris. She turned her face to the wall and began to pray.

Later she would remember momentary flashes of Royal straining to hold the door against the brunt of the storm. The pain of exertion contorting his features as his body threatened to give way. Of the wind drowning out the sounds of their screams. And just when she thought he might disappear before her eyes, that sudden and awful silence.

Royal dropped into the cellar as the door came shut with a thud. He sprawled on the steps. It was all he could do to stand.

"Oh, God," he muttered, and bent forward, clutching his knees and praying for strength.

For once, Maddie was too traumatized to speak. Her little blue eyes were wide with shock, her lips trembling as she clung to Angel's arms. She whimpered once and then was silent as Angel began to rock.

"Thank the Lord," Angel whispered.

Royal straightened and turned, fixing her with a weary stare.
"Keep Him on hold," he said. "It's not over."

Angel's eyes widened as a new fear began to spread. "But
the wind…the sounds…"

"It's the eye."

Angel groaned. He was right! Already she could hear the
wind beginning to pick up force. She looked at Royal, expecting to see defeat.

But she'd read him wrong. He wasn't defeated. He was mad.
He grabbed the flashlight from the floor and began sweeping
the darkened corners, searching for something, anything that
might help. As the wind turned into another long wail, he spied
a rusting crowbar on the lowest shelf. In a frantic lunge, he
thrust it through the iron handle on the underside of the door,
then jammed it into the groove between the door facing and
the wall of the cellar.

Like Excalibur, it seemed to have pierced the stone, but it
was enough of a wedge to give Royal added strength. It was
an extra pair of hands. He held on to the crowbar and rode out
the storm.

Maddie was silent, hardly moving, never taking her eyes
from her father. Angel felt the child's tension, but there was
nothing she could do except hold her close. Minutes passed.
They felt like hours. Then finally the storm began to lessen.
Angel didn't have to ask. She could see the answer on Royal's
face. It was passing.

A few minutes later Royal let go of the crowbar and sat on
the cellar steps, folded his arms across his knees and lowered
his head. Angel could see the muscles shaking in his arms.
Each breath he took seemed to come from deep, deep inside
him, as if he had to search for its source and then draw reserve
strength to claim it. Maddie wiggled to be put down, and Angel
turned her loose, then watched as she walked to Royal's side
and began to stroke his head as she did her kittens.

"Daddy…Daddy…"

Royal lifted his head. "What, baby?"

"Is it over?" Maddie asked.

He nodded, cupped her cheek and smiled wearily. "Yes, baby, it's over."

She leaned forward, as if what she had to say was a secret. "I want to go back to the house now."

Royal sighed, wondering if there was a house to go back to.

"I think you and Angel need to stay here for a minute while I go check on things, okay?"

It wasn't what she wanted to hear, but she nodded.

Royal started up the steps when Angel stopped him.

"Wait," she said, and handed him the flashlight, which he'd put on the shelf. "There will be damage. You need to see where you're going."

He frowned. "But that'll leave you two here in the dark, and Maddie's afraid of the dark."

Angel picked Maddie up. "So am I," she said softly. "But we don't want Daddy to get hurt, do we, baby?"

Maddie hesitated, and then shook her head.

Royal touched Maddie's cheek with the back of his hand, then he cupped Angel's shoulder. The look that passed between them was quick, but what Angel saw gave her strength. She nodded.

"I won't be long," Royal said.

Moments later, they were alone in the dark.

Chapter 10

Royal came out of the cellar braced for the worst. Although a steady rain continued to fall, the absence of wind seemed surreal. And it was dark. So dark. No security light. No intermittent flashes of lightning—just a curtain of water between him and what was left of his world.

Holding his breath, he lifted the flashlight, aiming the beam of light over the ground, then staring at broken branches, an uprooted tree, part of the pump house roof.

My God.

He clenched his jaw and aimed the beam toward the house, past the spiderlike roots of the upturned tree, past the roofless pump house. But it was raining hard, and the beam of light was too weak to pierce the darkness. He took a step forward, then thought of Angel and Maddie alone in the cellar. The idea of leaving them was repugnant, but he had no option. He stopped and turned, aiming the flashlight toward the cellar.

"You two okay?" he yelled.

Their voices echoed faintly in unison. "Yes."

"I'll be back soon."

Their answer was lost in the rain. Squinting against the downpour, he started toward the house, stepping around boards, over buckets, dodging whatever was in his path. He kept thinking of the generations of families who'd lived in the house before him, of the laughter and tears that had been shared behind those walls. Was it gone? Had it been damaged beyond repair?

He hadn't realized he'd been holding his breath until the beam of light caught and held on a corner of the house. He stopped, using the light to trace the angles of roof and walls. To his overwhelming relief, it was still standing.

"Thank you, God," he said softly, and moved up the steps into the house.

The first thing he stepped in was water. Expecting to see holes in the roof, he aimed the flashlight up. The ceiling seemed fine. He looked toward the porch and remembered running out of the house with Maddie in his arms.

The door! He hadn't closed the door behind him. The water had blown in with the storm. He aimed the flashlight to his left and started walking.

The living room had not fared well. A limb had blown off a tree and was half in and half out of the picture window. Sodden drapes hung askew, and the furniture near the window was soaked. The carpet squished as he walked across it, but it didn't matter. Things could be replaced.

He moved down the hallway, checking ceilings and floors, and entered Maddie's room. The window was broken, and the covers on her bed, as well as the floor around it, were covered in glass. He shuddered, then quickly moved away.

The door to Angel's room was standing open. Torn curtains and broken glass marked the beginning of the storm's entry there, as well. It was as if a madman had gone through the room, tossing things awry. Pictures had fallen off the walls. Lamps were on the floor. He aimed the flashlight to the ceiling, to the spreading water stain above Angel's bed.

He backed out and aimed the beam of light down the hall. One more bedroom to go. His.

Expecting more of the same, he was stunned when he pushed the door open. Everything was as intact as it had been when he'd left it, even the covers he'd tossed aside as he'd bolted out of bed. He whistled beneath his breath and shook his head. It didn't make sense, but he was glad to know there was one dry place they could spend the rest of the night.

The sound of glass breaking sent him across the hall. He shone the light. The big limb poking through Angel's window was closer to the floor. Everything was settling, including the weather.

He leaned against the doorjamb and sighed. Water was running out of his hair and into his eyes. Shivering from the cold, he swiped a weary hand across his face. There was plenty of damage, but nothing that couldn't be fixed. He shifted the flashlight to his other hand and started out of the house. It was time to bring his family home.

It didn't dawn on him until he started down the cellar steps that he had thought of Angel as part of his family. The ramifications of that simple acceptance didn't hit him until he shined the light in her face.

There in the dark, in the depths of the cellar, she sat—with his sleeping child in her lap and an expression on her face that stopped him cold. It was something he would have sworn he'd never see. But it was there just the same.

Trust. By God, she trusted him.

There had been times over the past few weeks when he'd pushed her too far, and he knew it. There were times she'd taken his guff without comment, but there were other times she'd given it back to him in spades. There had been times when he'd felt her fear, both of him and of the uncertainties in her life. He had not known how to make it better, and so they had kept their mental distances.

But tonight she'd done all he'd asked of her and then some. Because she had followed his lead so quickly, they'd gotten out of the house alive. He knew, as well as he knew his own name, that he could never have held Maddie and lifted the cellar door against the storm. And he could not have put Maddie down to do it, because the wind would have blown her away.

Royal's gaze blurred as he stared at his daughter's sleeping face. He couldn't begin to understand Maddie's dreams about a lady on her bed and the promise of angels, but by God, his doubts were over. Tonight Angel Rojas had lived up to her name. She'd been afraid of the storm and afraid of the dark, and yet she'd stifled her fears in order to protect his daughter, trusting him to take care of them both. Humbled by her faith, he shifted the light so it was out of her eyes. He started down the steps.

Angel knew her lips were trembling, but her composure had not shattered. All the while she'd been sitting in the dark, she'd been thinking of the path that had led her to this place. Only a few weeks ago she hadn't known these people existed, and now they were the most important people in her life. She thought of the storm that had raged over their heads and of the home they had abandoned. She saw the beam of Royal's flashlight as he started down the steps. He was back, and she was afraid to ask if there was anything left.

"Royal?"

"It's still there," he said.

"Thank God," Angel whispered, and then looked down as Maddie suddenly whimpered in her sleep. "Poor little girl," she said softly. "She's had a very rough night."

"We all have," Royal said and bent to lift her from Angel's arms as Angel looked up.

In the act of scooping Maddie and her covers, the backs of his hands slid the length of Angel's thighs. He clenched his jaw and closed his eyes. Her skin was warm and soft...so soft. Then he looked up. Their gazes met and held.

Even though the rain was still pouring down, he heard the rhythm of her breathing shift to an uneven gasp. He was close, too close to that sensuous mouth. All he would have to do was lean forward and he would know how she tasted. And then Maddie cried out in her sleep. He jerked and stood up, and the moment was gone.

An awkward silence ensued. It was all Angel could do to look at him, and Royal was at a loss as to what to say. It was the cold sifting into the cellar that prompted his return to sanity.

"Here," he said shortly, handing Angel the flashlight and then pointing to his sleeping daughter. "Trade me."

Angel stood. Once again the transfer was made. The moment Maddie was taken from her arms she felt weightless, as if the anchor holding her to earth had suddenly disappeared.

"Is it okay to leave?" Angel asked.

"Yes, and when we get out of the cellar, be careful where you walk. There's quite a bit of debris."

Angel nodded and thought of her shoes once more. Then she started up the steps, pausing at the top and aiming the beam of the flashlight into the cellar to light Royal's way.

The downpour had lessened to a drizzle. The thunder and lightning were moving away. As she waited for Royal to ascend, she shivered. She was wet and cold and about as tired as she'd ever been in her life.

"Do you want me to close the cellar door?" she asked as Royal cleared the top step with Maddie in his arms.

"Can you?" he asked. "It's pretty heavy."

"I'll try."

She laid the flashlight down, aiming it toward the opening. A few seconds later, the door fell shut with a thud.

Once again, Royal's estimation of this woman had to shift to make way for another fact. Angel Rojas was physically stronger than she looked. She stepped backward to pick up the flashlight, and he saw her legs, then her feet.

"My God, woman, you're barefoot! What were you thinking?"

The abruptness of his shout startled her, and she stumbled.

Burdened with Maddie's sleeping body, he had to watch her struggling to catch her balance.

"Be careful!" he cried. "There's all kinds of debris out here. You could cut your feet to shreds."

She picked up the flashlight and turned, aiming it to the right of his face, pinning him in the beam. The sarcasm in her voice was impossible to miss.

"I know that," she said, enunciating each syllable slowly and precisely. "I'm not stupid."

"Then why—"

"I couldn't find them. So I decided I'd rather be alive and barefoot than well-dressed and dead. Now for Pete's sake...and Maddie's...will you be quiet? You're going to wake her up."

Without waiting for his permission, Angel waved the flashlight at him, indicating he was to follow, and took off across the yard.

Even in the dark, even in the rain, Royal felt the heat rising on his face as he followed her. All he could see was her silhouette, but it was enough to know she was ticked off. Maddie whimpered again, and his focus shifted to getting them all inside the house, into dry clothes and into bed.

"You might want to wait here," he said as they stepped on the porch.

"Why?" she asked.

"Because there's broken glass all over the place. Give me the flashlight. I'll put Maddie in bed and then I'll come back for you."

"But I..."

Before she could argue, he disappeared. All she could see was a faint trail of light and then nothing. Struggling against the urge to throw something, she folded her arms across her chest and slumped against the doorjamb. There were times when that man's attitude got on her last nerve, and this was one of them. She stared into the kitchen, peering through the darkness and telling herself she didn't see anything broken.

Testing the theory of possible exaggeration, she took a tentative step into the kitchen and felt nothing but floor beneath her feet.

"Humpf," she snorted, and tried another step.

It took a second for the cold water to register, and when it did, she gasped and bolted outside. Her heart was pounding and she had the makings of a headache when she finally got her bearings. She hated to admit it, but it would seem that he'd been right. So she would wait. No big deal.

When she heard him coming, she braced herself for another confrontation. It never came. Before she knew what was happening, he handed her the flashlight and scooped her off her feet.

"I couldn't find your shoes, either," he said. "So don't wiggle. I'm too tired to argue."

Angel looked at him. At the hard angles of his face and the glitter in his eyes. She remembered how fiercely he had fought the storm to keep the cellar door shut and them from being sucked out into the storm.

"I'm sorry you have to do this," she said quietly.

As soon as she spoke, the tension on his face disappeared. He sighed. "And I'm sorry I snapped at you. I wasn't mad, just worried."

"I know. I shouldn't have been so defensive," she said. "I've depended upon myself for so long that I've forgotten how to accept help."

Royal nodded and kicked the door shut behind them after they entered the house.

"Aim the light straight ahead," he said. "And don't worry about what you see. There's nothing that can't be fixed."

She did as he said, absorbing the chaos of the house in the bits and pieces the light revealed. Although it was still standing, there was enough obvious damage for her to realize how dangerous it would have been had they stayed inside. She knew that most people killed in tornadoes were killed by flying debris, rather than by the twister itself.

"Oh, Royal," she said softly, and went limp in his arms.

He felt her shock. "Don't worry about it," he said quietly. "All that matters is that we're safe."

She nodded, but the images stayed with her. He passed her bedroom.

"Wait," she said. "You missed my room."

"You can't sleep in there," he said shortly. "The windows are broken. There's glass and water all over the place, and it's the same in Maddie's room. But we got lucky. Somehow my room escaped being damaged. We'll be able to spend the rest of the night in there."

Lucky? She was going to sleep in his room and this was lucky? Crazy was more like it.

"All of us?" she asked.

He set her down just inside the doorway.

"All of us. Right there in my bed, with you on one side of my daughter and me on the other. And before you balk on me, consider the situation. It's after three in the morning. If you're as tired as I am, you won't care who the hell you're in bed with as long as they leave you alone."

Angel bit her lip. A thousand questions were begging to get out, and she didn't have the guts to voice a one.

Royal leaned forward, pinning her with a cool stare.

"Do we have a problem?"

She glared at him. "No."

"Is there something you want to tell me?" he asked.

She clenched her jaw. "Like what?"

"Do you snore?"

"No!"

"Then we have nothing further to discuss." He thrust the flashlight in her hand. "We need to get dry. I've already changed Maddie's clothes. My clean T-shirts are in the bottom drawer. Get one on and then get in bed. I won't be more than a couple of minutes behind you."

"Uh, um—"

"On a practical note," Royal added, "if you need to use the

bathroom, don't flush. The power's off, and that means the tank won't refill.''

"Right," Angel said, and was thankful for the darkness because her face was flaming.

Having said all he needed to say, Royal stood, waiting for her reaction. When she neither moved nor spoke, he sighed in weary defeat.

"Woman, what the hell are you waiting for?"

She was as tired as Royal and probably twice as cold. Her feet felt as if they'd never be warm again. But she would have died before giving him a reason to complain.

"I guess nothing," she said shortly, and then turned her back to him and started pulling her wet T-shirt over her head.

"Oh, yeah, right," Royal muttered. "I was just leaving." He bolted out the door.

Long after they were both in bed, with Maddie sound asleep between them and the sound of rain falling softly on the rooftop, Royal lay without moving, staring through the darkness to the place where Angel slept. Even though the circumstances were extraordinary that had led to this event, he couldn't quit thinking that he'd never slept with another woman in his life except Susan. He'd had plenty of what he liked to call "encounters," but to lie down and sleep with someone was invoking a trust he held dear.

After a while, the uniqueness of the situation became less and less important. He closed his eyes. When he opened them again, it was morning.

Somewhere between a dead sleep and light slumber, Royal heard someone calling his name. He groaned and shoved his nose into the pillow. All he could think was that he ached all over and hoped he wasn't getting sick.

Then he heard it again and rolled over on his back. Whoever it was was persistent, he would give them that. He yawned and stretched, and as he did, felt the shape of little feet digging into his side. He frowned. Maddie? Why was Maddie sleeping in his bed? And then he remembered.

The storm.

He sat straight up in bed.

The door flew open. Roman's wife, Holly, burst in. Her short dark hair was loose and flying, her eyes filled with fear. When she saw them, the look on her face was somewhere between shock and relief. She turned in the doorway and shouted down the hall.

"Roman! In here! They're in here!"

At the noise, Angel woke with a start, and like Royal sat straight up in bed.

"What's happening? Is it storming again?" she asked, and started to reach for Maddie.

"No," Royal groaned. "It's my brother."

"Good Lord." Angel sighed and fell back to the bed with a thump, her hand plastered over her chest in dramatic fashion. "That probably shortened my life by a good year."

Royal grimaced. He knew just how she felt. But he should have known that Roman would come. The Justices had a way of looking out for each other. He was crawling out of bed as Roman ran into the room.

Roman's face was pale and his voice was shaking as he gave Royal a fierce hug.

"We heard about the storms when we woke this morning. Four people died and more than a dozen houses were destroyed. It's all over the news." He glanced over Royal's shoulder to the bed, and his eyes widened perceptibly.

Royal lifted a sleepy Maddie into his arms as she began to come to. "We're fine," he said. "Luckily this room escaped damage. The other rooms were uninhabitable."

Roman nodded. "We noticed," he said softly. "When I topped the rise leading to the house, I was afraid to get out of the car. And when you weren't in the cellar and you didn't come out when we called, we started to worry."

Holly leaned against Roman and sighed. "Actually, it scared

us silly. I was afraid to look and afraid not to,'' she said, and started to cry.

Maddie frowned. "Don't cry, Aunt Holly. I don't like it when you cry.''

Holly lifted Maddie out of Royal's arms and hugged her tight. "You've got quite a cleanup job ahead of you. Let us take Maddie. At least you won't have to worry about her getting hurt during the repairs.''

Maddie's lower lip slid forward. "I want to go home with Uncle Roman and Aunt Holly. This house scares me.''

Royal didn't bother to hide his relief. He glanced at Angel.

"It *would* make things easier for us.''

Angel wished she could disappear. Nothing in her past had prepared her for the embarrassment of lying in her boss's bed, in full view of his family, while a disaster cleanup was being discussed.

"Is there anything you need?'' Roman asked.

Royal nodded. "Yes, call the electric company and the phone company for me. I left my cell phone on the table last night. Needless to say, the tree limb and the rain didn't do it any good.''

Roman whipped out his cell phone and handed it to his brother. "Use this one until you get yours back on. You'll need to make all kinds of calls. And as soon as I get Holly and Maddie into Dallas, I'll come and help.''

"Bring breakfast when you come,'' Royal said.

Roman grinned. "Done.''

"I want breakfast, too,'' Maddie said.

Holly grinned. "We'll stop at McDonald's, okay?''

"Yeah!'' Maddie shrieked. "Beanie Babies.''

Royal frowned. "I thought you were hungry.''

In total female fashion, Maddie ignored the absurdity of her father's remark. Everyone knew that toys came with food at McDonald's.

Holly looked at Angel, feeling sympathy for the predicament she was in. "Are you all right?'' she asked.

Angel nodded and ventured a look at Royal. "Thanks to him, we're all okay."

A little embarrassed, Royal shrugged off the compliment. "I'm glad I woke up in time. Just let me get my boots on and I'll get Maddie some clothes."

"Let me," Holly said. "I know where most of her clothes are kept."

"I'll show you!" Maddie said.

"No, baby. You can't go in your room until we get it all cleaned up," Royal said.

Maddie frowned. "I didn't mess it up, Daddy, honest I didn't."

Royal grinned. "I know that. Now let's get you to the bathroom and your hair brushed. As soon as Angel and I fix the house, Uncle Roman and Aunt Holly will bring you home, okay?"

Maddie shrugged. "Am I staying all night with them, too?" she asked.

Roman tweaked his niece's nose. "Yes, Little Bit, you're staying all night. Now quit worrying and do what your daddy says."

Royal and Maddie disappeared into the adjoining bathroom, and Holly went to Maddie's room to search for clothes. Angel was trapped beneath the covers and Roman's all-seeing gaze.

"Rough night?" he asked.

Angel glared. "I've had better." Then she added, "Maddie has some chigger bites on her leg."

Roman nodded. "We'll see to them."

"Don't forget to take her chewable vitamins. They're in the kitchen on the shelf to the right of the sink."

Roman nodded again, but his estimation of this woman had just gone up five notches. In spite of everything that had happened, her worries seemed focused on Maddie.

"Got some at the house," he said softly.

Angel sighed and looked away. "I just…"

"Don't apologize to me," Roman said. "I'm with you.

Along with Holly, Maddie is one of the most important females in my life.''

Angel almost smiled. ''Well, then,'' she said softly, fidgeting with the covers and wishing someone would hurry up and come back. To her relief, Royal and Maddie emerged from the bathroom.

The silence in the room was impossible for Royal to mistake. He stared at the blush on Angel's face and gave Roman a hard-edged glare.

''Roman?''

Roman met the glare with a cool, unaffected stare. ''Yeah?''

''Are you messing in my business again?''

Roman winked at Angel and grinned. ''Nope.''

Angel slid a little deeper beneath the covers and wished herself invisible.

''Surely there are more important things to dwell on this morning than this,'' she snapped.

Both men jerked as if they'd been slapped. Before they could respond, Holly was back with Maddie's clothes. A few minutes later they were gone, and Angel was left with the growing feeling that she'd just lost her safety net.

Wearing a pair of Royal's boots, she picked her way through what was left of her bedroom to find some clothes of her own. In the process, she stumbled. When she looked down, she saw the toe of her shoe sticking out from beneath the dust ruffle on her bed.

''Finally,'' she muttered, and gathered the shoes up with the rest of her things.

Dressed and shod, she began searching for Royal. She found him standing on the porch. She paused in the doorway behind him, absorbing his stillness. He stood with his feet apart, his shoulders back, as if bracing himself for a blow. She smiled. Just as she might have expected. The storm had passed, but if need be, Royal Justice was still ready to go to war.

Chapter 11

"What do we do first?" Angel asked.

Startled by the sound of her voice, Royal spun around. Separated by a yard of space and the screen on the door, he still felt as if she'd invaded his skin.

Do first?

He wondered what she'd say if he told her the truth of what he was thinking. With her, he didn't know where to start…or even if he should.

Angel pushed the door open and walked outside. His silence was unnerving, as was the look in his eyes.

"Royal? Is something wrong? Did the storm—"

"No," he said, and looked away. "My mind was somewhere else."

That she could understand. There was debris as far as she could see. One of the small outbuildings had completely disappeared, and others were missing roofs. There was a section of rafters lying across part of the main corral fence. The large tree at the edge of the yard was missing several large limbs, one of which had gone through her bedroom window. It was such a mess, and Royal seemed so solemn, her compassion overruled her head. She walked to where he was standing and took his hand.

"It will be all right," she said softly. "We'll have this place back to normal before you know it."

Breath caught in the back of Royal's throat as the scene before him suddenly blurred. He didn't look at her and couldn't bring himself to acknowledge her presence. Her tenderness was his undoing.

We? She said we?

He gave her a quick glance, nodded and looked away. The task of putting everything back to rights didn't seem as insurmountable as it had moments earlier.

"What do you want me to do first?"

Royal turned, and the urge to take her in his arms made him weak. He managed a grin.

"Hell, honey, even *I* don't know what to do first."

"Then we need to make a list," Angel said. "Wait here. I'll be right back."

She went into the house and came out with a pad of paper and a pen.

"Let's start with a tour," she suggested. "When you see something that needs to be fixed or replaced, I'll write it down. Then we'll go from there."

She looked up, waiting for his approval. "If that's okay with you," she added.

Royal hugged her. He knew it could be a mistake, but he didn't give a good damn. He'd made plenty of mistakes in his life, and if holding her this close was going to be another, then so be it.

Angel was taken unaware, but before she could think what to do, he'd let her go and turned away. She stood in silence while her heart hammered wildly against her chest, then watched as he bent to lift a small piece of corrugated tin from the flower bed and toss it over the fence.

"Machine shop roof," he said shortly, and turned to see if she was following. "Angel."

She blinked as if coming out of a trance, then managed to answer.

"What?"

"Machine shop roof. Write it down."

"Oh…yes," she said, and so the morning began.

By noon, the rural electric company had restored power and the phones were working. An insurance adjuster had come and gone, giving Royal leave to commence repairs. One of Royal's friends was a roofer, and he'd come within an hour of Royal's call. They were both on the roof assessing the damage to the house while Angel waited below. The inconsistent murmur of voices could be heard inside the house, and she knew Roman was on the phone talking to a contractor regarding other repairs. As she stood at the foot of the ladder, she heard a car coming down the drive. She turned to look.

It was a black pickup.

And just for a minute, her heart stopped. She was halfway up the ladder and heading for Royal before it dawned on her what she was doing. She stopped in midstep, took a slow, deep breath and made herself go back the way she'd come. By the time she reached the ground, the pickup was parked. The man who got out wasn't wearing a beard, nor was he short and skinny.

Well over the age of seventy, he rolled when he walked and was so bald that the sun reflected off of his head when he took off his hat. He gave her a wink and a grin, then glanced at the roof where Royal and the insurance adjuster were standing.

"Been up there long?" he asked.

"A while," Angel said.

"Then they oughta be just about through."

"Yes, sir."

He smiled and offered his hand. "Name's Waycoff, Dan Waycoff. I guess you'd be Royal's new housekeeper."

Angel nodded as her fingers were engulfed by a large, callused palm.

"I neighbor the Justice ranch to the west. Real pleased to meet you," Waycoff said. "Been tellin' the missus that little Maddie is gettin' to be a handful for one man to handle alone, what with her startin' to school and all this fall."

"Yes, sir," Angel said.

"Hope you'll be happy here," Waycoff said. "Royal's a good man. Ain't many like him left in this world."

"That's true," she said, and looked up. To her relief, the men were coming down.

She held the ladder until they were clear, then started to make herself scarce. Royal stopped her with a look.

He was weary. She could see it in his eyes. And there was a smudge of dirt along the edge of his chin that she wanted to wipe away. Instead, she stood, waiting for him to make the first move.

Royal sighed, wishing he could call back that moment this morning when she'd taken him by the hand. He could still remember the softness of her skin and how firm her grip was. In a way, it was indicative of the woman herself. At first glance she seemed small and helpless, but he'd seen firsthand the strength, both mental and physical, that she continued to exhibit.

"Are you hungry?" he asked.

She started to lie, then knew it would serve no purpose. "Yes."

To her surprise, he grinned and tugged at her braid. "Then what are you waiting for?" He pointed at Dan Waycoff. "As soon as I get rid of this squatter, we're going to town to eat lunch."

Waycoff laughed. "You mean I'm not invited?" he teased.

Royal grinned. "Not unless you've taken a vow of fasting."

All the men, including Waycoff, laughed.

Angel smiled. She supposed it was a joke between old

friends. Then she remembered that the man who was coming to replace the glass in the windows had yet to arrive.

"But what about the glass man," she said. "Shouldn't I stay and..."

Royal frowned. "Hell, no. I've already talked to him at length. The place is a mess. I told him to fix it. If he can't find the stuff that's broken on his own, then he doesn't need to be here. Now go do whatever you need to do, and tell Roman to finish what he's doing if he wants to come, too. We're leaving in five minutes."

"Yes, sir," she said, and started up the porch steps.

Royal frowned. She'd done it again.

"I thought I told you to quit calling me sir."

Angel turned. Her voice was steady, but there was an edge to it he didn't miss.

"When you quit giving me orders, I'll quit calling you sir."

Then she went inside, leaving him standing in the yard to make what he chose of her answer. He was muttering beneath his breath when he suddenly remembered he wasn't alone. He rolled his eyes and turned around. Both men were grinning.

"Quite a little lady you got there," Waycoff said.

Royal snorted. "She's something, all right, but I'm not sure *lady* is the right word. She doesn't pull punches, and the hell of it is, most of the time she's right."

Waycoff slapped Royal on the back. "Then you better be watching your backside, boy, 'cause that there's the kind of woman you don't want to play loose with."

Royal glared. "I'm not playing anything with her, including loose, and I'd better not hear anything to the different," he warned.

Both men looked suitably chastised and got to the business at hand. The roofer left with a promise to be back early tomorrow, and Waycoff left a couple of minutes later, after having delivered the news that his wife was bringing them food for their supper.

As the last man drove away, Royal felt the burden of re-

building had lightened a bit. Plans were in motion. Decisions
were being made. And friends were coming through for him
in every way.

The main street of Alvarado was busy. Royal circled the
block twice before a parking space became available. He
wheeled to the curb, parked and pocketed his keys as he helped
Angel out of the cab. Roman got out on the passenger side,
and together the trio entered the local café.

The noise level was just below a roar. To Angel, it seemed
that the customers all knew each other and no matter where
they were sitting kept a running conversation going between
bites.

Royal spied a table being vacated and started across the room
with Angel behind him and Roman bringing up the rear.

It didn't take long for Angel to be noticed. A stranger's face
was always fodder for comment, and when she was keeping
company with one of the area's most eligible bachelors it was
worth remembering. Royal felt the stares and knew, when the
laughter shifted to whispers, that it was probably about Angel.
He stopped at the table and pulled out her chair. She hesitated,
then quietly took her seat. Roman dropped into the chair opposite hers and reached for the menus propped between the
napkin holder and a bottle of steak sauce. He handed one to
Angel with a wink, opened his own and began to read.

Royal lowered himself into his seat, grunting as his muscles
protested. Angel heard him and looked up.

"I think I have some aspirin in my purse."

Because it was second nature to deny anything regarding
weakness, Royal started to argue. But she'd offered without
malice or jest, and his macho was just about gone, thanks to
last night's wind.

"Don't mind if I do," he said shortly, and held out his hand,
watching as she shook three tablets into it. When the waitress
brought glasses of water and left with their orders, he downed
the aspirins in one gulp.

"Hey, Angel."

She looked up.

"Thanks."

"It was nothing," she said.

"You noticed," he argued. "That's something."

Roman eyed his brother, then Angel, then his brother again.

"Have I become invisible?"

Neither answered him.

Roman grinned. "Now I know how a boar hog feels about tits," he drawled.

Angel frowned. Royal narrowed his eyes to a condemning stare.

"I don't get it," she said.

"Damn it, Roman," Royal muttered.

But Roman wasn't through having fun at his brother's expense. He and Ryder had endured enough bossing from Royal through the years to last several lifetimes, and seeing his brother tied up in knots over a woman was too good to let pass.

Roman leaned forward. "Tits on a boar hog—out of place and completely useless?"

Royal's face turned dark red. Angel could tell his well-frayed emotions were about to explode. The urge to protect him came out of nowhere, and she reached across the table to Roman, her fingers curling around his wrist. She was smiling, but her grip on his arm was not friendly.

"Royal is your brother. And since I have no siblings, I can't say I know what sibling rivalry is like. But I don't like being the butt of jokes between you two. Added to that, you don't know how close you came to losing him last night. But for the grace of God and Royal's refusal to quit on us, you could have been planning his funeral today, not helping him clean up. So I suggest you shut up." She picked up her purse. "Now if you'll both excuse me, I'm going to powder my nose. When I come back, I expect peace and quiet at this table. If I have to eat my meal alone to get it, then I will do so. Do I make myself clear?"

Suitably chastised, Roman managed to nod.

It was hard to say who was more shocked, Royal or Roman. They sat in total silence, watching as Angel made her way through the maze of tables to the rest rooms near the front door. Anger was evident in the force of her stride. For a minute, neither of them moved.

When she'd lit into Roman, Royal had been too surprised to speak. Now he felt as if he'd been sideswiped. His ears were ringing, and he wondered if his face was as red as it felt.

"Well, damn," he said softly, and looked at his hands because looking at his brother was impossible.

Roman took a deep breath and grinned. "You're done for," he said softly.

Royal focused immediately. He spit his words out in short, angry jerks.

"Roman, just for once, like she said, will you shut the hell up?"

Roman lifted his water glass, making an anonymous toast, and took a deep drink.

"What was that all about?" Royal muttered.

Roman's grin widened. "Just drinking to your health. Like the lady said, I'm damned glad I'm not planning your funeral."

Royal leaned forward, making sure their neighbors at the nearest table didn't overhear what he said.

"If you don't shut that smart mouth of yours, you'll be worrying about your own funeral, not mine."

Roman laughed and drained his glass. Their food—and Angel—arrived at the same time. They ate their meal in total silence.

Angel was still shaking when she laid down her fork. Her plate was empty, and she had no idea what she'd just eaten. Her head was spinning, and all she could think was, *What have I done?* It had taken all her willpower to come back to the table and face them. She'd made a fool of herself, but she knew in her heart she would do it again. In her entire life, she hadn't admired many men. But after last night, Royal topped that short list by far. He'd put himself at risk time and again for her and Maddie. The way she looked at it, she owed him a debt she could never repay. Speaking up on his behalf was little reward, but it was the best she could do.

The waitress laid their bill at the edge of the table. Royal was reaching to get it when Roman slipped it from beneath his fingers.

"This one's on me," he said. "I'll meet you at the truck."

Royal nodded his thanks as Roman got up and headed for the cashier. He took a deep breath and ventured a look at Angel. She was fiddling with her purse and looking everywhere but at him.

"You ready?" he asked.

To his surprise, she met his question with a straightforward gaze.

"Yes."

He hesitated, distractedly chewing on the edge of his lip. It had to be said. There was no use waiting.

"Uh, Angel."

She froze. *Oh, no. Here it comes.*

"About earlier…"

She waited. All she could think was, *Please don't fire me.*

"It wasn't necessary…but thanks."

She went weak with relief. "It was no big deal. Just something I needed to do."

That was something he understood.

They exited the café, and the sultry air enveloped them. Angel dug in her purse for her sunglasses as Royal unlocked the truck. A few yards away, three men were leaning against the side of the building beneath a tattered awning, taking the offered shade for themselves with no regard for passersby.

"Hey, Justice," one of them called.

Angel looked up as Royal turned. She could tell by the expression on his face that he wasn't pleased to see them.

"Duke," Royal said, acknowledging the other man's presence as he sauntered toward them.

Duke looked from Angel to Royal and back again. The smirk on his face aggravated Royal even more.

"Well, now, I heard you got hit pretty hard last night," Duke said.

"We're still standing," Royal said shortly, and wished Roman would hurry.

Duke nodded and grinned at Angel. "You ain't too choosy about the company you keep, are you, darlin'? When you get tired of old Justice there, you come on into town and give me a try. I'm real partial to brown-eyed señoritas."

Angel froze. It wasn't anything she hadn't heard a thousand times before, but for Royal, once was obviously too much. One second Duke was grinning at her and the next he was sitting on the sidewalk with his hands across his face. Blood was oozing between his fingers, and there was a stunned expression in his eyes.

"Well, hell, Justice, I think you broke my nose."

"And you're damned lucky that was all I broke," Royal said softly. "She works for me, and she's proved herself to be a damned good friend, which is a whole hell of a lot more than I can say for you. And if I hear of you, or anyone else, saying anything off-color about this woman, that won't be all I break. Do we understand each other?"

Suitably corrected, Duke sat quietly, holding his nose and afraid to so much as look in Angel's direction.

But Royal wasn't through with him yet. "Don't you have something you'd like to say to Miss Rojas?"

Duke nodded, dripping blood all over his shirt and pants. "I'm real sorry, ma'am."

Angel stared in disbelief. Before she could answer, Roman came out of the café and stopped in midstride.

"What the hell happened?" he asked.

The two men who'd been standing with Duke shrugged. They wanted no part of Duke's folly.

Roman headed for Royal. "Is everything okay?"

Royal gave Duke one last look. "It is now," he drawled.

Then he turned, yanked open the door to the truck and stepped aside, waiting for Angel to get in. She slid into the middle of the seat, then watched as Royal circled the truck while Roman crawled in beside her.

"You okay?" he asked.

She arched an eyebrow and nodded as Royal slid behind the steering wheel. The door fell shut with a thud. There was a long moment of silence while Royal fumbled with the keys. Angel sighed. There was no use waiting. It had to be said.

"Uh... Royal."

He paused without looking at her.

"Yeah?"

"It wasn't necessary...but thanks."

He jammed the key into the ignition. "It was no big deal. Just something I needed to do."

Angel laughed.

The sound of her laughter was balm to his soul. Royal looked at her and grinned.

The shared moment bonded them in a way nothing else could have done. Resisting the urge to trace the smile on her lips, he started the engine.

Roman stared at them both as if they'd suddenly gone mad. "Have I missed something?" he asked.

"Yes," they said in unison.

He waited for an explanation that never came. "Well, then," he finally mumbled. "That's what I thought."

Angel was quiet all the way to the ranch. Satisfied with listening to the two brothers talking, she let her thoughts go free. It wasn't until later, when Roman and the workmen were gone and the sun was starting to set, that she realized it was going to get dark. And that meant going to bed. Without Maddie to lie between them, where would she sleep? Her mattress had been ruined by the rain, and Maddie's was still filled with shards of glass. Tomorrow new ones were being delivered, but tonight, the only place still in one piece was Royal's room...and Royal's king-size bed. Before her worry could fester, she heard a vehicle coming down the driveway. Royal was at the barn feeding Maddie's cats. She went to the door and recognized the black pickup from earlier in the day. That would be Dan Waycoff's wife with the supper she'd promised, Angel thought.

Hurriedly, she brushed wayward strands of hair from her face and smoothed the front of her shirt. There was no way to look good after a day like today. She'd been up to her knees in mud and water, and there was a small tear at the hem of her shirt from some of the branches she'd carried away. She sighed, hoping Mrs. Waycoff wasn't big on first impressions. When the woman crawled out of the truck, Angel began to relax.

Almost six feet tall and as thin and rangy as an old muley cow, the woman lifted a long arm in a friendly wave and hefted a box from the seat beside her. She started talking before the truck door was shut.

"Hello, there," she yelled. "I'm Myra Waycoff. Hell of a way to meet, isn't it, girl? Dan says you all were real lucky last night. We got side winds but nothing direct. Loosened a few shingles on the roof and rained in around the chimney, but shoot, I been tellin' that Dan for almost three years to fix it, and he hasn't done it yet. Do you like fried chicken?" She laughed and continued her spiel before Angel could answer. "Hell, what am I asking? Everyone likes fried chicken. Brought some potato salad and biscuits, too. And a pie. Royal likes my pies."

She was on the porch and walking through the door Angel held open. She set the box on the table with a thump, stood back and dusted her hands on the seat of her faded jeans.

Angel couldn't stop smiling. Never in her life had she met a woman as lacking in subterfuge as this one.

"It's nice to meet you, Mrs. Waycoff. My name is Angel Rojas."

"Have mercy, child. Call me Myra."

She enveloped Angel in a smothering hug, which Angel found strangely comforting. A combination of scents clung to her old plaid shirt. Angel recognized hay and sweet feed and, if she wasn't mistaken, ginger and cinnamon. Her grin widened as Myra launched into a barrage of questions she didn't seem to want answered.

"Angel, is it?" Myra said as she turned Angel loose. "Is that your real name? Lord have mercy, I'd never be able to live up to such a name. Dan says I'm hell on wheels." She threw back her head and laughed, making the short gray curls on her head bounce with vigor. "But when you get my age, if you're still kicking, I figure you ought to be able to be any damned thing you want. Know what I mean?"

The question wasn't anything more than punctuation, a way for Myra to catch her breath. She launched into another subject without batting an eye.

"You got hit hard," she said. "But not as hard as the Deevers down the road. Their whole house is gone."

Angel's heart went out to those people. Even if she didn't know them, last night they'd shared a terror no one should know.

"Oh, my," Angel said softly. "If they were as afraid as I was, then bless their hearts."

Myra beamed. "I knew before I met you that we were going to get along," she said.

"Why?" Angel asked.

"Because Dan came home laughing about how you put Royal in his place."

A slow flush spread up Angel's neck and face as she remembered. *I'll quit calling you sir when you quit telling me what to do.*

"I shouldn't have lost my temper like that," Angel said. "Royal is my boss."

"Pooh," Myra said. "He's still a man, isn't he?"

Definitely. But Angel kept the thought to herself.

Myra slapped Angel on the back. It was a comforting thud. The grin on Angel's face spread wider.

"Men are like range steers. They need boundaries or they'll

run wild all over the place. Give 'em plenty of rope. Don't want 'em to feel like you've got 'em tied down. But for God's sake, make sure that rope is tied to something solid.''

Myra Waycoff's analogies were priceless. Angel knew she shouldn't be discussing her boss like this, but she couldn't help herself. ''Why?''

Myra grinned. ''Because eventually they're gonna run out of rope, and when they do, they'll buck like hell before they realize they like being roped and they like being tied.''

Angel was still laughing when Royal came in the back door.

He liked Myra Waycoff, but he was aware of her verbal tendencies. He shuddered to think what she'd been telling Angel.

''What's so funny?'' he asked.

Myra gave him a hug similar to the one Angel had received. ''You, boy. Just you.''

Royal rolled his eyes and gave Angel a nervous look, wondering what family secrets the old woman had revealed. But Angel wasn't talking. In fact, she wouldn't even look Royal in the face. That was enough to make him worry, but he wasn't deterred for long. When he frowned at Myra, she slapped his rear. He grinned and kissed her soundly on the cheek before dancing her around the kitchen floor.

Angel was stunned. She'd never seen Royal so playful. A part of her rejoiced in the sight and a part of her felt guilty that she'd done nothing to make him happy. Even if he was her boss, their relationship should be comfortable. They should not constantly be at each other's throats.

''Quit, you damned fool,'' Myra finally cried, and thumped Royal on the arm. ''I'm too old for such carrying on.''

She grabbed Angel by the wrist and yanked her forward. Before either Royal or Angel knew it, they'd been thrust into each other's arms.

''Dance with her, boy. I'm going home. Nice to meet you, Angel, girl. I'll be back in a couple of days to pick up my dishes.''

She was driving away before they had the good sense to move. Royal looked at Angel. Her eyes had the look of a doe caught in the headlights of an oncoming car. As much as he might like to explore the softness of her skin and the textures of the hair brushing across the backs of his hands, he knew it was time to let her go.

"She's something, isn't she?"

Angel swallowed, trying to find words in her brain that would make any sense. But coherence was lost to her. The feel of Royal's hands at the middle of her back and the solid length of his body pressed too intimately against her own was making her weak.

Then suddenly she was free and Royal was at the sink, washing his hands and whistling beneath his breath. Bereft by the abrupt abandonment, she turned and began taking out the food that Myra had brought. She didn't know Royal was standing at the sink and shaking or that the water he was using was deep-well cold to keep his mind off dragging her down the hall and taking her to bed. All she knew was that he'd let her go.

"Smells good," Royal said, as she began to take covers from bowls.

"Yes. If she cooks as well as she talks, it will be wonderful," Angel said.

Royal laughed, and the tension between them was broken. But all the way through their meal, she kept glancing outside to the ever-growing darkness.

Night.

What would it bring?

Chapter 12

The house was quiet. Only the sounds of running water from the adjoining bathroom could be heard. Angel sat on the edge of the cot Royal had set up. There were no words for the relief she felt when she walked into the room and saw it there, waiting to be made up. She'd done so quickly, claiming it as hers before Royal emerged.

She'd bathed while Royal had been on the phone. She stared at the closed door between them, then the few yards of space separating her cot from his bed and knew it would never be enough. Something was happening between them. Something she wasn't ready to face. Something she didn't know how to stop.

The water stopped. Her pulse skipped a beat and then accelerated. He would come out and she didn't know what to say. Too much had gone on between them to ignore. After the way Royal had decked that man on the street, people would obviously talk. She sighed. The only thing she had to her name was a good reputation. She didn't want to lose it. Not even for Royal. He'd hired her as a housekeeper, not a whore. She wouldn't be any man's whore, but dear God, she would be Royal's love.

Afraid to face him, she laid down on the cot, pulled the covers over her breasts and pretended to be asleep. The bathroom door opened. Willing herself to a calm she didn't feel, she heard him pause, then sigh. Her heart went out to him, but she didn't move.

Royal knew she wasn't asleep. And she was in the wrong bed. He hung his wet towel on the doorknob and turned back the covers on his bed. Without raising his voice, he calmly announced his intentions.

"I'm going into the living room to watch the evening news and weather. When I come back, you'd better be in this bed or I'll put you in it myself."

Angel's eyes flew open in sudden shock, but it was too late to argue with him. He was already gone. She heard the muted voice of a local newsman. She threw back the covers and sat on the side of the cot, contemplating his threat. His voice had been too calm, too matter-of-fact to ignore.

She stared at the wide, inviting surface of the bed on the other side of the room, then at the cot, and shook her head. He was too tall for the cot. He would be miserable.

"Fine," she muttered, and traded beds. She slid beneath his sheets with trepidation, but soon began to relax.

Her eyelids fluttered as she drifted in and out of reality. One arm slipped off the side of the bed as she rolled onto her stomach. She'd braided her hair to keep it from tangling in her sleep, and it was wrapped around the arm on which she pillowed her head. The room was quiet, so quiet. And she was so very, very tired. There was a light under the crack in the door, and every now and then she heard a phrase or two from the newscaster.

"...under an overpass in some weeds. The body has been identified as Darcy Petrie, a waitress at an Amarillo truck stop. Authorities have linked it to..."

Angel should have been listening, but she'd fallen asleep.

* * *

Royal came in and let his eyes adjust to the darkness. A slight smile broke the seriousness of his expression as he saw the way she was sleeping. Like Maddie, she was half in and half out of the bed. Carefully, he unwound her from the covers. His voice was just above a whisper as he leaned down.

''Angel, sweetheart, roll over.''

Without waking, she sighed and did as he'd asked. As soon as she was in the middle of the bed, Royal straightened her covers.

Never in his life had he wanted anything as badly as he wanted to lie down beside her. Not to make love, just to hold and be held. He turned toward the cot, and seconds later was shifting the pillow beneath his neck to a more comfortable position.

A faint glow from the security light illuminated the room in shades of black and gray. He kicked at the sheet, trying in vain to lengthen the covers on his legs, but gave it up as a lost cause. He was too tall for the cot. But the code of honor with which he'd been raised had precluded him from taking the bed. He wouldn't have slept a wink if he had. Angel Rojas was tough, but only in spirit. There was a fragility to her stature that sometimes scared him. And then he remembered the way she'd stood by him through the storm and how she'd sheltered Maddie when he could not. He closed his eyes, trying to block out the images of dark eyes watching him...of her soft hands touching him...of her mouth and the way it looked when she smiled. A knot came in his gut as he admitted that his housekeeper meant more to him than she should.

When he heard her roll over, he turned until he was facing the bed, then lay watching her sleep. He stared so long his eyes began to burn and he told himself he'd close them. Just for a minute. Just to let them rest.

And then it was morning.

Tommy Boy Watson had been on the road too long. He was sick of getting lost and taking wrong turns. These days, the only face he recognized was his own when he looked in the mirror. He was tired of being a stranger in a strange place. It had been over a week since he'd performed a cleansing, and the voices were quiet inside his head. He hadn't dreamed about his daddy since that night in Amarillo. That had been a very close call. His first. He intended it to be his last. Tommy Boy was through with his mission and on his way home. He was satisfied his father would have approved of his final act of retribution.

The waitress who called herself Darcy had been all her reputation had promised. She'd taken his order and his measure at the same time. Between bites of his burger, he'd asked if she liked to party. She'd winked and she'd smiled and she'd named her price. He hadn't counted on the fact that she would tell anyone where she was going.

He was waiting for her in the parking lot under the broken security light when she got off at eleven. He watched the front door with interest, wondering if she would scream as the last one had or if she'd go mute with terror as he put the knife to her throat. His fingers curled around the steering wheel in anticipation. He would soon find out.

He saw her emerge from the café. To his dismay, she wasn't alone. Another woman was walking with her, and they were chattering away as if they hadn't a care in the world.

His first instinct was to leave. He was reaching for the keys to start the ignition when the two women veered away from each other. One went toward a small brown car parked a few yards from his. Darcy continued toward where he was parked. He sighed with relief. They'd taken the decision out of his hands.

A few sprinkles of rain were dotting the windshield of his truck as she opened the door.

"Still in the mood, honey?" she asked.

"Get in and find out," Tommy Boy said.

She giggled as they drove away.

He'd been wrong about her. She hadn't screamed and she

hadn't frozen in fright. She'd fought him, and fiercely. His groin was still sore where she'd kicked. And when he pulled out the knife, she'd pulled out a gun. It was only by sheer luck that he'd slit her throat before she could pull the trigger.

Here he was, looking for a road that would take him north. He was heading home. Someone in a BMW whipped past him as if he was sitting still. But he didn't take it personally. Some people got high on fast cars. Tommy Boy preferred good music. He reached toward the dash and upped the volume on his stereo. The mournful wail of a sad country song filled the interior of his truck. He stroked his beard in thoughtful fashion and leaned back in the seat, uplifted by the music and the words.

About an hour later, he pulled off the highway to get some fuel and something to eat. By his best estimation, he was about seventy-five miles from the western edge of the Oklahoma border. The cloudless sky was a white-hot blue, and he reached for his cap before he got out of his truck. A stiff breeze lifted the edges of his untrimmed beard as he started toward the small café. As he crossed the parking lot, he heard a car pulling up behind him. He glanced over his shoulder, making sure he would be out of the way.

His heart skipped a beat. Texas highway patrol. He pulled the brim of his cap down and kept on walking.

Stay cool. Stay cool. It's no big deal. They have to eat, too.

A door slammed behind him. He could hear the crunch of gravel beneath the officer's boots. Tommy Boy hunched his shoulders and kept on going. Inside the café, Tommy Boy chose a seat at the counter. The officer sat in a booth. Tommy Boy reached for a menu, quickly gave his order, then downed the glass of water the waitress had given him. On the wall to his left, the noise from a small black and white television added to the busy hum of voices. He glanced up. A local anchorman was updating the latest reports on the aftermath of the tornado that had swept across the northern portion of the state, ending near Dallas. He remembered the night all too well. He'd been holed up in that Amarillo motel and had experienced moments when he'd believed the roof would go.

The waitress slid his order in front of him.

"Be needin' anything else?" she asked.

"Bring me a Coke. A large one," he added.

It appeared, along with a bottle of steak sauce and a bottle of ketchup.

Tommy Boy grabbed his fork and dug into his food like a starving man. Only after he'd taken a few bites did he think to slow down. He reached for a knife to butter his roll, listening absently to the broadcast still in progress. They flashed a picture onto the screen, and he didn't have to hear what the newsman was saying to know who she was. It was Darcy Petrie, and her body had been found. The knife slipped from his fingers and fell onto the plate with a clatter. The bite of food was still in his mouth, forgotten in his need to hear. There was a terrible fear in the pit of his stomach that hadn't been there before. But there had never been a witness before.

Calm down, Tommy Boy.

The voice came out of nowhere, and he gasped, then choked on his food. He took a big swallow of his drink and made himself relax.

I hear you, Daddy. I'm being calm.

But he couldn't help looking over his shoulder to the booth on the other side of the room. Just to make sure the patrolman was where he'd seen him last. Just to make sure this wasn't a trap. The officer was cutting into a piece of pie with relish, completely oblivious to Tommy Boy's anxieties. Tommy Boy sighed and turned to the broadcast.

"Last seen getting into a late model black pickup on the night of..."

"Son of a—"

The blood drained from Tommy Boy's face. It was just as he'd feared. Although they hadn't seen his face, they knew what he drove. The skin on the back of his neck began to crawl. Any minute now he'd feel the cold, hard press of a gun barrel.

He stared at his plate, at the way the pea juice was running into his mashed potatoes and gravy. He wished he'd ordered a hamburger. He didn't like his food to touch.

He sat for a good two minutes without moving, without taking a bite.

"Somethin' wrong with your food, mister?"

He jumped, then looked up. The waitress was standing before him with a half-empty coffeepot in her hands.

"No," he muttered, and picked up his fork, trying without success to stop the tremble in his fingers.

She shrugged and walked away, leaving Tommy Boy with a sick, sinking feeling. He laid down his fork and turned, staring past the customers, past the booths lining the walls where the patrolman was seated, then through the windows to the parking lot.

His gaze went straight to his truck. A shiny black Dodge extend-a-cab with chrome running boards. His pride and joy. And it had been Darcy Petrie's last ride. His gaze shifted to the next row of cars, to a dusty black truck with a trailer. And then to his right, to a small black Nissan with a camper. And then to a large black four-by-four pulling a horse trailer.

See, Tommy Boy. I told you to relax.

"Yeah, Daddy, I see. I see," Tommy Boy muttered.

The man on the stool beside him looked up and stared.

"You say something to me, mister?" he asked.

Tommy Boy grinned and shook his head. "Nope. Just talking to myself."

The man shrugged and went back to his meal. Tommy Boy picked up his fork and cut off a big bite of chicken-fried steak. It was okay. He should have known it would be okay.

Three days after the storm, the house was almost back to normal. Angel had been relegated to the porch while new carpet was being laid. There were brand-new mattresses leaning against the south kitchen wall. Tonight she would sleep in her own room, and in her own bed.

Her eyes darkened as she gazed toward the barns and the men working there. Royal and two hired hands were still fixing fence. Even though they were a distance away, it was easy to tell which one was Royal. His shirt was bluer, and he was taller by half a head than the other two.

She sighed. Last night had been endless. They were both suffering the effects of close proximity. He'd fought the covers on his cot until two in the morning. She knew because she'd been awake. Finally, she had grabbed her pillow and rolled out of bed.

"I'm going to the bathroom," she said. "When I come back, I expect you to be in this bed and quiet. If you're not, I will put you there myself."

She dropped her pillow by the bathroom door and disappeared.

Royal yanked his pillow from the cot and threw it on his bed before falling onto it with a thump. The mattress gave only slightly, supporting his long length to perfection. He groaned in ecstasy and stretched. Covers were still on his feet, and he was not falling off of the sides.

The bathroom door opened. Angel picked up her pillow and headed for the cot.

Royal heard her straightening the covers, then heard the slight creak of wood as the cot gave to her weight. Guilt hit him. He sighed.

"Uh, Angel."

"Go to sleep," she said shortly.

He rolled on his side, bunched the pillow beneath his neck just right and did as she'd ordered.

And they'd finally slept.

Angel smiled, remembering what she'd found on the kitchen table this morning.

The note was still in her pocket. The flower, a lone purple iris that had miraculously escaped the storm, was in a vase and sitting in the kitchen window. She touched her shirt pocket, hearing the crackle of paper beneath her fingertips, then looked toward Royal, who was almost a quarter of a mile away.

You were aptly named.

A film of tears suddenly blurred her vision as she looked away. She kept reminding herself not to make more of the note than it really meant. So he thought she was an angel. No big deal. It was a word often used lightly. But there was the flower. Society today kept advocating men to say it with flowers, and he had. Exactly what had he been trying to say?

The phone rang. She ran into the kitchen to answer. To her delight, it was Maddie, wanting to know if her room was fixed and if her kittens had all been fed.

And so the morning passed. As she prepared the noon meal, her gaze kept straying to the delicate petals on the purple iris. It had survived so much, and yet there had so much beauty yet to give.

It hit her then, with a paring knife in one hand and a tomato in the other, that people could be like that. That they could endure without breaking many times over, yet when it came time to give, those who had endured longest often gave the most.

I could be like that, Angel thought. *If anyone wanted me as much as I wanted them, then I would give everything... if anyone cared.*

Royal was at the kitchen sink washing his hands and Angel was putting the finishing touches on lunch when Roman walked in the back door.

"Come on in," Royal said dryly, aware that Roman always made himself at home.

"Thanks," Roman said, and winked at Angel, who was already setting another place at the table.

"How's Maddie?" Angel asked.

Roman grinned. "You talked to her this morning. She's in perpetual motion." Then he added, "What you don't know is since then she's been invited to a birthday party of some kid in the apartment across the hall.'' He glanced at his watch. ''In fact, if I remember correctly, she and Holly should be in the middle of pizza with seven other kids and their parents. After that, someone said something about swimming.''

Royal reached for a towel to dry his hands as he turned. ''I don't think I packed her swimsuit.''

Roman grinned. ''I know. She and Holly have already been shopping.''

''Lord,'' Royal muttered. ''She won't be fit to live with by the time I get her back.''

Angel interrupted. ''Iced tea or coffee?'' she asked.

''Tea,'' they both answered.

She started to get the glasses. Royal reached over her head and took them out of her hands.

''I'll do it,'' he said.

''But that's what you pay me to—''

Royal began putting ice in the glasses. ''Something's burning,'' he said, ignoring her comments.

''Oh, great,'' Angel muttered, and grabbed a couple of pot holders.

Roman silently watched them in action. A slow grin began to spread on his face. It was like watching a mating ritual, but without any touch. He shook his head and sat at the place Angel had set for him. The way he figured, it was just a matter of time before one of them lost total control. And if he was a betting man, his money would be on his brother. He'd always been short on patience.

''Smells good,'' Royal said, as he set the tea-filled glasses at their places.

''Enchilada casserole,'' Angel announced as she transferred the hot dish from the oven to the table.

Royal stopped what he was doing and leaned over the food, giving it a long, testing sniff.

The gesture was so blatantly rude, Roman couldn't help but comment.

"For Pete's sake, Royal, Mom would have had your head for that. What are you doing?"

Royal sat and picked up his fork. "Just checking," he said.

Angel started to grin.

Royal gestured to Roman. "Guests first," he said, and watched as his brother dished a generous helping onto his plate.

"It's very hot," Angel warned him.

Roman nodded and picked up his fork. "I'm letting it cool."

Royal looked at Angel. "Will it?" he said.

"Will it what?" she asked.

"Cool?"

She threw back her head and laughed, and the sound filled the room and Royal's heart.

"I don't get it," Roman said.

"Habeneros," Royal said.

Roman's nostrils flared as he looked at his plate in dismay. He could eat Mexican with the best of them, but over the years, he'd learned that Habenero peppers should be measured in voltage, not weight.

"Oh, that kind of hot."

"For very big men, you two are certainly concerned with your poor little tongues."

Royal snorted, "Well," he persisted, "will it cool, or should I just dig the hole now to save you the trouble, and crawl in before I die?"

"Have we been in disagreement?" she asked.

"Well, no."

"Then you have nothing to worry about."

Satisfied that she had not booby-trapped his food, Royal took a generous portion of the casserole, then filled her plate, as well.

"Is that enough?" he asked.

Angel was suddenly embarrassed that she'd been so unprofessional with her boss.

"Yes, sir," she said.

He frowned. "Hell, we've just spent the better part of three nights together. Don't go all prim on me now."

Her mouth dropped, and Royal knew if looks could kill, someone would be planning his wake.

Angel was on her feet, her voice shaking with anger as she stared him in the face.

"Listen to me, your royal highness! How dare you insinuate that anything has been—"

Ignoring Roman's snort of laughter, Royal grabbed Angel by the hand before she could bolt.

"Sorry," he muttered. "I don't know why, but you bring out the absolute worst in me. I didn't mean to be so disrespectful. And I didn't mean that the way it sounded. I was just trying to say that I thought we'd gotten past all the formalities. Okay?"

Angel glared, first at Roman, who was past being able to eat, and then at Royal, who looked as if he'd willingly shoot himself if someone would just hand him the gun.

She threw up her hands and sat, muttering in rapid Spanish.

Royal looked nervous as he picked up his fork. He didn't know whether to be relieved that she was still here or nervous that this would be his last meal. He glared at Roman, who was still laughing.

"Oh, shut the hell up," he muttered, then gave Angel another nervous look. "What's she saying?" he asked.

Roman wiped the tears from his eyes and shook his head in disbelief. "You don't want to know." He choked, then started laughing again. "Royal highness...Lord, that's a good one."

They ate in silence. Angel forked her food in angry jerks. Royal ate in nervous haste, and Roman snickered between bites. Royal noticed the time and got up to turn on the television.

"Weather report," he announced to no one in particular and poured himself some more tea.

But it wasn't weather that flashed on the screen. It was a picture of Darcy Petrie, late of Amarillo, and mother of two.

After the first couple of sentences, they watched without speaking.

"Last seen with a man in a black late-model pickup truck. Darcy Petrie is survived by a four-year-old daughter and a two-year-old son. Authorities believe that her death is linked to the deaths of eight other women in four different states. If anyone has any information regarding the…"

"Oh, my God," Angel whispered, and stood with a jerk, spilling tea across the table and onto the floor. She kept seeing that bony face and those pale green eyes.

Roman grabbed a hand towel from the counter and began mopping it up, but Royal's attention was pinned on Angel. He reached for her a second too late. She slid to the floor in a slump.

Chapter 13

Angel came to in Royal's arms, but she couldn't remember what had put her there.

"What happened?" she asked, struggling to get up.

"Easy, now," he said gently. "You're all right. You just fainted."

A frown creased her forehead. "I've never fainted in my life."

"Except today," Royal said, and circled his thumb gently at a spot just above her ear. "You hit the floor pretty hard. Do you hurt? Are you sick?"

She winced at his touch. Her head *was* sore. Hurt, she supposed, when she'd fallen. Other than that, she didn't feel any different.

"I don't think so. I feel fine now. Please help me up."

"Fine does not faint," Royal said. "Lie still until you get your bearings." When she looked as if she might refuse, he added a small grin. "Please?"

It was too good an offer to ignore. Lifting a shaky hand to her forehead, Angel relaxed against the cradle of his elbow.

"This is so unlike me. I've never..." Memory hit. "Dear God...the man on TV."

Royal frowned. "Man? What man?"

Angel rolled off his lap and onto her feet. The abruptness of the motion made her sway unsteadily. Royal tried to pull her onto the sofa. She reached for his hand, trying to pull him up, instead.

"No, no, you don't understand. I think I saw him."

Royal glanced at Roman, who was coming into the room with a cold, wet cloth for her forehead.

"Saw who?" Roman asked. "What have I missed?"

"I don't know," Royal said. "Let her talk."

Angel was shaking as fear surfaced, reminding her how afraid she'd been and how certain she was that he'd been following her.

"In the kitchen when we were listening to that news bulletin—"

Roman interrupted. "Angel, honey, you're not making any sense. What news bulletin?"

But Royal remembered because he'd been thinking of Maddie, and that once upon a time, all the women who died had been someone's little girls.

"The murder victims in the interstate killings," he said.

Angel turned, her face alight with relief that someone was willing to listen.

"Yes," she cried. "That one." She pressed a shaky hand to the middle of her belly, making herself calm when she felt like screaming. "Oh, Royal, I could have been one of those victims. I saw him." She added, "At least I think it was him."

Royal undid himself from the sofa in slow, measured steps. Like a cat moving toward a cornered prey, he took her by the shoulders. "What the hell are you saying?"

Desperate that they believe her, she gave both men a beseeching look as she began to explain.

"When I was hitchhiking, before you and Maddie picked me up, a man at a truck stop offered me a ride." She blushed and looked away, suddenly ashamed to say it, although she had nothing to be ashamed about. ''I think he thought I was a prostitute. He offered me money. When I turned him down, he got very angry.''

The investigator in Roman began to take notice. Granted, her experience was frightening, but either there were huge gaps in her reasoning or she hadn't told them everything yet. He put a hand on Angel's shoulder. She jumped.

''Sorry,'' he said softly. He hated to push, but they needed to know everything. ''Can I ask you some questions?''

Her chin was trembling as she nodded.

But it wasn't okay with Royal. Everything inside him was going haywire. He kept looking at her and trying to remember that he'd hired her to take care of his daughter and his home, not wring his heart into knots. But it didn't do any good. The longer he looked, the worse he felt. From the moment she'd hit the floor until he had her in his arms, he'd felt weightless. As if his world had suddenly come undone from its anchor. Only after he'd felt the steady beat of her pulse had he begun to relax. Her eyes were filled with tears and her lower lip kept trembling. It was more than he could stand.

''Come here, girl,'' he said softly, and wrapped her in his arms as he might have Maddie. ''You're not in this alone.''

His gentleness was her undoing. Silent tears slipped from her eyes, tracking the contours of her cheeks and then falling onto Royal's arms. Encircled within his embrace, her back against his chest, she felt capable of almost anything.

Roman gave her a long, steady look. ''You okay?''

She took a deep breath. Bolstered by Royal's strength, she lifted her chin defiantly. ''I am now.''

He nodded. ''Now then. This man, the one who tried to pick you up. Did he threaten or harm you in any way?''

Angel thought, slowly shaking her head. ''No.'' Then she added, ''But it was broad daylight and there were lots of people around the parking lot.''

Roman frowned. ''So what makes you think that he's the

one who's been killing the women? There are lots of crazies
in the world. What makes you think this is the same man?''

Her stomach knotted as she remembered the fear and panic.

''Because after I refused him, he followed me. Every time I
got a new ride, he was there. When I stopped to eat, he would
show up at the same café.''

Royal flinched. ''The sorry son of a—''

''Easy, brother,'' Roman said.

Royal clenched his jaw, swallowing a rage born of helpless-
ness as he realized how close she'd come to dying. He thought
of that woman's picture they'd flashed on the screen. He didn't
even remember her face. Would he have noticed if it had been
Angel's instead? He doubted it. He hadn't known she existed
until she crawled into his truck, wide-eyed and nervous and
soaked to the skin.

She stood within the shelter of his arms while her lifeblood
flowed beneath his fingers, rapidly when she was frightened,
more measured when she thought to take a breath and slow
down. In a swift moment of revelation, he knew how spare his
life would have been without her.

A false quiet descended upon him as his heart raged for
revenge. As the eldest Justice, he'd been born to inherit what
Anson Justice had started and what their father, Micah Justice,
had continued to build. His values had been forged by men
who believed in dying for what was right. He'd been raised
with the knowledge that a Justice takes care of his own.

Granted, Angel was only the housekeeper, and technically
that *did* put her under his concern. But she'd long ago become
more than an employee. He just hadn't faced it until now.

After more questions from Roman, an uneasy silence fell
upon the room. In the face of what Angel had told them, there
wasn't anything left to say.

Angel was pacing between the sofa and the door, trying to
remember everything. Although it was hot and sunny outside,
she felt cold.

Poor Darcy Petrie. Poor little kids. Their mother was dead.

She stopped suddenly and turned, almost shouting as she remembered.

"His truck. I almost forgot to tell you about his truck."

"What about his truck?" Royal asked.

She was shaking all over, and Royal could tell that she was about to come undone. "It was a new one, and black. Shiny and black, just like they said on TV. And Royal, you know that day in the rain, the day you picked me up?"

Royal waited.

"He passed us while we were parked on the side of the road. That's why I agreed to go home with you. Right then, total strangers were more appealing than being on the highway with him."

Royal's fear for her grew. If he'd been a little bit later, they would never have met. That man would have gotten to her first.

"That does it for me," Roman said. "I'll be right back." He walked out of the room, leaving Royal and Angel alone.

She shuddered then moaned. "What if it's him? What if he's still out there looking for me?"

Royal held her, cupping the back of her neck and pulling her into a fierce embrace. Holding her close—but not close enough. His voice was full of anger, and Angel could feel the tension in his body.

"Look at me." He tilted her chin until their gazes were locked. "I won't let him hurt you."

She shuddered as his hand centered in the middle of her back. It was only a hand, but right then it felt like a shield between her and the world.

"I am so scared."

"So the hell am I," Royal said softly, and laid his cheek against the crown of her hair.

Slowly, her arms slid around his waist. His strength became her strength. The rhythm of his breathing her marker for survival. As long as he was with her, she would be safe. She kept seeing that woman's picture as it had flashed across the screen.

Darcy Petrie.

Mother of two.

She started to cry.

The tears tied Royal in knots. That she was crying was more than he could bear. She was his Angel of the laughter and the quick, hot temper. Not these deep, choking sobs. Not this blind, stark fear. He rocked her where they stood.

"It will be all right," he said. "I promise you, Angel, it will be all right."

Roman strode into the room. "I called the FBI."

Startled, she drew back from Royal's arms. "The FBI?"

"We're talking about a possible serial killer who's strung victims in several states. That drops him under the jurisdiction of the federal government."

Angel groaned. This was going from bad to worse.

Royal looked at his brother. "Murder is out of my league," he said quietly. "I'm asking you to stay with us on this."

Roman nodded, then gently patted Angel on the back of the head as he might have done Maddie.

"You couldn't drive me away," he said. "Now I'd better call Holly and tell her I'm going to be late."

Angel looked at Royal, wishing she could read his mind. He was her boss. He had a child to raise and a ranch to run. And because of her presence, something ugly had come into their world.

"I think it would be better for you and for Maddie if I left the ranch. You both need someone to depend on. This could get ugly," she said.

Royal tightened his hold on her, but his grip was far gentler than his voice. "Like hell." He looked at Roman and grinned. "And ugly doesn't scare me. I've been dealing with ugly brothers all my life."

Roman arched an eyebrow. Angel laughed. It wasn't much, but it was enough to make them all feel better.

A horn sounded. They jumped, and Royal strode to the window.

"Great," he muttered. "Finally. The plumber."

"What about the FBI?" Angel asked.

"If they show up on time, we'll give 'em a hammer and put 'em to work," Royal said.

Angel smiled. A few minutes earlier she wouldn't have believed it possible, but she was starting to relax. The shock of her discovery was settling in. The authorities had been notified. They would come. She would talk. And please God, they would catch the killer before anyone else died. It was simple…and it was out of her hands.

Roman stepped into the hall to make some calls. After he checked in with Holly, there were some things he needed to set in motion. He doubted it had occurred to either of them just yet, but if word got out that there was a witness, her life wouldn't be worth a damn.

Angel stared at the face on the paper, then took a deep breath. It was him. From the thin, angular face and pale eyes to his unkempt beard and graying ponytail. She could almost hear the nasal intonation of his proposition.

"What do you think, Miss Rojas?" the sketch artist asked.

She looked at Deaton, the agent who'd taken her statement, then at the face the police sketch artist had made.

"It's him."

"You're sure?" Deaton asked.

"Yes."

Deaton nodded at the officer who'd done the drawing. "I want this face on the evening news and every broadcast afterward until he's caught." He looked at Angel. "Down the road, we'll need you to identify him. Are you willing?"

She gave Royal a nervous glance. But when he winked at her and nodded, she knew it would be all right.

"I'm willing to do anything to help stop the killings," she said softly.

"Yes, ma'am. And if he turns out to be our man, you are one lucky lady to have escaped." Deaton's cool demeanor shifted noticeably as he remarked, "His victims did not die an easy death."

She flinched.

Royal saw her reaction. He'd had enough. He unfolded himself from a nearby chair. "You through with her now?"

Deaton nodded. "We'll be in touch."

Roman was leaning against the doorjamb, where he'd been standing and listening. "I can assume you have taken measures to insure that her identity is not revealed?"

Royal looked at his brother and froze. *Oh, God. I didn't think.* The bland expression on Roman's face was for him a dead giveaway. Roman had tuned into something neither he nor Angel had considered. If the killer knew there was a witness...

Deaton gave Roman a curious glance. "Of course."

"Just checking," Roman said.

Angel's back was to the men, but there was something in Roman's voice that made her turn.

"What?" she asked.

"There's nothing for you to worry about, Miss Rojas," Deaton added. "You've done your part. Now let us do ours."

"Like hell," Royal said. "She's just put her life on the line. You better make damn sure she's protected in every way, or I'll take care of it myself."

Deaton frowned. He had no patience with attitudes or loose ends. But there was something about Royal Justice that made him nervous. If ever there was a man less likely of following orders, he would be it.

"We don't need any unnecessary heroics," Deaton growled.

Royal wasn't about to be deterred by a man in a three-piece suit. He didn't budge an inch when Deaton pointed in his face.

"Keeping her safe is necessary to me," he said shortly. "Besides, we take care of our own."

"Speaking of own," Roman said, "I'd better head into Dallas. I promised Maddie and Holly I'd take them out to dinner tonight."

Royal sighed. He'd hated sending Maddie into Dallas, but it had been necessary after the storm. He missed his daughter like crazy. It was the first time they'd been apart for this long, and while Maddie wasn't having any problems, he was feeling rejected.

"Is she all right?" Royal asked.

Roman rolled his eyes. "Does a bear—"

"Never mind," Royal muttered, then grinned. "You can bring her home tomorrow. The house will be ready by then."

Roman nodded, then gave Angel a lingering look before leaving.

The last of the agents was getting into a car when Royal turned to Angel.

"Feel like getting some air?"

Air? After what he'd just said, she felt as if she were already flying. *We take care of our own.* She wanted to laugh. She wanted to cry. She did neither.

"What about the plumber?" she asked.

"He knows what to do. He'll leave when he's through."

She nodded, then followed him out the door.

Royal glanced toward the sky out of habit, checking the weather. It was hot, clear and cloudless—a good day to cut hay. Instead, he was dealing with federal agents and talking about serial killers, and he felt as if he'd walked into a nightmare.

The chains on the porch swing creaked as Angel sat down. He turned, his hands stuffed in his pockets, his gaze fixed upon her face. That beautiful face. Her lips were swollen from crying, her eyes red-rimmed and brimming with unshed tears. She was in shock, and he knew just how she felt. Hell, he'd been in shock for all of three hours now—ever since he realized that he'd fallen in love.

He kept staring at her, willing her to look up—to look at him. But she seemed bent on staring at the floor of the porch and the toes of her shoes. He sighed.

Angel knew he was staring. Her skin felt hot—her breasts

felt achy and heavy. But she was afraid to look up. Afraid if she did he would see her true feelings. And that couldn't happen. She was nothing to him but the woman who took care of his child. It wouldn't do to let her imagination run wild. Yes, he'd been more than supportive, and yes, he'd comforted her in a way she hadn't expected. And yes, Royal Justice was possessive about things that were his. She kept reminding herself it was nothing but duty and honor that had made him say what he had to Deaton.

She worked for Royal. In a way, that made her part of the Justice family. He had given her plenty of grief, but he was a man who had honor. She couldn't deny him that. But love her? No way.

His family ties and family roots were deep and true. She had none. When he picked her up on the side of the road, she had no destination in mind. This ranch, this man and his child had become the most important things in her life. The last thing she wanted to do was lose them. And the best way to keep that from happening was to stay in her place. It was bad enough that she'd brought all this danger into their lives. Bringing shame to herself would be the last straw.

Royal wanted to shake her. She'd withdrawn into that damned expressionless shell again. He hated when that happened because he didn't know how to react. He could handle her fury. At least it was an emotion he recognized. Even her tears, as much as they tore at his heart, were easier to take than this wall of silence. He combed his fingers through his hair in sudden frustration and strode toward the swing.

"Talk to me," he growled.

She looked up. "About what?"

His control snapped. He yanked her out of the swing and into his arms before she could argue.

"About anything, damn it. You hide yourself from me behind those big brown eyes. You look at me, but you won't say what you're thinking."

Angel twisted out of his hold, her voice shaking with frustration.

"You know something, Royal? Not everyone has the luxury of saying what they think."

"And why the hell not?" he growled. "I never let anyone's opinion stop me from voicing mine."

She smiled bitterly. "And you're coming from a different place than most. You are your own boss. You don't have to answer to anyone to depend upon putting food in your mouth and a roof over your head."

He groaned. "That isn't what I mean." Then he turned and walked to the edge of the porch. "I didn't mean to make you angry. I don't want to fight. I know you're scared. Sometimes talking helps."

"Talking won't change what's happened," Angel said.

"You were a witness, for God's sake," Royal said. "Not a participant in the crimes."

Angel sighed and nodded. "You're right. I just can't get over feeling guilty about involving you in any way."

He wanted to hold her and settled for the olive branch she'd offered instead.

"So absolve your guilt and talk to me," he muttered.

She managed a smile. "Can we walk?"

He held out his hand.

By the time they reached the barn where Dumpling and her kittens resided, Angel felt better. But Royal was impatient. He didn't feel better. In fact, he was feeling decidedly worse. The closer they were, the harder he got. It was uncomfortable as hell and just that little bit disconcerting to know that a woman had that kind of hold over his emotions. Finally, he'd had enough.

"I'm still waiting," he said.

Angel paused at the granary door, where the sacks of horse feed were kept, then poked her head inside.

"Look. Flea Bit is sleeping with Dumpling and her babies."

Royal took her by the arm. "Look at me," he said softly.

Angel bit her lip and turned, meeting his gaze without blinking. It was the hardest thing she'd ever had to do.

Her skin was soft beneath his fingers, her mouth slightly parted and tilted upward as she looked at him.

"I'm looking," she said.

He exhaled softly. *God, so am I.* "What do you see?"

She answered without hesitation. "My boss."

"Is that all?" he asked.

Her gaze slipped.

"Don't do that," he said harshly, and laid the palm of his hand against the side of her face, making her look at him again.

"Don't do what?" she asked.

His voice lowered. "You know."

Her pulse skipped a beat. For a long, silent moment, they stared into each other's faces, taking comfort in the familiarities. Twice she tried to look away, and each time Royal forced her back. His gaze raked her face, and she could feel the warmth of his breath upon her cheek. There was a muscle jerking at the side of his jaw and a promise in his eyes she was afraid to believe. She moaned beneath her breath and then started to shake.

"What?" Royal whispered.

Her answer came out on a sigh. "You know."

He took a step closer. "I want to hear you say it."

Her nostrils flared in sudden anger. "Why?" she cried. "Why do you need to see my weakness? You already know my shame."

"There is no shame in loving, Angel, girl. Only in letting it go to waste."

She started to cry, soft, silent tears that spilled out of her eyes and onto his fingers as they cupped her cheeks. He lowered his head until their foreheads were touching and their lips were only inches apart.

"Angel Rojas, you're everything I ever wanted in a woman. You're beautiful and gentle and you have a temper that matches mine to a T. You make me laugh and you make me crazy. You may not be ready to hear this, but it has to be said. I'm in love with you, girl. And it's a damn good thing that your bedroom is going to be ready tonight because there's not enough will-power left in me to spend another night just listening to you sleep."

Angel was stunned. Her ears were ringing from his words. She saw the truth in his eyes and still she couldn't bring herself to move.

Royal groaned. Her silence was his undoing. "I won't ever say this again," he said shortly. "But I won't say I'm sorry, either."

"Thank you, God," she whispered, and moments later was in his arms.

Royal caught her to him. Burying his face against her neck and then brushing his mouth against the warmth of her skin, he groaned. It was just as he'd feared. She tasted as good as she smelled.

"Ah, God, I want to make love to you."

His words were nothing but an echo of her emotions.

She leaned back in his arms until she could see his face and the fire blazing in his eyes.

"Then do it," she said.

His nostrils flared. It was his only response. Angel found herself in the hayloft, watching as Royal stripped off his clothes, making a bed on the hay for her to lie down. It was just as she'd dreamed. His body was beautiful in every way.

He turned to her. She pulled her T-shirt over her head. Al-ready aroused, he gritted his teeth against a flood of emotion.

"Hurry," he growled.

"Then help me," she whispered.

She stood naked before him, waiting for the first steps of the dance to begin.

He reached for her, palming her breasts, then rubbing her nipples until they were hard, aching buds. She swayed on her feet, then gave up the fight and reached out to him.

He took down her hair, combing his fingers through the long, silken strands and letting it spill across her shoulders and upon her breasts. Her head lolled in silent ecstasy. Their gazes met and held.

He lowered his head.

Her breath caught. His mouth. God, his mouth. It was there on her lips, stealing her breath…and her heart. She wrapped her arms around his neck. She never knew when he pushed her down upon the bed he'd made in the hay. A pencil-thin ray of sunlight was shining through a small nail hole in the roof above them. After that, Royal was all she saw.

Chapter 14

The ranch had grown quiet. Everyone was gone. The soft mewling of Dumpling's kittens could be heard as the old cat left on a hunt. In the rafters above their heads, a roosting pigeon cooed softly to its mate circling the sky outside the barn. And in the loft, in the loose, sweet hay, a man and a woman were making slow, sweet love.

Their bodies were slicked with sweat, their hearts hammering against their breasts. Locked into the age-old rhythm, Royal rocked within the cradle of her hips. Lost in the sounds of her soft gasps and small cries, he kept driving them both toward a spiraling heat.

Angel moaned beneath her breath as a short burst of pleasure sent her arching toward his downward thrust. Good. So good. She bit her lower lip to keep from crying aloud and closed her eyes, concentrating on the feeling centered between her legs. Ah, God, she wanted more.

He gave her what she wanted.

And then it was coming.

Blasting through her body like a heat wave. Nailing her

where she lay and rendering her helpless to move. At that moment, willing to die from the joy, she felt it sweep through her system, leaving tiny aftershocks of the pleasure he'd given her to remember him by.

"Oh, Royal."

She felt empty and at the same time complete. She lifted her hands to him, sliding them up the sides of his face.

He was shattered by her complete capitulation. Her touch was the trigger that detonated the last of his control.

"Ah, God," he groaned. Thrusting in one last time, he let himself go, sliding deep inside her and spilling his seed…and his soul.

Afterward, they lay in silence, absorbing the enormity of what they'd done. For Royal, there was no turning back. He did not give his love lightly, and today he'd given his all.

As for Angel, she, too, had crossed a bridge. This wasn't the first time she'd shared her body with a man, but it was the first time she'd shared her heart. And while there was a part of her that feared this might not last, she was so much in love she was willing to take the risk.

Royal brushed his mouth against the base of her throat, then raised himself until he could look at her.

"Are you okay?"

Angel cupped the sides of his face with her hands. "I may never be okay again."

His heart skipped a beat. He knew just what she meant. And while he would still do what they'd done all over again, there was something he had to get said.

"This isn't over."

Her heart fluttered within her chest. "What isn't over?"

"The lovemaking…and the love. Today was a beginning, not an interlude."

She smiled and wrapped her arms around his neck.

He bit his lip and groaned when she pulled him to her.

"I have something I need to say to you," she said.

There was a gleam in her eye that was making him nervous.

"This isn't over," she said softly.

He started to grin. "What isn't over?"

"You." She rolled, pinning him to the floor and straddling his hips. "Me." He was getting hard all over again, pushing against her. She shifted quickly, impaling herself. "This."

Tilting her head and closing her eyes, she braced her hands against his chest and began her ride.

Royal watched her body undulating upon him until he began to lose focus. He fisted his hands into the long lengths of her hair and held on for dear life until it was time to let go.

Tommy Boy Watson's belly felt as if it was splitting in two. Twice in the past hour he'd been forced to pull off the highway to seek relief from the gripe centered in his lower regions. He didn't know whether it was caused by the food he'd been eating or the stress he was in. It was difficult to stay focused when he would have sold his soul for a roll of toilet paper and a bottle of Tums.

He'd been driving since daybreak, heading north on Interstate 35 through Oklahoma. He'd come this way before. It felt good to be retracing his steps. It felt right to be going home. Just as he topped a small rise, his belly knotted in a new fit of cramps. Frantic, he began searching the roadsides and the horizon for a place that would provide some privacy. There was none. The ache twisted deeper. Wild-eyed, he took the next exit, uncaring where it would lead, as long as it was away from civilization.

The speedometer was on seventy-five when he came over the hill. To his left was a large stand of trees and a herd of cattle grazing in the pasture beyond. A little farther down on the right, the roof and company sign of a rural gas station were just visible. His brain went in overdrive as he weighed his options. Stop now and brave the woods and the cows. Hold off a few seconds longer and opt for an outhouse with walls and a roof. He flew by the trees in a blur of black.

The station it was.

He saw the bathroom doors as he slid to a stop outside the station. One marked His. The other marked Hers. He headed for the one that was standing ajar. That it was the one set aside for the female sex no longer mattered. It was as far as he could go.

He emerged from the small, unlit room pale and shaken. For now, the pains were gone. But his legs felt as if the bones had turned to mush. He wiped a shaky hand across his face, feeling the wiry brush of facial hair against the palm of his hand. He sighed. His beard needed a trim.

"Anything I can do for you, mister?"

The unexpected voice made him jump. He turned, coming face to face with a teenage girl. He wouldn't have put her at more than fifteen. She was tall and gawky, her oversize clothes conveniently hiding the evolution of her femininity. Her hair was short and greasy, her skin marked with acne, both old and new. Tommy Boy looked at her and, except for the fact she was of the opposite sex, saw himself in her. A misfit. It was instant empathy.

"No. I was just resting myself a bit," he said.

She shrugged and started into the station.

As she reached the corner, Tommy Boy thought. "Hey, girl."

She stopped and turned.

"You happen to have anything for an upset stomach?"

She shrugged. "Just some of that pink stuff."

"That'll do," Tommy Boy said, and followed her inside.

She dug through a shelf behind the counter. Tommy Boy strolled to an old red pop box beside the door and opened it up. He grinned.

"Man, I haven't seen one of these in years," he said, looking at the cans of pop floating in the ice.

The girl didn't bother to answer. It didn't matter. Tommy Boy's remark had been more to himself than to her.

He thrust his hand inside, digging through the numbing water for a red and white can containing his favorite drink.

"Whoo, that's cold," he mumbled, as he pulled up his prize and carried it to the counter.

"Need any gas?" the girl asked.

Tommy Boy shook his head. "Nope, this'll do me."

"That'll be three dollars and twenty-seven cents," she said.

Tommy Boy reached into his pocket, pulling out a handful of bills and some change. A couple of quarters fell to the floor. He stomped on them quickly, trapping them beneath the soles of his shoes before they could roll under the counter. He tossed her some money and bent to pick up his coins as she began to make change. His gaze absently slid to a nearby newspaper rack. It took a couple of seconds for the face on the front page to register, and when it did, he stood with a jerk.

The girl was waiting. He held out his hand in a daze. She handed him his change.

"How much for a paper?" he asked.

"Fifty cents."

He laid two quarters onto the counter with quiet precision. His mind was racing as he watched her drop them into the register.

It was his face. The image was unmistakable. The headline beneath was even worse.

Have you seen this man?

His belly rolled and he broke out in a cold sweat, uncertain if it was nerves or another wave of peristalsis. Condensation from the can of pop was dripping through his fingers onto the floor. He kept staring at the young girl's face. At the expression in her eyes. Was she faking it until he drove out of sight? Would she tell? Did she know? His fingers twitched beneath the chill of the can. The switchblade in his pocket was heavy against his thigh. It would be an easy kill. Just set down the can and pop the blade. One swift, clean cut was all it would take. She wouldn't suffer, he'd see to that.

While he was thinking, the phone rang. He watched, his heart in his mouth, as she lifted the receiver. It still wasn't too late. He set the can on the counter and stuck his hand in his pocket. *Do it now, before she can tell.*

As his fingers closed around the shaft, a feeling of power came over him. He was in control. It was in his palm, the weight of it making his pulse accelerate. He shifted from one foot to the other, testing his balance, testing his nerve.

"Yes, Momma. See you in a little bit, and I love you, too," the girl said, and hung up the phone.

Tommy Boy froze. Her voice had lost its sullen tone. Her acne-scarred face had taken on a beauty he wouldn't have believed. When she turned, she was smiling to herself. He saw the child she had been and the woman she could be.

"Anything else?" she asked.

He looked at the medicine on the counter beside his pop. He rolled the knife in his palm one last time and then let it drop into the depths of his pocket.

"Nope. I guess I've got everything here that I need."

"Come again," the girl said.

Tommy Boy dropped the medicine in his pocket, took his pop in his hand and lifted a paper from the rack on his way out the door. He never looked back.

Night came, and Tommy Boy was low on gas and afraid to stop. The newspaper had been brutally frank about the way the women had died, but he was angry they hadn't told all of the facts. No one had seen fit to mention what they'd done for a living. No one had seen fit to add that they had ruined good men's lives. In his eyes, their deaths had been righteous. They hadn't suffered nearly as long as his daddy had. It didn't matter to him that their bodies had rotted before they'd been found. At least they'd been dead before the rotting occurred. His daddy's flesh had come away from his bones while his heart was still beating.

But how? he wondered. Who had seen his face? Not the other waitress at the Amarillo truck stop where Darcy Petrie

d worked. It had been raining, and dark. All she'd seen was
s truck. Then who?

Giving the gas gauge a nervous look, he pounded the steer-
g wheel in frustration. Only a few miles from the Kansas
order, and he was running on empty. He was going to have
chance a stop. The only satisfaction he had was that his looks
d altered dramatically since this morning.

About an hour after reading the paper, he'd pulled to the
de of the road and hacked off his ponytail with his knife. It
d hurt like hell, but not nearly as much as when he'd tackled
is beard. Two hours later, he was minus all but a thin, scraggly
rowth, nothing a good razor and a can of shaving cream
ouldn't fix.

The only decision he had left to make was what to do about
is truck. The description in the paper fit his rig to a T. And
hile it wasn't the only black truck in the country, he felt like
e was driving a big neon sign that said, Here I Am. Come
nd Get Me.

But he'd taken the risk and crawled inside. And here he was,
ill driving north and almost out of gas.

A green highway marker pointed east. Medford Blackwell
xit. He took it without slowing down, rounding the sharp
urve and sliding to a stop. He sat with his engine idling, read-
ng the road signs and deciding where he would spend the
ight. Medford was twenty-two miles west, Blackwell only
ree east. Blackwell it was.

But first things first. He turned right and right again, coming
 a stop at the self-service pumps of a busy gas station. He
ot out with a groan, stretching his legs and rocking his head
rom side to side on his neck. Bones popped. His head felt
nusually light. He attributed it to the missing ponytail, which
ormally hung down his back. As he reached for the hose, a
ark-haired woman walked into his line of vision. Her hair was
ong and pulled from her face with a thin, red ribbon. Her
horts and T-shirt were white, offsetting a well-oiled tan. He
tared, trying to remember where he'd seen her before. Then

he shrugged, stuck the nozzle into the tank and released t
flow.

Gas fumes rose between him and the truck bed. He wrink
his nose and stepped to one side, taking advantage of an inte
mittent breeze. It wasn't until he started inside to pay that
hit him. He stopped and spun, staring in the direction whe
the woman had been. But she and her car were long gone.

"Oh, man," he muttered. "Oh, man."

He'd just remembered why the woman had seemed so f
miliar. She looked like the whore down in Texas who h
refused his ride. She'd seen his face. And she'd probably se
what he'd been driving. It had to be her. She was the on
person who'd seen him up close and personal and then walk
away. But where the hell was she now? He wanted to puk
Instead, he went in and paid for his gas.

Maddie burst into the house a few steps ahead of Roma
She flung her overnight bag aside and jumped into her daddy
arms.

"I'm back," she cried. "Did you miss me?"

He laughed and kissed her soundly. "No. Not me. I didi
miss you at all." Then he looked at Roman. "Thanks for e
erything."

Roman shook his head. "Don't thank me. And I'm sorry
dump and run, but I've got to meet a client in a couple
hours. See you guys later."

He was gone.

Maddie was unfazed by what she knew to be a monument
lie. She knew good and well that she'd been missed. She gi
gled and returned his kisses twofold. Everything was back
order. Then it dawned on her that her welcoming party w
one person short. Her smile shrunk and a frown slipped in
place.

"Daddy?"

"What, baby?" he asked.

"Where is my angel?"

"She's in the—"

Angel interrupted. "I'm right here," she said. "Do I get a
ug, too?"

Maddie squealed and laughed as Royal pretended he wasn't
*oing to give her up. By the time Angel got her kiss and hug,
*Maddie was weak from giggling. She leaned into Angel's em-
*race, melting against the loving welcome she knew was there.

"I missed you," Maddie said softly.

Angel's heart skipped a beat as her arms tightened. "Oh,
*aby, I missed you, too."

Royal watched them, his heart too full to speak. Maddie
*urned, her face alight with joy. Her world was back in its orbit.

"Did you take good care of my kitties?" she asked.

Royal rolled his eyes and pretended disgust. "If that isn't
*ust like a woman."

Maddie giggled. "Daddy. I'm not a woman. I'm a little
*irl."

"Oh, well, then," he said. "I suppose it's still all right. And
*es, I fed your damned cats, every morning and every night.
*They are so fat now that their bellies drag the ground. Are you
*appy?"

Angel arched an eyebrow at him, as if to say watch your
*anguage, but it was obviously a case of too little, too late. And
*t wasn't as if Maddie was paying attention. She'd heard his
*ussing too many times before.

"I want to go see them," Maddie shrieked. "I want to see
*f their bellies really do drag the ground."

"Why don't you take your bag to your room first?" Angel
*uggested. "You have a new bed and new carpet and curtains."

"Yeah!" Maddie shrieked, and darted toward her room.

"Your bag," Royal shouted, but it was too late. She was
*lready gone.

Angel picked it up and handed it to him as he started out of
*he room. He took it without thinking and was halfway down
*he hall when he suddenly stopped. He dropped the bag where
*e stood and went to Angel.

"Did you forget something?" she asked.

"Hell, yes," he said softly, and scooped her up, leaving he
feet dangling as he planted a hard kiss in the center of he
mouth.

By the time he turned her loose, his ears were ringing an
he had an itch he sure couldn't scratch.

Angel was reeling from the unexpected pleasure when sh
suddenly remembered that Maddie was just a short distanc
away. She glanced over his shoulder, making certain they we
still alone.

"It doesn't matter if she sees," Royal said.

Angel looked startled. "But she will—"

"Look, lady," he said softly, and cupped the side of he
cheek. "I wasn't playing games when we made love. I full
intend that it will happen again." He leaned down and kisse
her. "And again." He kissed her again. "And again." Her sig
was warm against his face as he kissed her one more tim
"And again."

Angel was still standing with her head tilted and her eye
closed when Royal lifted his head.

"Do you have anything to say?"

"Again," Angel whispered.

He obliged with a grin.

A week came and went without disaster. Maddie was in he
routine, down at the barn with her kittens or begging Ange
for afternoon treats. Royal had begun cutting hay, and onl
now and then when they happened to catch a newscast woul
either one of them remember what had transpired. The FBI ha
not called. Angel liked to tell herself that her part in the dirt
business of murder was over. In the back of her mind, she kne
there might come a day when she would have to pick him ou
of a lineup or even testify against him at a trial. But those day
were so far out of the realm of her reality that she let the ugl
thoughts slide.

At night, after Maddie was asleep, Royal would come to he

oom and lie beside her. The gentleness with which they made
ove was coupled with the growing bond between them. The
imes when he would just hold her brought tears to her eyes,
and the nights as they planned the next day were the most
precious to Angel of all. It was for her proof that she'd become
a real part of his world.

On the days she was alone in the house, she let herself pre-
end this was her house she cleaned and her family for whom
she prepared meals. Because even though she knew Royal
loved her, he had yet to say the words she longed to hear. To
belong, truly belong to this man and his child, she needed to
be his wife.

And then the day came when she turned on the television
and sat down to rest. She had a glass of iced tea in one hand
and a freshly baked cookie in the other. Lunch was ready and
waiting, but Royal and Maddie had yet to come back from
town.

Condensation from the glass was making a wet spot in her
lap, but she didn't care. She took a bite of the cookie, savoring
the burst of brown sugar and chocolate chip in her mouth. The
show in progress was interrupted for a bulletin. She listened
absently, mentally preparing what would need to be reheated
first upon their arrival, when the announcer's words began to
sink in. Stunned, she laid her snack aside and leaned forward,
focusing on every word.

"Today it was revealed that there may be a mystery witness
to the interstate killings. Through unimpeachable sources, we
have learned there was a woman near Dallas who narrowly
escaped the killer's knife, and that she is working in conjunction with authorities to see that the killer is brought to justice."

Angel stood and screamed Royal's name. Only after she
heard the echo of her voice in the silence of the house did she
remember that he and Maddie weren't home.

"Oh, God, oh, my God."

Her hands were shaking as she locked all the doors. Before
she could think what else to do, the phone began to ring.

* * *

Royal was at the feed store, arguing with Maddie as to why she couldn't have a grape sucker from the jar on the counter when he heard the high-pitched beep that was the local television's signal of an upcoming bulletin. He looked at the small black and white television.

"Hey, Will, turn that up, will you?" he said.

The owner of the feed store picked up his remote and aimed it at the screen.

Royal's face turned pale and then a dark angry red. He heard enough to know that Angel's safety had been seriously compromised. Without asking for permission, he reached for the office phone and started punching in numbers.

"Daddy, who are you calling?" Maddie asked.

He yanked a grape sucker from the jar on the counter and all but stuffed it into her mouth.

"Here," he said. "Don't talk. Suck."

Her eyes alight, Maddie grinned. For one of the few times in her life, she did as she'd been told.

The phone rang once, then twice, then again, then again. Royal's belly was in knots. He didn't know what she would do if she saw it, but he kept remembering that once she'd offered to leave. Dear God, if she got it in her head that the killer would come looking for her, she might up and run.

"Come on, baby," he muttered. "Pick up the phone. Pick up the phone."

Angel closed her eyes and said a quick prayer as the phone continued to ring. It rang so many times the sound became human. But was it a warning—or was it a threat? Finally, she couldn't stand it any longer. Her hands were shaking and her throat was burning as she lifted the receiver to her ear. When she spoke, all she heard was her voice, high-pitched and tinny, and the fear coming out in a single word.

"Hello?"

Royal heaved a great sigh of relief. "Angel, thank God. Are you all right? Why didn't you answer the phone?"

She started to cry.

He cursed beneath his breath. It was just as he feared. She'd heard the broadcast.

"Angel...sweetheart, listen to me."

She choked on a sob. "What?"

"I'm on my way. No one's going to hurt you. I promised, remember?"

She nodded, then realizing he couldn't see her response, she said yes.

"That's a great big area they named. There is no way anyone could know it was you. Right?"

She shuddered. He was right. She'd panicked too soon. "I guess," she said.

A little of the tension went out of his body. Without missing a beat, he pointed a warning finger at Maddie to keep her sucker away from the feed store cat while adding a footnote to his call.

"Angel."

She sounded small and lost, and he wished to God he was there with her.

"We're on our way."

"Okay."

"I love you, baby."

A fresh set of tears spilled down her face. She squeezed the receiver tightly, holding on to her man in the only way she could.

"I love you, too," she said softly.

"You'd better," he growled. "We've got at least a good sixty years ahead of us, and some good loving, too."

She was smiling when she hung up.

The click sounded in Royal's ear and he hung up with a sigh. When he turned, he realized that Will had long ago hit the mute button, and every ear in the store, including Maddie's, had been trained on his end of the conversation.

"Uh…" Will began.

Royal's jaw slid forward in a mutinous thrust as he reached for Maddie's hand.

"If you want any more of my business, Will Smith, then you won't bother to finish what you started to ask." He looked around the feed store to the half dozen men gathered there. "That goes for the rest of you, too."

None had the guts to look him in the eye.

Will had known Royal Justice for more years than he cared to count. He'd seen him deck a man for raising his voice in front of his wife. But that had been before his wife died. After that, old Royal had kept to himself. He grinned. Maybe the gossip he'd been hearing was right, after all. Maybe Royal Justice *was* sweet on his housekeeper. And wouldn't that be fine.

"I ain't sayin' a word," Will muttered, pretending great indignation. "Alls I was goin' to ask was do you want to charge the feed you picked up?"

"Yes," Royal said, and started out the door. But he should have known his Maddie would have the last word.

"Daddy, are you in love with my angel?"

He groaned and slammed the door behind him.

Chapter 15

Angel heard Royal's truck coming down the driveway and ran out of the house. She was standing on the porch when it came to a sliding halt. He got out before the dust had settled, set Maddie on her feet with an order to go wash the grape sucker off her face and hands and headed for Angel with single-minded intent.

Angel met him at the steps. Within seconds, she was in his arms, her face buried against his neck. Safe. She was safe.

Maddie stared intently at the couple, drawing her own conclusions to what she was seeing. At that moment, Flea Bit came sauntering around the corner of the house with its tiny tail straight up in the air like a flag at full mast.

"Flea Bit," Maddie squealed, and held out her hands.

Royal turned. The word no was at the edge of his tongue when she picked the cat up. By then it was too late. Cat and girl were now stuck to each other with a thick, grapey glue.

"Well, damn," he muttered. But the look on Maddie's face was priceless. He couldn't help it. He started to laugh.

Laughter was the last thing Angel expected to hear, but when she turned to look, she started to grin.

Maddie was trying to let go, but every time she lifted her hand, a new patch of kitty hair got caught in the mess. The cat was squalling in pain and climbing the front of her shirt in a futile effort to get free. The closer it got to her face, the wilder Maddie's expression became.

"Daddy!" she screeched.

Angel was laughing as she ran to help. "Wait, honey," she cried. "Don't move. Let Daddy and me help you."

Maddie was considering the wisdom of a real good cry to offset the fact that she hadn't done as she'd been told, then decided it wasn't going to be necessary after all.

Her daddy was on his knees, trying to peel the cat's claws from the front of her shirt, while her angel was trying to unstick the hair from the palms of Maddie's hands.

"We're all stuck," she announced.

Royal paused and looked up. In every way that counted, Maddie was right. She was stuck to the cat. The cat was stuck to her shirt. Angel was getting sticky from both cat and Maddie, and intermittently, the cat stuck its claws into him.

"Yeah, honey, we sure are," he said, then grinned at the look on Angel's face as Flea Bit's little tail hit her square in the face.

Flea Bit hit the porch running and didn't look back. Maddie looked at her hands and sighed.

"Daddy?"

"Hmm?"

"Will the hair grow back on Flea Bit?"

Angel sat on the porch, folded her arms across her knees and dropped her head. Her shoulders were shaking uncontrollably.

Guilt hit Royal belly-first, and he started to panic as he realized he'd completely forgotten why they'd rushed home. He dropped to one knee and cupped the back of her head.

"Angel, honey, I'm so sorry. It's not that I didn't think of your feelings, but Maddie was…uh, well, the cat was so…"

"Oh, God," she gasped, and fell backward onto the porch with her arms out and her face streaked with tears. But they weren't tears of sorrow. She was laughing so hard she couldn't stop.

"If you could have seen your face," she mumbled, then rolled onto her side and laughed even harder.

Relief settled. All he could think was, thank God she wasn't mad.

Maddie started off the porch in the direction the cat had gone. Royal grabbed the tail of her shirt and gave it a yank.

"Inside. Now," he said shortly. "And don't come out until those hands are clean and shining."

She disappeared, leaving them alone on the porch.

"Here," Royal said. "I'll help you up."

Angel shook her head and held out her hands. "Don't touch me," she said, and laughed even harder. "I'm all catty, too."

He stood with a silly grin on his face, staring at her while the last empty place in his heart slowly filled. She had become his touchstone to sanity—his friend and his love. As he watched her, still trying to come to terms with her hysteria, she suddenly blurred before his eyes. It came to him then that without her beside him, his life would be far less than it was meant to be.

"Marry me."

The words silenced her as nothing else could have done. She rolled on her back, the last of her smile still fixed on her face.

"What did you say?" she asked, and heard the panic in her voice.

"You heard me," Royal said.

"Say it again," she whispered. "Say it while I'm looking at your face."

He squatted beside her. "Marry me."

She sat with a jerk. "Just like that? Without an I love you or I can't live without you? You say marry me just like that?"

His voice was shaking. "I love you. I can't live without you."

Angel started to cry. But not like she had before. Not because she was afraid of the killer. But because she was afraid she was dreaming.

"I don't know what to say."

Royal felt sick. He didn't know where this was going, but he would have liked a resounding yes.

"Say I love you. I can't live without you," he said.

Angel pressed a hand against her chest. The pain in there was so great that she thought she might faint. If this didn't work out, it would kill her.

"I love you."

He rocked on his heels and started to grin.

"I can't live without you," he prompted.

She bit her lower lip and took a deep breath. "I can't live without you," she echoed.

The grin widened as he stood and pulled her to her feet.

"My hands," she muttered, trying in vain to wipe the cat hair from her palms.

Cat hair was the farthest thing from Royal's mind. He lowered his head, nipping at the edge of her lower lip, then kissing the tears on her face.

"Angel, sweetheart..."

She felt rootless, as if she could take wing and fly. It was all she could do to answer.

"Hmm?"

"Isn't there something else you've forgotten to say?"

Her mind was racing. To the best of her knowledge, she'd said enough already.

"Like what?" she murmured, then groaned when he backed her against the wall of the house.

"Like yes."

If he'd just take his hands off her breasts, she might remember what they'd been talking about.

''Yes, what?'' She sighed as her nipples peaked beneath his caresses.

''Yes, you will marry me.''

''Yes, you will marry me,'' she echoed.

He lifted his head. There was a devilish grin on his face. ''Well, now, Miss Rojas, don't mind if I do.''

Royal was red in the face and way past congeniality. His last ounce of patience had run out the moment the federal agent had started to mouth weak excuses.

''Look, Deaton. I don't give a tinker's damn whose fault it was. The fact is that someone leaked the information to the media about Angel's existence. If you don't find out who did it and put a stop to it, the next thing will most likely be her name and address running on a crawl at the bottom of the screen. And if that happens, you better start running. And don't bother with a forwarding address because I'll be right on your ass.''

Deaton winced. He'd known from the start that Justice could be trouble, but he didn't much blame him. He had no idea who'd leaked the information to the press, but he would find out. He'd already accessed the bank accounts of everyone who'd had seen to the files. If anyone tried to claim receiving a recent inheritance, they'd better have a dead body to back it up.

''Look, Justice, all I can say is I'm sorry. And you know as well as I do that it would be next to impossible to find Miss Rojas based on the information the media put out. There's what? A million people living in the Dallas area alone?''

''Hell if I know,'' Royal said shortly. ''All I'm saying is, you screwed up. Don't let it happen again.''

He slammed the phone down in disgust and picked up a paperweight from the desk.

''If you throw it, something will break,'' Angel said calmly. ''And if it does, you're cleaning it up, not me.''

Royal dropped the paperweight to the desk and reached for her, pulling her into his arms and hugging her close.

"Okay, okay," he said softly. "I hear you. I'm calm."

"And I'm Snow White," she said.

A frown creased his forehead as he gave her a cold, hard stare. "Was that a crude ethnic joke I didn't get?"

She grinned. "So I'm not lily-white and we're missing a few dwarfs, but there's still Maddie…and you."

This wasn't the first time he'd heard her make a remark about the color of her skin, something she should have been proud of. Then he remembered what she'd told him of her past. When life was a struggle, sometimes ethnicity got lost in just trying to survive.

"If I'd wanted lily-white, I could have had lily-white," he muttered. "Personally, I like my women like I like my toast. Hot and brown all over."

Angel's mouth dropped open. "Toast?" She started to grin. "Toast. Well now, you sweet-talking man, how can a woman resist after a compliment like that?"

Still grinning, she hooked her fingers in the belt loops of his jeans, pulling him closer and stealing a quick kiss.

Before he could follow through on the notion she'd put in his head, she spun out of his arms and headed for the door.

"Hey!" he called. "Where are you going?"

She stopped in the doorway. "To see if Maddie is asleep."

"Why?"

A wicked smile tilted the corners of her lips. "Because I can't seduce you if I don't have you all to myself."

All things considered, it was a long, eventful night.

Tommy Boy Watson sat on his motel bed, staring blankly at the television. A young, dark-haired man was walking the fields with a journalist, pointing out the recent damage done to this year's wheat crop. From what Tommy Boy gathered, Grant County had been hammered by the storm that passed through, and the current crop was shot. He sighed. If things didn't change, he was going to be next.

He closed his eyes and laid on the bed, trying to recall his daddy's face. It wouldn't come. All he could see was that dark-haired bitch turning her back on him and hitching a ride with that trucker.

It was her fault. Even though they hadn't said her name, he knew it had to be her. They'd talked about her on the six o'clock news, and he knew they would repeat it on this broadcast. Because of her, every lawman in the country would be looking for him. Then he reminded himself they'd be looking for the old Tommy Boy. He looked different now. He rubbed his hands up and down the length of his face, testing the baby-soft skin that had been underneath his beard. It made him feel strange, almost nude. His father, if he'd still been alive, wouldn't know him. When he looked in a mirror, he didn't know his face. They would never recognize him as the man in the sketch.

But there was his truck. The bitch had described it. And he had hauled the bodies in it until he found a place to dump them. He'd washed it out good, but with today's technology, if he missed so much as a hair or a drop of blood, his goose would be cooked. He frowned. As much as he hated to face it, he had to at least consider the wisdom of getting rid of his truck.

The sun was high in the sky the next day when Tommy Boy pulled into the street from the parking lot of Melvin's Used Cars. He adjusted the rearview mirror as he drove and fiddled with the radio stations until he had them all set to his liking. The interior of the little red Toyota pickup smelled like lemon oil and Armor-All. There was a cigarette burn in the seat, and one of the floor mats was missing. The right window was hard to roll down, and there was a faint scratch across the tailgate. The grudge he had against that bitch kept growing. Because of her, he'd had to give up his pride and joy—his new Dodge truck. His gaze slid to the dusty red hood. He narrowed his eyes. The paint job on this truck would never hold a shine.

He drove west out of Blackwell, heading toward the interstate. He'd been thinking all night about what he should do. He could go home. But if he did, he would spend the rest of his life looking over his shoulder, waiting for the day when that bitch would show up, pointing her finger at him and screaming, "It's him." Or he could go to Texas and find her, like he should have done before. It would be a pleasure to shut her up once and for all.

He kept heading west. Either way he went, it was a long drive.

The interstate appeared. His belly knotted with uncertainty. Which way? A bridge was imminent. If he took the on ramp before he crossed it, he'd be in Kansas in less than half an hour. If he crossed the bridge and headed south, it would take a good day's driving to cross the Red River into Texas.

If he hadn't been so ticked off about the situation in general, he might have laughed at the incongruity of his dilemma. What was that old saying? Something about crossing bridges when you got to them? Well, here he was, facing the biggest bridge of his life and he couldn't make up his mind.

Make her pay. Make her pay.

Tommy Boy jerked when the voice echoed inside his head. A slow smile spread across his face as he gunned the little red truck across the bridge and took the southbound ramp.

"I hear you, Daddy. I hear you loud and clear."

Maddie was digging holes in the dirt at the edge of the garden with a stick as Angel picked ripe tomatoes from the vines. Every now and then she would jump up and run down the row, pointing to one Angel missed. After the third time this happened, Angel set down her bucket.

"Come here to me," she said softly, then hugged the little girl tight. "You know what, Maddie mine?"

Maddie grinned. She loved the nickname Angel had given her. It made her feel as if they all really belonged together.

"What?" Maddie said.

"You are the best helper anyone could have. I don't know what I'd do without you."

Maddie threw her arms around Angel's neck and closed her eyes in pure delight as Angel kissed her all over her face. Still giggling when Angel turned her loose, Maddie dropped to her knees and began fiddling with a bug running through the dirt.

"Angel?"

Angel stopped and turned. The plaintive note in Maddie's voice was unexpected.

"What is it, honey?"

"Are you and my daddy going to get married?"

Again, Angel set the bucket aside, but this time she sat down in the row and faced Maddie. She took her by the hands and pulled on the ends of her fingers until she had Maddie giggling.

"What would you say if we did?" Angel asked.

Maddie's eyes rounded, and her forehead wrinkled in a thoughtful frown. Finally, she answered.

"I do?"

Angel grinned, and then, ignoring the dirt and the proximity of the tomato plants, she lifted Maddie into her lap and pulled her close against her breasts. At that moment, the scent of little-girl sweat and freshly turned earth seemed sweeter than any flower could have.

"So you think it would be a good thing?" Angel asked.

Maddie nodded as she leaned against the softness of Angel's breasts. "The lady told me you would be my mama." She looked at Angel, testing her…judging her…waiting to see if she got that same look Daddy did when she talked about the lady who sat on her bed.

Angel shivered. There was so much going on with this child that neither she or Royal understood. But she had enough faith in herself and in God to know there were some things one didn't question.

''You still haven't told me what you think,'' Angel persisted. ''I would live here for always. And your daddy and I would sleep in the same bed. But that wouldn't mean that your daddy didn't love you as much as he used to. It would mean you would have two people, not just one, who loved you most of all.''

Satisfied with what Angel had told her, Maddie nodded, then sighed. A few moments later, her eyes began to droop, then her head lolled against Angel's shoulder.

And so they sat between the rows of ripening tomatoes. A small sweat bee buzzed around a skinned spot on Maddie's knee. Angel waved it away as she bent and kissed the edge of her ear.

''I love you, Maddie mine,'' she said softly.

Maddie was silent for so long, Angel thought something was wrong. She looked down and smiled. Madeline Michelle was asleep.

Angel looked up. Royal was standing at the end of the row. She smiled and motioned him forward.

''She's been playing so hard,'' Angel whispered as he bent to lift his daughter out of her arms.

Royal nodded. At that moment, words were beyond him. When he'd first come out of the house and seen their heads above the rows in the garden, he thought someone had been hurt. The closer he'd come, the less his worry had been. He'd seen them laugh. He'd seen them hug. He'd watched Angel's tenderness as she'd settled Maddie close in her lap. And then he'd watched his daughter's eyes droop, secure in the knowledge that if she was with Angel, she was safe.

Angel watched Royal striding away with his child in his arms, then sighed and got to her feet to finish what she'd been doing. There was a satisfaction within her that hadn't been there before. An affirmation that what they were doing was right. Not just for the passion that bound her and Royal, but for the love she also felt for his child. She palmed a warm, red tomato and tugged, then set it in the bucket with the others she'd picked. She smiled. And her child, too.

By the time she looked up again, Royal was coming back.

"Look," she said, holding up the bounty for him to see. "You and Maddie sure know how to plant a garden. Just look at what you've—"

He took the bucket out of her hands and set it on the ground, then put his arms around her waist and lifted her off her feet. His face was buried against the heat of her neck, his body trembling against hers.

"Woman, you are breaking my heart."

Tears shattered Angel's vision as a burst of love for this man hit her square in the belly. One of her shoes dropped to the ground.

"Wait, Royal. My shoe."

He set her down, but instead of retrieving the shoe, he took the other one off, too. Then he scooped her into his arms and started toward the house, carrying her as if she weighed nothing at all.

Surprised by his intensity, she brushed her hand against the side of his face.

"Where are we going?"

He paused and closed his eyes, turning his face so his mouth was centered in the middle of her palm. The scent of the earth was on her—from the land on which they were standing to the pungent odor of crushed tomato leaves from the crop she'd been harvesting. He shuddered with longing.

"Inside. If I don't make love to you within the next five minutes, I might not come out of this day alive."

She smiled, then playfully rubbed her hand across the breadth of his chest.

"I never thought of myself as medicine before, but if I can help a good man with a great big ache..."

His eyes narrowed dangerously. There was a muscle jerking at the side of his jaw.

"You ever made love in the dirt before?"

She shook her head, her eyes widening nervously. All she could think was he wouldn't dare.

"Then don't mess with me, woman, until I get you behind closed doors."

Four days passed. Days in which joy came to the house in myriad ways and cemented Angel's presence in their lives. Angel hugged the memories to her, and each night before she went to bed, she stood before the mirror and looked at the woman she was becoming. Her hair was still the same. Long, thick, and black—sooty black. Her eyes were still large and brown, her brows finely arched. Her nose was still small and straight with a slight flare at the nostrils. Her lips had not changed. They were still shaped in a perpetual pout.

But the differences were there. In the glow in her eyes. In the tilt of her smile. In the tenderness of her touch. In the way her heart beat. Rock steady. Like the love she had for Royal Justice and his child.

The Angel Rojas who'd left Fat Louie rolling on the floor of his bar—defiant, disbelieving, distrusting of anyone or anything except herself—was gone. And each day that dawned brought a finer sense of purpose to her life. Since the day they'd put her mother in the ground, she'd been searching for a place to call home. It was now within reach. She'd accepted shelter from Royal, then a job. Now she was about to become his wife. Her life was full. Her heart was content. The only shadow on her horizon was the distant threat of having to one day face a killer. But it was so far removed from the life she was living that she gave herself permission to forget. Only now and then, when she happened to catch an update on the investigation and the drawing was flashed on the television screen, did she let herself remember the loose ends of her past.

But Royal hadn't forgotten a thing. When it came to the women he loved, he went all the way and then some. He had not forgotten that Angel was the only witness in a federal investigation, and while the chance that she would be in danger was remote, the fact that it was there was enough for him to act upon.

When a graying, middle-aged wrangler showed up on the Justice doorstep looking for a job, Angel thought nothing of it. His truck was old and rusting. Besides a suitcase, there were a couple of saddles and some tack in the truck bed. Nothing but a cowboy looking for work. When Royal hired him on the spot, she still didn't wonder. After all, he'd hired her with far less need and reason.

His name was Rusty. He tossed his meager belongings into the two-bed bunkhouse and went to work the same day. He ate meals with them, and in the rare times when there was nothing to do, he could be found sitting in a shady spot, whittling on a small piece of wood.

Maddie was fascinated with him…and with the knife. It took an entire day for Royal to impress upon her the trouble she would be in if she ever tried it herself. After that, everything settled. On August the first, just over a month away, Maddie would turn five. And before that month was out, she would be going to school. Everything was moving at an unstoppable pace.

Royal stood in the hallway with his Stetson in his hands. He'd been ready for the better part of thirty minutes waiting on women of all ages to get ready, too. Angel had poked her head out her bedroom door, blown him a kiss and waggled two fingers at him as an indication of how much more time she needed. His daughter wasn't any better. She'd dawdled on the porch with the kittens too long. And while he could have followed her in her room and done it all for her, it wouldn't have taught her a thing. So he'd taken a deep breath and calmed his frayed nerves and bellowed instead of screamed.

"Madeline Michelle, if I have to tell you again to brush your teeth—"

Maddie was running before he finished. She didn't have to

hear the rest of it to recognize the implied threat. She'd never had the nerve to test her daddy that far and see what he *really* would do.

"I'm brushing. I'm washing. I'm changing my clothes," she shrieked.

He jammed his Stetson on his head and pivoted sharply. Out. He needed out.

"I'll be waiting on the porch," he yelled to anyone in general.

The door slammed behind him and hot air hit him in the face. Tomorrow was the first of July. He had hay on the field drying, and it looked like rain. And while he had some control over the women in his life, there was nothing he could do about the weather. Until the hay was dry enough to bale, there it would lay.

He caught movement out the corner of his eye and turned. It was Rusty coming from the back yard.

"We're driving into Dallas," Royal said. "Maddie starts school in a few weeks." He rolled his eyes and shook his head. "Buying clothes for school. My God, I knew this day was coming, and I'm still not ready."

Rusty nodded. "Mine are grown and gone for more than ten years now," he said. "But I remember how it was. It's hard to let go."

Royal glanced over his shoulder, making sure they were alone. "We should be back before three. If something happens, I'll call."

The older man's smile shifted. It wasn't much, but his expression had hardened.

"I suppose I'd better get at that tack," Rusty said. "There's a couple of bridles that need mending."

Royal nodded. "See you later. Oh, and don't forget. Angel said to tell you there's plenty of leftover roast and some of her chocolate pie in the refrigerator. Help yourself."

Rusty's smile shifted again, rekindling the light in his eyes.

"I'll be doing just that," he said, and waved as he walked away.

The door opened behind Royal, and he turned. Angel was coming out the door, holding Maddie's hand. She was wearing gauzy white pants and a loose matching top, a recent purchase from a mail-order catalog. White backless sandals flopped against her heels as she walked.

Royal whistled appreciatively and winced when Maddie, wearing red shorts and a red and white top, put a matching sway in her walk as she headed toward the truck. It reminded him of the day she'd gone to Paige Sullivan's party with the nail polish still wet on her fingernails. He groaned beneath his breath and sighed as Angel slipped an arm around his waist.

"Poor Daddy. It's going to be all right."

"Oh, I know that," Royal said. "It's simple, really. She just won't be allowed to date until she's twenty-one."

Angel giggled and squealed with delight when he spun her off her feet and planted a swift, hard kiss upon her lips.

Maddie stopped in midsway and spun, her foray into adult behavior instantly forgotten. She was giggling and squealing along with Angel before she reached Royal's side.

"Do me next, Daddy! Do me!"

Royal laughed. His world was complete.

Chapter 16

The light was turning red as Tommy Boy braked to a stop on the outskirts of Dallas. He had seventy-five dollars in his pocket and less than four hundred in the bank back home. It was as close to broke as he'd ever been in his life.

For the last two days, he'd been so mad at himself for turning south instead of north that it was all he could do to keep driving. He'd never listened to his daddy all that much when he'd been alive. He didn't know why he was listening to him now.

The engine in his pickup coughed and sputtered, and he gunned the accelerator to keep it from dying right there in the street.

"Sorry ass piece of junk," he mumbled.

If it hadn't been for that black-haired bitch flapping her mouth, he would still have his good truck. Better yet, he would already be home. The engine sputtered again, and this time it died.

The light turned green.

Tommy Boy cursed.

Behind him, cars began to honk. He rolled down the window, stuck out his arm and flipped everyone off before popping the hood. His stride was short and jerky, evidence of his anger.

Waves of heat washed over his skin as he leaned inside. He turned his head, squinting to protect his eyes from a stream of escaping steam, and that's when he saw her. In the left-turn lane, sitting in the front seat of a late-model pickup. At first he thought he was dreaming. He'd looked for her for so long. He stood and stared. There was a child in the seat beside her, and a big cowboy behind the wheel. His heart leaped. It *was* her—the bitch who'd gotten away. By God, he'd found her.

He started to run for his truck and then remembered the piece of junk wouldn't start. He watched in horror as the light changed to green. They started to turn away from Tommy Boy, moving into a thick stream of traffic.

''No,'' he shouted, and clapped a hand over his mouth in shock.

He didn't want her to see him. He couldn't let her go. Frantic, he began to run behind the truck as it moved into traffic, ignoring the shouts and honks from other drivers as they swerved to miss him. He was looking for something—anything—that would tell him what he needed to know. A tag number wouldn't do. He certainly had no way to access the records. And he would have bet his life that wasn't the only blue Chevy truck in the state of Texas. Desperation kept him moving when the logical thing would have been to give up. But he couldn't. His life depended on ending hers.

He kept running. His lungs began to burn, and there was a stitch in his side. To make matters worse, the truck was stretching the distance between them. Out of nowhere, a man on a motorcycle roared past him. It was reflex that sent him diving into the grass in the center median. When he looked up, the truck was turning a corner.

''Oh, no,'' he groaned. They were gone.

And that's when he saw it. There on the side, in neat white letters on that dark blue paint.

Justice Ranch, Alvarado, Texas

He started to grin. Another car honked at him as he crawled
to his feet. He grinned and waved, then started hoofing it toward his down-and-out truck. The smile on his face didn't fit
his situation. But Tommy Boy knew something no one else
did. His luck had just changed.

School clothes weren't all Royal bought at the mall. While
Angel and Maddie were in the bathroom, he'd slipped into the
jewelry store and bought Angel a ring. All the way home, one
scenario after another ran through his mind about how he
would give it to her. It had to be special. And the timing had
to be right.

There was a smile on his face he couldn't control. After
tonight, there would be no more misunderstandings about what
Angel Rojas meant to him. The ring was his brand. The woman
was going to be his wife.

He grinned again.

His wife.

They topped the hill above the ranch. Out of habit, his gaze
raked the area for anything out of place. Roman's car surprised
him. Although they talked on the phone every day, he hadn't
seen him since the day he'd brought Maddie home.

"Uncle Roman's here," Maddie squealed.

"So I see," Royal muttered.

Surprised by his tone, Angel stared. "Is something wrong?"
she asked.

Royal hesitated, then told himself he was just borrowing
trouble.

"No, I doubt it. He usually calls before he comes, that's
all."

Angel nodded, but she had picked up on the hesitation in
Royal's voice and couldn't help but wonder.

Roman was sitting on the porch with Maddie's kitten in his
lap. He stood as they parked, and the cat scampered off the
porch and under the lilac bush.

"Uncle Roman!" Maddie shrieked, and ran with her arms outstretched.

He caught her on the run and hugged her a dozen times over, kissing her between each embrace.

Madeline Michelle, princess of it all, soaked up the love like a sponge. It was no more than she expected.

"Aunt Holly sent you some brownies," he said. "They're in the kitchen. Ask Daddy if you can have some."

Maddie hit the door running and didn't look back.

Royal rolled his eyes and announced to anyone who cared to hear, "Yeah, sure, Maddie, you can have a brownie. Don't forget to wash your hands first."

Angel laughed. "She ate all her lunch, remember?"

He was smiling when Roman stepped off the porch.

"Rusty's gone," Roman said.

Royal pivoted. "Why and where?"

"Appendicitis. He called me over two hours ago. Said he was driving himself to the hospital." He glanced at his watch. "In fact, I'd be guessing he's probably going into surgery about now."

"Oh, no," Angel gasped. Her face fell. "Oh, Royal, he was all by himself."

Roman started to say more, but something made him look at Royal. Royal was frowning slightly and shaking his head. It wasn't much, but Roman realized Angel didn't know about Rusty's real identity or why he'd been hired.

"Well, I just wanted to let you know," he said.

"I guess I'd better get Maddie's packages," Angel said, and started toward the truck.

Royal caught her by the wrist, then cupped the back of her head in a tender gesture. "No, baby, I'll get them," Royal said. "You go check on Maddie. And if she's had more than two of those brownies, put the damned things away."

"Or maybe I'll get a glass of milk and join her," Angel said. "Chocolate sounds just about right." She started toward the house then stopped and turned. "Roman, tell Holly thank you."

"Sure thing, honey," he said, smiling. The moment she was out of sight, he turned. "What do you want me to do? I'll hire someone else today."

Royal sighed, stuffed his hands in his pockets and walked away from the house. Roman followed.

"What are you thinking?" Roman asked.

Royal turned. The wide brim of his Stetson was shading his face from the rays of the sun, but Roman could see the worry on his brother's face.

"About what I'd do if anything ever happened to her."

Roman stood watching Royal struggle with his emotions.

"You're in love with her, aren't you?"

Royal took off his hat and combed his hand through his hair. "Oh, yeah, big time," he drawled.

Roman grinned.

"If we didn't have bigger fish to fry, I'd say I told you so."

Royal set his Stetson on his head and then looked at the house. It was so familiar…so safe. He'd been born here. He'd brought his first wife here. And God willing, he would grow old and die here someday. And yet as comfortable as this place was to him, there was a pall on his soul. Something kept pushing at him to take his family and run. If he'd been another sort of man, he might have done so. But Royal had never run from a fight in his life, and he wasn't about to start now. He clenched his jaw and curled his hands into fists, then turned to Roman.

"Get someone else out here as soon as you can. If not tonight, then tomorrow at the latest. I've got a feeling in my gut that won't go away, and until that son of a bitch is caught and put behind bars, I won't feel right."

"Consider it already done," Roman said. "But how are you going to explain another hired hand to Angel? She's not stupid, you know."

Royal nodded. "It's her life that's on the line. I won't lie to her again."

A few minutes later, Royal was alone, watching the dust settle in the driveway and wondering where to go from here. As he started toward the house, the bulge of the ring box in his pocket reminded him of better things. When he entered the house, there was a grin on his face.

"Did anyone save me some brownies?" he yelled.

Two voices in the back of the house shouted no.

He was still laughing when he tackled them both on the bed.

All good plans and intentions were subject to change. Finding the right moment to give Angel the ring kept coming and then going without it having been done. Royal's frustration was mounting, and by nine o'clock, if he'd had a cage, he might have put Maddie in it. It was almost as if she sensed something was up and didn't want to miss it happening. They'd put her to bed twice already, and he could still hear her singing to her teddy bear.

He aimed the remote at the television and hit the mute button. "That little wart is still awake," he muttered. "Probably all that damned chocolate."

Angel looked up from a shirt she was mending. "Maybe I should read her another story."

He shook his head. "Knowing her, that's what she's angling for. How many did you read earlier?"

"Only two."

Royal grinned. "You, my love, are a pushover. I never read more than one."

"That's because you fall asleep first," Angel said.

He pretended to frown.

Maddie was beginning the second stanza of "Colors of the Wind," the theme song from the Disney video *Pocahontas*. It was loud and a little off key, but it was obvious by the way she was belting out the lyrics that she was into the moment.

Angel started to laugh. Not loud, and not at Maddie, just at the situation. Here they were, two reasonably sensible adults, fitting their lives to conform to a child's.

Royal studied her face as she sewed, watching the dexterity of her fingers as the needle went in and out through the holes in the button she was sewing on his shirt. Her face was in profile, highlighted by the reading lamp beside her. He stared for so long his eyes started to burn. She was so damned beautiful.

Before he knew it, he was out of his chair and on one knee in front of her.

"Hey," she said, when he took the needle and shirt out of her hands.

Then he took the ring box out of his pocket and set it in the center of her palm and closed her fingers over it. His voice was rough with emotion as he looked at her.

"If you'll have me."

Angel's heart skipped a beat. Even though he'd already proposed and she'd said yes, this made everything official in the eyes of the world.

"Oh, Royal," she said softly.

"Open it," he urged.

She laid it in his hand. "You do it," she begged.

A little nervous, he took out the ring, then slipped it on the third finger of her left hand.

"If it doesn't fit…"

He needn't have worried. It slid down her finger like pearls against silk. He looked at the diamond solitaire shining on her finger like a piece of morning sky. His eyes darkened. "I love you, girl. Marry me soon."

The weight felt strange upon her finger as she slid her arms around his neck.

"Name the day, and I'm yours."

He groaned softly and leaned forward. "You're already mine, lady, and don't you ever forget it."

"Daddy, whatcha doin'?"

Royal rocked on his heels and stood up with a jerk.

"What the hell are you doing out of bed?" he growled.

But Maddie wasn't about to be deterred. She pattered across

the floor and crawled into Angel's lap as if Royal wasn't even there.

"You and my daddy were kissing, weren't you?" she asked.

Angel was trying hard not to grin. "Yes, we sure were," she said. "Want to join us?"

The idea obviously had merit. Maddie giggled and threw her arms around Angel's neck and planted a kiss on the side of her cheek.

"My turn," Angel said, and kissed the little girl.

"Now you do it, Daddy," Maddie demanded, and lifted her arms to be held in Royal's arms.

He sighed and did as she demanded. After all, she *was* the princess of it all.

Four kisses and a giggle fest later, Maddie was in bed with her teddy bear tucked under her chin. Royal was about to turn out the light. Angel was sitting on the side of the bed with a book in her hand.

Maddie peeked out from beneath heavy eyelids, checking one last time to see if they were still there. Then she sighed.

"Angel."

"What, darling?" Angel asked.

"You're sitting beside my lady tonight."

It was all Angel could do not to bolt. The thought of sitting next to a ghost, however imaginary, was a little unnerving.

"That's nice," she said, darting a nervous look in Royal's direction. As she suspected, he was frowning.

"I'm going to sleep now," Maddie said.

"It's about damned time," Royal muttered, but not loud enough that anybody heard.

He turned out the light and stood aside, waiting for Angel. The night-light was on by Maddie's bed. Her teddy was tucked under her chin. Angel blew him a kiss as she headed for the kitchen to make them some coffee. Royal watched her go, savoring the comfort that comes from knowing that for once, he was doing everything right.

He turned and gave Maddie one last glance. And just for a

second, before he focused and blinked, he thought he saw the silhouette of a woman, head bowed, hands folded in her lap, sitting at the foot of Maddie's bed and watching her sleep. But the moment was fleeting, and when he looked back, she was gone. Angry with himself for even thinking it, he strode away.

At four minutes after three in the morning, the wind began to blow. A low rumble of thunder could be heard in the distance, and Royal rolled to the side of the bed and sat up. Almost at the same moment, Maddie began to cry. Royal heard her first and was out of bed and halfway down the hall before Angel knew what was happening. She followed.

The light from Maddie's room spilled into the darkened hall. When she entered, Royal was sitting on the side of the bed with Maddie in his lap, and it looked as if there was no consoling her.

"What's wrong?" Angel asked, as she sat beside them and began stroking Maddie's hair. "Did you have a bad dream?"

Thunder rumbled again, closer. And then it dawned on Royal. The storm. Maybe she was afraid it would storm like it did before.

"Are you afraid it will storm?"

"No," she sobbed, and surprised them both by crawling from Royal's arms into Angel's lap. Angel held her close and rocked her where she sat.

"Don't cry, sweetie," she whispered. "Daddy and I are right here. There's nothing to be afraid of, right?"

"She said he was coming to get you," Maddie sobbed.

Angel's heart skipped a beat, and she tried hard to smile. But there was a part of her that already knew what the child was going to say.

"Who, darling?"

"The lady. She said the man was coming to get you. I don't want you to go. I want you to marry us and stay here forever."

Royal was starting to get scared. Between the look on Angel's face and Maddie's tears, it was more than he could handle.

"Damn it, Maddie, there is no lady. You're just having a dream."

Angel wasn't so sure. That sick feeling in the pit of her stomach was growing stronger.

"Royal, would you bring me a wet washcloth? We're going to wash away all these tears. And when they're gone, the bad dream will be gone, too."

Glad to have something to do, Royal stalked into the bathroom. As soon as they were alone, Angel cuddled Maddie close. It took her a minute to find the right words, but she knew they had to be said.

"Maddie, sweetheart?"

"What?" Maddie asked.

"What man is coming to get me?"

"I don't know," Maddie muttered, her eyes already closing in weary defeat. "Just the man. The man from the road."

Angel clenched her jaw to keep from screaming. When she looked up, Royal was standing in the doorway with the washcloth in his hands. Water was dripping onto the floor. He looked as if someone had unloaded a shotgun into his belly and he was waiting to feel the pain.

"Hellfire," he muttered, then turned and flung the washcloth into the tub. "Isn't this ever going to end?"

"Do you believe her?" Angel asked.

"Do you?" Royal countered.

Angel was too scared to cry. "Yes. God help me, I do."

Royal lifted Maddie out of her arms and started down the hall toward his bedroom. Angel followed. Maddie roused only slightly, settling as soon as he laid her down.

"What are you doing?" Angel asked as he set Maddie in the middle of his bed.

"Get in," he said, pulling back the other side of the covers and motioning for her to lie down.

"All of us?"

Royal's expression darkened. "Until I figure out what the

hell's going on, I don't want either one of you out of my sight.''

Angel crawled in beside Maddie, who was already asleep. Royal touched Angel's hand, gently fingering the diamond.

''Angel.'' His voice was quiet, just above a whisper.

''What?'' Angel's voice was low, too, so as not to awaken Maddie.

''I won't let him hurt you.''

She shuddered, drawing comfort in the warmth of his touch.

''I know.''

The thunder came and went. Not a drop came from the moisture-laden clouds. Sometime before daybreak, Royal slipped out of bed and went into his office. He unlocked his gun case, loaded a hunting rifle and carried it to his truck.

It was against the law to carry a loaded gun in a vehicle, but he didn't give a good damn about laws. All that mattered to him was keeping Angel alive.

It took Tommy Boy the rest of the day to get his truck fixed. When he finally left Dallas, it was getting dark, and from the looks of the sky a storm was brewing. He didn't care. In fact, he welcomed it. People died in the rain just as easily as they died on a clear day—and it was easier to hide the evidence.

When he drove into the outskirts of Alvarado, he realized he should have waited until morning. Everything in the small town was closed. He peered into one storefront after another, reading the signs.

Open at Eight.

Open at Nine.

He sighed. He wouldn't get anywhere until morning.

A police car turned a corner at the end of the block. His pulse accelerated. No need calling attention to himself. He got into his truck and started out of town. He'd seen a picnic area at a roadside park a few miles back. Good a place as any to spend a long night.

When the clouds rolled over and thunder rattled the windows

in his truck, he rolled on his back and looked out the windshield to the dark sky above. Every now and then a periodic flash of lightning would show, but the rain never fell. When he looked up again, it was morning.

It was easier to find the Justice ranch than Tommy Boy would have believed. All he did was drive into Alvarado, order breakfast, then pump the skinny little waitress for information. He got more than he bargained for.

She said Justice, the man who owned the ranch, was well-to-do. People were saying the woman he'd hired as housekeeper was going to be his wife. And his little girl was starting kindergarten in the fall. He paid for his food and walked out of the café with one purpose in his mind.

So maybe the black-haired woman hadn't been a whore, after all. That would explain why she'd been so angry about his offer. Then he reminded himself she'd still taken a ride with a trucker. Maybe she was living a decent life and wasn't out infecting the good men of this world with her disease, but she'd still seen his face. She was the only witness who stood between him and safety. Tommy Boy was short on sympathy. She had to die.

He got in his truck and started out of town. All the way to the ranch, he kept discarding one scenario after another as to how he would effect what he'd come all this way to do. Maybe she'd be the only one in the house. If so, all he'd have to do was knock on the door.

Then he reminded himself there was the man to consider, this Justice man. Tommy Boy had seen him in the truck. He appeared quite large. Maybe even larger than his daddy had been. If the man was still at home…

Tommy Boy's fancy wandered. He finally decided he would play it by ear.

Royal was nursing his third cup of coffee and pacing the kitchen floor waiting for Roman to call. He could hear his daughter giggling as she and Angel made up the beds. His thoughts were on what was going on in Maddie's head, not what was happening in the real world, and how much, if at all, the two were connected. As much as he was opposed to the idea and as difficult as it was for him to believe, he would be crazy to ignore all the signs. Whether he understood it or not, something out of his control was choreographing his world. It was all he could do to keep up.

He drained the last of his coffee from the cup and turned to set it in the sink when the phone rang.

"Finally," he muttered, and answered. "Hello?"

"It's me," Roman said. "I've got a man on the way."

Royal went weak with relief. "Thanks, brother," he said softly. "I don't know what I would have done without your help on this."

"Don't mention it," Roman said. "Besides, I'll remind you of that next time I want a favor."

Royal grinned, and then got to business. "What's his background?" he asked.

"Retired undercover narc. He's a funny-looking little guy, but he knows his stuff. He'll be there before long and asking for work. Oh, yeah, you should know that he can't ride, so don't put him on a horse."

Royal laughed.

Roman added, "Just don't worry. You can trust him. He's the kind of man who blends into the background. You won't even know he's there unless it matters."

A phone rang in the background. Royal heard his brother talking to his secretary, then he came on the line.

"Look, Royal, I've got to take this call. If you have any concerns, don't hesitate to let me know."

"Thanks again," Royal said. It wasn't until they'd disconnected that he realized he hadn't asked for the man's name. Then he shrugged. What could it matter? How many funny-looking little guys were going to show up today on the pretense of asking for work?

* * *

Tommy Boy topped a low hill and whistled between his teeth as he slowed to absorb the size of the ranch in the valley. Money. The man had money. He reminded himself why he'd come, and accelerated. The sooner this was over, the sooner he would be home.

He pulled up to the main house and parked. That blue Chevy truck was off to one side. He frowned. That probably meant the cowboy was home. A small delay, but nothing he couldn't handle. He got out and glanced in the mirror on the door of his truck, making sure his hair was slicked back and his cap was on straight. His narrow angular face was shiny in the early morning sun. He rubbed a hand over his chin, savoring the lack of whiskers, satisfied he was unrecognizable. He hitched his pants a little higher over his bony hips and started for the porch. The heavy weight of the switchblade bumped the outside of his leg as he walked. It was a good feeling to know that help was so near at hand.

He knocked, bracing himself for the moment of confrontation, practicing what he would say. A few seconds later, the door opened, and his first thought was that the cowboy looked even bigger without his hat, which seemed silly.

He yanked off his cap, revealing his thinning hair and high, shiny forehead.

"Mr. Justice?"

Royal glanced over the man's shoulder to the little red truck he was driving, then at him. He nodded.

Tommy Boy wadded his cap without thinking. That hard blue gaze was intimidating, and it was all he could do to stare him straight in the face.

"My name's, uh, Wilson, Fred Wilson. They said in town that you might be needing help. I'm a hard worker, and I need the job."

Royal frowned. Boy, Roman hadn't been off the mark on this one's description. He *was* a funny-looking little fellow, and if ever someone could blend into the background, he would be it. He glanced at the dusty red pickup and then stepped onto the porch. Time enough later to explain to Angel what was going on.

Justice's exit from the house was unexpected. Tommy Boy took a step back and grabbed his pocket in self-defense. But when the man started talking, Tommy Boy let go of the knife. He felt as if he'd fallen down the rabbit hole with Alice. Nothing made sense.

"So when can you start?" Royal asked.

Tommy Boy looked startled. "Start?"

"Work."

"Oh, uh, now."

Royal nodded. "My brother filled you in on what's going on, didn't he?"

"Uh, yeah, right," Tommy Boy mumbled.

"Roman said you don't ride, which is just as well. I don't want you far from the house. Just find yourself some things to do around the barn and keep an eye on my family."

Tommy Boy didn't know what the hell was going on, but he'd landed on his feet with this one.

"Yeah, sure," he said quickly. "I can do that."

Royal nodded and pointed to a small, whitewashed building on the south side of the barn.

"That's the bunkhouse. Just unload your stuff. You're the only one who'll be staying there."

Tommy Boy nodded. Speech was beyond him.

"You'll eat your meals with us. Breakfast at seven. Dinner at twelve. Supper at six." Then he added, "I like to eat with my daughter, and she goes to bed around nine."

Tommy Boy's head was bobbing like a float on the end of a fishing line.

"Yeah. Right. Seven. Twelve. Six. Got it."

"Then I'll let you get at it," Royal said. "If you have questions, I'll be around."

Tommy Boy bolted for his truck and crawled inside. His hands were shaking as he started the engine and drove toward the bunkhouse. All he could think was that he must be dreaming and that he wanted to get this over before he woke up.

Chapter 17

"Hey, Angel," Royal called as he went in the house.

She came out of Maddie's room carrying a load of laundry in her arms.

"Yes?"

"I just hired a new man to take over Rusty's job," he said.

"Oh?"

"His name's Fred Wilson. He's an odd little duck, but don't let it worry you. Roman vouched for him."

Angel nodded and started toward the laundry room when something Royal said registered. She stopped and turned. Royal was still there, watching.

"Why would you need Roman to vouch for a man you hire?"

He hadn't meant to get into this now, but as he'd said before, he wouldn't lie to her again. Maddie came out of her room carrying a coloring book and a box of crayons. He frowned, trying to find a way to answer Angel without saying too much in front of Maddie.

"I hired him to, uh, take care of you two when I'm not around."

Her eyes widened. She would have asked more, but Maddie spoke.

"Daddy, come watch me color," she begged.

"I can't, honey. I've got to check on some cows in the north pasture. Want to come with me?"

"Yeah!" she yelled, pivoted and ran toward the door, still holding her crayons and book.

"I won't be gone more than half an hour or so," Royal said.

Angel nodded. "It will be all right," she assured him. "I know how to use a phone...and my fists."

Royal hugged her. With the laundry between them, it was hard to get close. She laughed when his hand got tangled in a sheet. He lowered his head, tasting the sweetness of her skin and breathing in the soft sigh that escaped her lips.

"You know something?" he whispered.

Mesmerized by the heat she saw building behind his eyes, she shook her head in slow denial.

"No, what?"

"The luckiest day of my life was the day you got caught in that rain." Then he kissed her.

Angel dropped the laundry. It fell on their feet as she slid her arms around his neck.

He groaned and pulled her close, then closer still, and it wasn't enough for what he wanted to do.

"Daddy!"

He groaned again. "Duty calls," he said softly, then brushed one last kiss against her mouth. "Hold that thought."

Angel sighed. "For how long?" she asked.

He grinned. "For as long as it takes. Trust me. I'll make it worth your while."

She was still smiling when the back door slammed. She bent, gathered the laundry she'd dropped and headed for the washing machine.

* * *

Tommy Boy never bothered to unload his stuff. It was risky enough just being here. He didn't plan to be around long enough to need a change of clothes. All he knew was that opportunity had been dumped in his lap. It was up to him to take advantage. He stood at the window, peering through a dusty pane and watching the house. Sooner or later the cowboy would surely leave. When he did, Tommy Boy would be in and out long gone before they knew what hit them. It did occur to him that he would be leaving more witnesses behind. But he'd figured that all out. After this was over, he was thinking of going to Canada. He'd lived in Chicago all his life. Maybe going home wasn't so good, after all. Maybe it was time for a change.

His persistence was rewarded. Justice and the kid he'd seen yesterday got into the blue Chevy truck. He didn't see the woman anywhere. He grinned. That meant she was in the house alone. When they headed his way, he stepped back from the window, unwilling for them to see him staring. To his relief, they kept on going, past the bunkhouse and the barns and up through some gates in a pasture above the main house. He patted the side of his pants, feeling the bulge of the knife in his pocket. No time like the present.

Royal's attention was divided between Maddie's chatter and the cattle he needed to move. But the farther he got from the ranch, the more anxious he became. He glanced at the picture she was drawing and managed a grin. He recognized Flea Bit. That was the one with a tail and four legs. The rest of them were up for grabs.

Sensing she was being observed, Maddie tried extra hard with what she was drawing, but the pickup was bouncing too hard to be very exact.

"Daddy, you need to slow down. I'm having a very hard time."

"Sorry, honey," he said. "But we're almost there. As soon

as I stop, you can crawl in the truck bed and draw all you want, okay?''

"Okay." She sighed, set down her crayons, then got on her knees to look out.

A couple of unusually quiet minutes passed with Maddie staring intently out the back window and Royal growing more and more uneasy.

He kept thinking of last night and the dream Maddie had. The man on the road. She'd said the man on the road. Why would she have worded her warning exactly that way? It had to have been something she overheard. Something to do with Angel's testimony to the FBI or something he and Roman had said. But what? They'd been so careful every time the subject came up.

He glanced at Maddie. She was crying. Not loudly, just big silent tears running down her face. He hit the brakes and parked, then pulled her into his lap.

"Baby, what's wrong?" asked. "Are you sick?"

"I want to go home."

He frowned. Not once in her entire life had Maddie ever wanted to stay in the house in lieu of a trip to the pasture with him.

"But we're almost there," he said. "It won't take long to get the cattle moved into the other pasture. You know. You've watched me do it before."

But her story didn't change and her tears wouldn't stop. "I want to go home."

Exasperated, he made her look at him. "Can you tell me why?"

"I don't know," she sobbed and hid her face on his shirt. "I just need to go home."

He heard it then. It was a small change in words, but a whole different meaning from want to need.

"What do you mean, you *need* to go? Are you afraid Angel is going to bake cookies without you?"

"No, Daddy, no." Then she started to sob. "I can't tell you or you'll get mad."

Guilt hit him hard as he swiped at her tears with his handkerchief. "Baby, no. You can tell Daddy anything you need to tell him. I promise it will be all right."

She sniffed loudly and blew into the handkerchief when he held it to her nose.

"You swear?" she asked.

"I swear."

"It's the lady. She wants me to come back."

A chill made the flesh crawl on the back of his neck, but he made himself stay calm.

"How do you know?"

"'Cause I saw her. She waved at me."

"Saw who, baby? Who was waving at you?"

Maddie looked at Royal, gauging his mood. Then she sighed. "The lady who sits on my bed."

He couldn't think what to say.

Sensing she was losing his interest, Maggie began to beg. "It's true, Daddy. I swear it's true."

Royal set her on the seat. "Buckle up," he said shortly.

"Where are we going?" she asked.

He wouldn't look at her because to do that would be to admit she was right.

"Hand me the phone," he said.

Maddie opened the glove box and dropped the cell phone into his hand.

He punched in the numbers to Roman's office as he was turning, telling himself he was doing this for Maddie and not for himself.

"Roman, it's me," he said when he heard his brother's voice.

"Glad you called," Roman said. "I was about to call you. Nathan Dean called about an hour ago. His flight was delayed in Denver. It will be sometime this evening before he can get to the ranch."

Royal felt sick. "Who the hell's Nathan Dean?"

"The man I hired to replace Rusty," Roman said. "Why? Don't you still want him?"

Royal hit the brakes and shoved the truck into park. It was all he could do to breathe.

"My sweet Lord," he groaned.

"What's wrong?" Roman asked.

"About an hour ago a man knocked on our door wanting a job. He said his name was Fred Wilson. I thought it was the man you sent. I left him at the house with Angel."

Roman was out of his chair and reaching for the gun he kept locked in his desk. "It may be nothing, but I'm on my way."

"It'll take me a good fifteen minutes to get back to the house," Royal said.

"I'll call Deaton on the way out," Roman added.

Royal's voice was shaking. "Call me back."

The line went dead in his ear. Royal looked at Maddie. She was staring straight ahead, wide-eyed and silent. If he needed proof of his daughter's sincerity, he had it. She was never quiet for long.

"Hang on, baby. The ride's going to be rough."

When her coloring book slid onto the floor, she ignored it. When the box of crayons went bouncing after it, she never moved. Her gaze was fixed on something the rest of the world couldn't see.

Angel reached above the washing machine to the soap box on the shelf. The box was in her grasp when she felt a draft at her back. Her first thought was that the door hadn't latched when Royal and Maddie left. She turned and froze, her hand on the soap box and the beginnings of a smile on her face. Her heart dropped. She was supposed to lock the doors.

He was different, but she recognized him just the same. And when he spoke, she knew she was right. That voice and those washed-out green eyes. It was him. She didn't waste her breath on a scream. She just threw the soap in his face and ran.

He had expected, at the least, a hello. Instead, soap powder went up Tommy Boy's nose and into his eyes. He heard her running and leaped, rather than stepped, in the direction of the sound. He fell flat on his face. While he was struggling for a foothold in the tiny white pellets of soap, he could hear her getting farther and farther away. It was just like that day in Dallas when he'd watched from the grass in the center median as they turned the corner and disappeared. Only this time there wasn't going to be any sign on the door of a truck telling him where she'd gone.

Finally, it was rage that got him past the soap. He ran through the house, searching room after room. She was no-where in sight. And while he knew there were probably places she could hide, instinct told him she was already gone.

He ran outside, the switchblade open and clutched in his hand. His eyes were burning unbearably, and there was a strong taste of soap on his tongue.

"You bitch!" he screamed. "You're gonna pay."

Angel was halfway up the ladder to the barn loft when she heard him shout. Even though the sound was far away, it star-tled her, causing her to miss the next step. Momentum slammed her body against the wall, and suddenly she was hanging by the tips of her fingers. Pain ripped through her leg as breath left her body. She bit her lip and groaned. Her grip began to slip. In panic, she clamored to regain a foothold. Only after she felt the wooden slat beneath her foot did she realized she could take a new breath. Desperate to get out of sight before he saw her, she resumed her climb. Blocking out pain, she made it to the top with less than a minute to spare.

In the loft, she frantically searched the flat, open spaces for a good place to hide. Except for a loose mound of hay toward the back and a dozen or so bales on her right, there was none. She glanced through a crack in the wall. He was coming this way. She stifled a groan. It was too late to find a new place. In another minute, he would be in the doorway.

She looked at the loose mound of hay. It was where she and Royal first made love, but there wasn't enough of it to hide in. Her only option was the bales. She darted toward them, crouched in the farthest corner and bit her lip to keep from crying. Her heart was racing, her muscles trembling from the massive adrenaline rush.

"You won't get away," he yelled.

She stiffened. He was here!

She closed her eyes, making herself focus until the sound of her breathing was almost nil. Then she waited, trying not to panic at the high-pitched, singsong voice of the man.

"It's all your fault, you know. If you'd just kept your mouth shut, no one would ever have known. But that's just like a woman. They never know when to shut up."

She shuddered and shrank into the shadows.

He was going from granary to granary, from stall to stall. She could tell by the sounds of slamming doors and muffled curses. And she was hiding above his head, trapped and weaponless. If only she hadn't climbed to the loft.

"They didn't matter. Not really," Tommy Boy called. "I only killed whores. Filth of the earth. Spreaders of disease. They destroy families, you know. If you'd left it alone, I would never have come back. But you saw me, didn't you?" He laughed. "You must have taken a good look at me then to have recognized me today. Not even my daddy would know me like this."

Something slammed. Angel winced. He was getting angrier, she could tell.

"Little Miss Do-gooder," he sneered, and threw a pitchfork across the aisle. It stuck in the dirt, swaying like a Saturday night drunk. "They deserved to die. They killed my daddy and lots of other good men like him. I made them sorry...then I made them pay."

Angel wanted to stand up and scream. The suspense of not knowing when or if he would appear was as frightening as the man himself. But she stayed. She couldn't give up on Maddie and Royal, and she wouldn't give up on herself.

Blood oozed from the wound along her shin, and she winced as she moved to an easier position. *Easy does it,* she thought, and made herself concentrate on something besides the pain.

"I never killed an innocent," Tommy Boy said. Then he chuckled. "Until you. Are you an innocent little Mex or are you a whore like the rest and just better at hiding your dirty little world?"

Angel shook her head. The man was crazy, and she needed a plan. It was silent. Too silent. She listened. Praying for the silence to continue, because she knew all too well that if he started up the ladder, she would know from the creaks and groans of the wood as it gave to the weight.

Tommy Boy had missed the ladder when he'd run into the barn. It wasn't until he was at the other end of the aisle and looking back the way he'd come that he saw it. When he did, he started to grin.

"Hey, missy, missy, missy," he called, giggling. He was calling to her like one would call for a cat.

He started to climb then realized that the open knife in his hand was a hindrance. Confident that he was in total control, he hit the lock on the switchblade and flipped his wrist sharply. The blade slipped into its sheath with a resounding click. He dropped it into his pocket.

"Now then," he muttered to himself and started to climb.

About halfway up he saw a dark splotch of red on the step. He touched it. It was wet. He grinned.

"Hurts, doesn't it?" he yelled, chiding her, goading her, feeling the power of total control. Then he looked at the opening above. Just a few more feet and he would be there.

Angel was shaking so hard her teeth were chattering. His taunts were like swords through her soul. As badly as she wanted to believe her life wouldn't end in this way, it was getting harder and harder to pretend.

She heard him calling out to her as if she were an animal. Kitty, kitty, kitty, as if she would have no better sense than to come running. Frantic, she looked around the loft, praying for an answer, for anything that would give her another way down.

Fur brushed her elbow, and it was all she could do not to scream. Her heart was pounding. She looked at the cat winding itself in and out of her arms as she braced herself on the floor.

Dumpling! It was Dumpling, probably searching for supper. With all those kitty mouths to feed, she was forever on the hunt.

She gathered the cat against her breasts and buried her face in the old cat's back, remembering the way Maddie would love her and talk to her as if any minute the old cat would stand up and talk.

A board creaked on the other side of the floor. He was here! Only God could help her now.

From the corner of her eye she saw a quick flash of gray and another of blue. Dumpling was starting to squirm in Angel's arms, and she realized the old cat had brought her kittens to the loft, probably teaching them to hunt. She hunkered down, waiting for Royal…waiting for a miracle.

Tommy Boy was getting antsy. He was tired of the games. He wanted them over, and now. The cowboy wouldn't stay away forever. He needed to be long gone before the cowboy came back. He palmed the knife and released the blade, taking comfort in the click as it locked into place. Once he realized she was in the loft, a new solution to his problem had come into play. He didn't have to cut her to kill her. He could break her neck. A headfirst dive through the opening in the floor would make her death look like an accident. He could leave in the middle of their grief and no one would be the wiser. It was perfect. All he had to do was get his hands on her, and it would be over.

"Here, kitty, kitty, kitty," he called, liking the way the words felt on his tongue.

He hadn't planned on getting the real thing, and in so many sizes. They came running out of the hay and out of the shadows. Two of them, then three of them, then five, crawling over his shoes and mewling at the top of their lungs. He didn't know they expected a treat.

"What the hell?" he shrieked, and kicked out, sending a kitten flying into the air. It landed with a squeak, then scampered away. "Get back! Get back!" he yelled, all the while moving to stay out of their way. It was an impossible feat.

He stepped on a tail first and then another's small paw. Two identical cries of pain sent old Dumpling scrambling out of Angel's lap and flying across the floor to her babies' aid. Snarling and spitting, she launched herself at the intruder, landing square in the man's bare face.

He screamed from shock and the sharp, ripping pains. The knife clattered to the floor as he reached for the cat with both hands. But it was too late. It was a hit-and-run affair.

He turned in a circle, screaming at the top of his lungs and looking for a cat to kill. Where there had been numbers, now there were none. At some silent message from Mama, every single kitten was gone.

Everything had turned into a blur of red as blood dripped from his scratches and into his eyes. He sank to his knees, trying to find the knife he'd dropped. Without it he felt undressed.

Angel stood as he screamed, quickly assessing his condition and her options for escape. He was on his knees between her and the opening in the floor. Her chance was slim, but thanks to Dumpling, it was better than it had been before.

She saw him searching for the switchblade while blood ran in both eyes.

God help me, she prayed, and bolted.

Tommy Boy heard her coming and started to stand. But she was too fast, and he was too blind to dodge what was coming. She hit him with her body, sending him sprawling again, and escaped through the hole in the floor.

"Son of a holy bitch!" he screamed, then saw the knife. Moments later, it was in his hand and he was flying down the ladder, half-blind and moving on instinct and rage.

Angel was running across the barnyard toward the back pasture. The way she saw it, she just might outrun him. And if she was lucky, she would run into Royal before the man ran her down.

It felt good to no longer be trapped. She wanted to shout from the excitement of the escape. Instead, she lengthened her stride, felt the wind in her hair and the sun on her face and knew that this wasn't the day she would die.

Royal was driving so fast, he wasn't even hitting the low spots. Foreboding rode beside him like a ghost, reminding him that he'd promised he would keep Angel safe. It had been such a stupid thing to do—driving away and leaving Angel with a man he'd never seen before. Rationally, he knew the timing of the incident had been perfect for deception. But he could have stayed. Should have stayed. He prayed as he drove that he would get a chance to tell her he was sorry.

Maddie clutched the door and her seat belt with an intensity he'd never seen. Her fear was palpable, but he already knew it was not for herself.

About half a mile from the house, she started to cry again. Royal groaned. Even if they survived this hell, would his daughter ever be the same?

"Hurry, Daddy, hurry. The lady says hurry."

He cursed. Because something was happening that he still couldn't see.

He came over the hill in the air, landing a few yards away with a thump, and gave Maddie a frantic look.

"Are you all right, baby?"

Maddie was staring at the glove box as if it was a television screen. Her eyes were wide and fixed and brimming with tears.

"She's running now, Daddy. She's running."

Royal jerked and looked out the windshield. He groaned.

My God, Maddie was right! It was Angel, coming uphill toward him at an all-out stretch. Her hair was flying behind her, and her arms were pumping frantically with every step. But it was the look on her face and the man behind her that stopped his heart. He didn't know how and he didn't understand why, but Maddie had been right. They had needed to go home.

"Hold on, Maddie. I see her now. Everything's going to be all right."

He mashed the accelerator to the floor. There was a closed gate and less than a hundred yards between them when he came to a sliding halt. If he'd been alone, he would have crashed through the gate without hesitation. But he'd already put his daughter through hell. The possibility of putting her in physical danger wasn't something he could consider.

He unbuckled her seat belt and pulled her to the floor.

"Look at me, Maddie," he yelled.

She looked, her eyes wide with shock and fear.

"You get on the floor and cover your head and don't get up no matter what you hear. Understand me?"

"I promise," she said.

Royal got out of the truck and reached behind the seat for the rifle he'd stashed. He vaulted the gate without bothering to open it, then started running.

When Angel saw them coming over the rise, it had been all she could do to keep moving. But the man was too close and she was too set on living to take the chance. Her legs felt like rubber, and it was hard to take the next step. Her lungs burned. She needed a breath. *Keep moving. Keep moving.* The words became a chant that kept her going.

She could hear the man shouting and screaming, and she wondered how he had the breath to do all that and still run. Adrenaline, she reckoned. She could do with a burst of it.

Royal was out of the truck. She saw him jumping the gate and running. She needed to stop. She needed a breath. She heard a grunt of rage as the man reached for her. Her T-shirt tightened around her throat. With a last burst of energy, she sprinted away, giving herself some space. But it didn't last long. She was at the end of her run. He would catch her, after all.

Royal could see it clearly. The man called Wilson was almost upon her. There was no way he could get to her in time. And there was no way he could take a clean shot without hitting her. In the time it took him to take a breath, he'd come to a stop and was waving his gun.

"Down!" he shouted, motioning for Angel to drop. "Get down now!"

She lurched forward, sailing out and down like a swimmer about to belly-flop. Royal watched it happening as he lifted his gun to his cheek. The rifle stock was warm against his face. The smell of gun oil and clover was in his nose as he lined up the cross hairs on the telescopic sight.

Angel was almost on the ground, her face contorted in a grimace in preparation for the pain of the fall. Her hair was flying behind her like a widow's veil, long and black. Then she was down. He saw the displacement of dust as she hit, then the face of her killer as it suddenly appeared in his site. The trigger was smooth against his finger. He squeezed off a shot.

Tommy Boy never saw it coming. One minute the woman was almost in his grasp, the next thing he knew she was on the ground and his brain was coming undone. Just before the lights went out, he thought he saw a quick flash of blue. Like the blue from that damned Chevy truck. The thought died as quickly as Tommy Boy Watson.

Angel was crying and couldn't stop. Royal rolled her over and lifted her off of the ground and into his arms. He kept kissing her face and wiping her tears and shaking so hard he thought they both might fall.

"Oh, my God, oh, my God," Angel kept saying. "I thought I would die. I thought I would die."

Royal held her. There was nothing he could say to take away the shock. Only time would heal her wounds. All he could do was apologize over and over for leaving her alone with the man.

"I didn't know," he kept saying. "I swear I didn't know. I thought it was the man Roman hired to keep you safe." He buried his face in her hair. "Instead I nearly got you killed."

"But you came," Angel cried. "You still came."

It was then Royal remembered his daughter, who was still lying on the floor of his truck. It was because of her that Angel was still alive.

He cupped Angel's face. "It was Maddie. She made me come back."

Angel shook her head. "I don't understand."

"Neither do I," Royal said. "But she said the lady told her to come back. She said we needed to get home. All the way here she was crying and begging me to hurry."

Angel was stunned. "Oh, Royal, she saved my life, didn't she?"

It was still difficult for him to say it. "I wouldn't have come back if she hadn't begged me so hard."

She realized Maddie was nowhere in sight.

"Where is she?" she asked.

"On the floor in the truck." He put his arms around her. "Come on, sweetheart, let's go get our girl."

A few minutes later, they were on their way to the house, leaving what was left of Tommy Boy Watson for Deaton to clean up. Angel was sitting close to Royal's side and holding Maddie in her lap with the little girl's face pressed against her neck. They didn't want her to see the man sprawled on the ground or the grass beneath him turning red from his blood. It was enough that she would know her daddy had used a gun that day to save an angel's life.

As they turned the corner by the bunkhouse, they saw Roman coming down the driveway in a cloud of dust. He skidded to a halt a few seconds ahead of Royal.

Royal glanced at Maddie, then Angel.

"Wait here a minute, will you?"

She nodded. There were things that needed to be said that a little girl didn't need to hear.

Maddie clung to Angel as if she'd never let go.

"It's over, baby," she said softly.

Maddie nodded.

Angel could see the two brothers, heads together and deep in conversation. She watched as Royal pointed toward the hill above the barn, then saw Roman jerk as if he'd been punched and turn to look at her. Their gazes met and held. Then he headed for his car with Royal right behind them.

She watched them taking turns on the phone, then saw the look on Royal's face when he headed her way. There was such a sense of completion within her, as if every loose end in her life had finally been tied and clipped.

Royal opened the door. "Come here, punkin," he said softly, lifting Maddie out of Angel's arms, then transferred her into Roman's.

Roman headed toward the house, holding her close and whispering sweet little nothings near her ear, trying to coax a smile from his girl.

Royal reached for Angel, taking care not to hurt her any more than she'd already been hurt. But the need to hold her was overwhelming. He'd come close...too close to losing her.

"Can you make it?" he asked, letting her pull herself out of the cab.

Angel slid free and into his arms.

"You know what, Royal Justice?"

"No, what?" he said softly, cradling her close.

"It feels good to be home."

Epilogue

"I need to build a bigger closet," Royal muttered, as he pulled things off shelves and tossed old clothes aside to make room for Angel's things.

Angel grinned. They'd been married for all of a week, and he was determined her clothes should hang next to his, even if there wasn't room, even if the closet across the hall was nearly empty.

"I'm sure it will be fine," she said, and knelt beside a box he'd taken from the shelf.

She opened it, expecting something ordinary like maybe a hundred socks with holes or ties he didn't like. She found pictures instead. More than a dozen. All sizes. Some framed. Some in old cardboard folders.

"What are these?" she asked, lifting one out.

She turned it over. An odd shaft of pain came and went in her heart as she realized this must be Susan. Maddie's mother. Royal's wife. Then she reminded herself, that *she* was his wife now. But there was little joy in the knowledge that this pretty young woman with the smiling face and big belly had to die before that could happen.

"It's Susan, isn't it?"

Royal turned, then dropped the handful of shirts he'd been holding and knelt beside her.

"Wow," he said softly. "I'd forgotten these were even here." He rubbed the dust off one, grinning as he tilted it to the light. "She was eight and a half months pregnant here. See that dress? It was green. She was so sick of that dress—she called it a tent—swore she'd never wear green again." He stared at the image. "Seems like all that happened to another me…in another life. Do you know what I mean?"

Angel nodded. When Royal handed the picture to her, she laid it aside and watched as he resumed what he was doing. A long minute passed. Finally, curiosity got the best of her.

"I never thought of it before, but you don't have any pictures of her anywhere, do you?"

Royal leaned against the bureau. "They used to be everywhere," he said. "But after she died…" He shrugged. "I missed her so much, but there was Maddie. I couldn't grieve and raise our child. One day I just put them away. After a while I forget they were there."

Angel frowned. "Has Maddie seen these?"

A strange look crossed his face. "Well, hell. I don't know." He looked embarrassed. "That sounds awful, doesn't it?"

Angel shrugged. "Has she ever asked about her, like what she looked like?"

Royal shook his head. "Hardly ever. Maybe because she's still so little. Maybe because she's never known what it's like to live with a woman." Then he added, "Until you."

Angel smiled, but she set another picture aside as well. "Maybe we'll keep these out…just in case," she offered.

Royal pulled her to her feet and into his arms. "I knew there was a reason I loved you," he said softly, and proceeded to kiss her senseless.

As Royal was considering the wisdom of locking the door

and taking Angel to bed, Maddie burst into the room with Flea Bit under her arm.

"Daddy, can I take the meat scraps from dinner to Dumpling and the babies?"

After the part Dumpling had played in Angel's escape, Royal was all for buying the cat ground sirloin and serving it up on a platter.

"Yes, but don't stay long. As soon as we get this closet cleaned, we're going to the mall."

"Yea!" Maddie shrieked.

Disturbed by the noise, Flea Bit wiggled to be put down.

Maddie started to give chase and stumbled.

Angel caught her before she could fall. "Are you okay, honey?"

Maddie nodded, watching intently as Angel began moving the box on which she had stumbled.

"What's in there?" she asked.

Royal rolled his eyes. "You know what curiosity did to the cat," he muttered.

"Considering the fact that Flea Bit is about her best friend, I don't think that's a good analogy to use on her," Angel said.

Royal grinned. "Right. What was I thinking?"

Maddie dropped to her knees and peered into the box. Angel watched, curious as to what her reaction might be. But neither she or Royal was prepared for what came.

Maddie rocked on her heels, her eyes alight with joy as she held a picture aloft.

"Look!" she cried, waving it in the air. "Look at this, Daddy, it's her! It's her!"

Angel knew what was coming before Maddie got it said. She started to shake.

"What is it?" Royal asked, and took the picture out of Maddie's hand.

Even now, after all the years that had gone by and the love he felt for Angel, he felt sorrow that his first love had died so soon. It was Susan, taken on the day of their wedding, just before they'd left for their honeymoon. He remembered the way she'd smelled, like gardenias. And the silken feel of that dress she was wearing, as blue as the bluebonnets she'd had in her bouquet.

"It's her!" Maddie cried, and tugged at his hand until he gave her the picture. "It's the lady who sits on my bed."

Royal sat down because standing was suddenly impossible. Maddie's words were ringing in his ears, but they didn't make sense.

"I told you she was real," Maddie cried as she crawled in his lap. "Now do you believe me?"

Royal was shaken to the core. He kept looking at Maddie and then at Angel, remembering what Maddie claimed the lady had said. Sending them an angel. That was it. She was sending them an angel.

Angel sat on the bed beside him. "It all makes an odd sort of sense now, doesn't it?"

He stared at the picture until the face began to blur. Then he looked at Maddie—at the expectation on her face. He had to clear his throat before he could speak.

"Yes, baby. I believe you."

"Yea!" she shrieked, and bounced off his lap, going in search of the cat who'd slipped away.

Angel waited, accepting the fact that somewhere within this revelation was a miracle. For reasons she would never understand, she'd been led to this place, to these people, to this home. Not only had she been sheltered here, she'd been saved by an angel of her own.

Royal was shaking as he set the picture aside and pulled Angel into his lap.

"Tell me I'm not crazy," he begged, then rolled over, taking her with him onto the bed.

"You're not crazy," she said softly, and held him close, cradling his head upon her breasts.

Outside their window, they could hear Maddie scolding as she dug poor Flea Bit out from under a bush. A few feet away a faucet dripped steadily, monotonously. The scent of dust was faint but unmistakable. Remnants of a past that had been disturbed. Royal sighed. She felt his body relaxing, heard his breathing shift as he drifted off to sleep.

Angel closed her eyes not to sleep, just to rest. With Maddie afoot, sleep was never an option. Quiet descended, followed by a peace unlike any she'd ever known.

It came then, faint, like a memory too old to retain but there just the same. Familiar, and yet hard to explain.

It was the scent of gardenia.

In that moment, Angel knew. She wouldn't look. Couldn't look, although she felt no fear. The communication was instant. Tears started to roll down her face and still she wouldn't look. There was no need. She'd heard in her heart all she needed to know.

"I hear you," she whispered. "Yes, I'll keep them both safe, just as you kept me."

And then the feeling was gone, and Angel knew that what had been left of Susan Justice would never come again. Not because she'd been replaced, but because there was no longer a need.

* * * * *

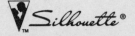

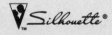

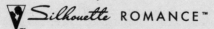

#919 THIS HEART FOR HIRE—Marie Ferrarella

Given the threats against him, Logan Buchanan knew he had no choice but to hire private investigator Jessica Deveaux, but seeing her again only reminded him of how much he'd once loved her. Now it was up to Logan to prove he'd changed, before someone took away his one last chance for happiness.

#920 THE FUGITIVE BRIDE—Margaret Watson
Cameron, Utah

FBI agent Jesse Coulton was having a hard time believing beautiful Shea McAllister was guilty of doing anything illegal on her Utah ranch. As he worked undercover to discover the truth, Jesse desperately hoped she was innocent—because the only place she belonged was in his arms!

#921 MIDNIGHT CINDERELLA—Eileen Wilks
Way Out West

After being accused of a crime he hadn't committed, Nathan Jones was determined to put his life back together. And when he met and fell for his sexy new employee, Hannah McBride, he knew he was on the right track. But then their newfound love was put to the test and it was up to Nate to prove that he was finally ready for happily-ever-after.

#922 THE DADDY TRAP—Kayla Daniels
Families Are Forever

When Kristen Monroe and her nephew Cody knocked on his door, Luke Hollister knew his life would never be the same. As she hid from Cody's abusive "father," Kristen shocked Luke with an incredible secret. And the longer they stayed, the more Luke fell in love—with the woman he desired and the son he'd always wanted....

#923 THE COP AND CALAMITY JANE—Elane Osborn

Bad luck seemed to follow Callie "Calamity Jane" Chance everywhere. But when she met sexy detective Marcus Scanlon, she knew her luck had changed. He was hot on the trail of suspected catnappers, and Callie was his only witness. Once the culprits were nabbed, would Callie accept Marcus's proposal—for a disaster-free future?

#924 BRIDGER'S LAST STAND—Linda Winstead Jones
Men in Blue

Detective Malcolm Bridger never thought he'd see Frannie Vaughn again after their one memorable night together. Then Frannie got mixed up in his current case. Suddenly Malcolm was falling for this forever kind of girl, and their near one-night stand was slowly becoming a one-*life* stand.